Paradise, New York

para

NEW YORK   a novel

 Temple University Press · Philadelphia

dise

Eileen Pollack

Temple University Press, Philadelphia 19122
Copyright © 1998 by Eileen Pollack
All rights reserved. Published 1998. Printed
in the United States of America. Book
design by Richard Eckersley. Set in Scala.
⊗ The paper used in this publication meets
the requirements of the American National
Standard for Information Sciences –
Permanence of Paper for Printed Library
Materials, ANSI z39.48–1984

Library of Congress Cataloging-in-Publication Data
Pollack, Eileen, 1956–
Paradise, New York : a novel / Eileen Pollack.
p.   cm.   ISBN 1-56639-657-3 (alkaline paper)
1. Jews – New York (State) – Catskill Mountains
Region – Fiction. I. Title.
PS3566.04795P37 1998 813'.54–dc21 98-33591

In memory of my grandparents, Anna and Elias Pollack
and Pauline and Joshua Davidson, none of whom are to be
found in this book, all of whom live in my heart

Dedicated to my son, Noah Elias Glaser

Acknowledgments

This book would not exist if not for the advice
and support of Marcie Hershman, Maxine
Rodburg, Suzanne Berne, Adam Schwartz and
James Alan McPherson. I also am deeply
grateful to David Gurevich, Sue Monsky, Lynne
Sharon Schwartz, Josh Henkin, Phil Brown,
Jerry Jacobs, Mary Jack Wald and Charles Baxter.

Blessed are the man and the woman
who have grown beyond their greed
and have put an end to their hatred
and no longer nourish illusions.
But they delight in the way things are
and keep their hearts open, day and night.
They are like trees planted near flowing rivers,
which bear fruit when they are ready.
Their leaves will not fall or wither.
Everything they do will succeed.

Translated by Stephen Mitchell

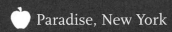 Paradise, New York

 Part One: Winter

If God had found a reason to take a snapshot of Paradise, it would have shown Main Street to be the trunk of an evergreen, roads sprouting like boughs so ragged and droopy the whole thing resembled a Christmas tree left by the curb. Once, fifty resorts had decorated the branches of Paradise. Now, the remains clung to the roads like cracked, fading baubles. That December afternoon in 1978, as I drove with my mother to our family's hotel, I counted nine victims of Jewish lightning, the freakish force that strikes only vacant resorts with no chance for profit except from insurance. ("Hey Solly, I was upset to hear about your fire." "Shh!" whispers Sol, "it's not until tomorrow.") Patches of snow drifted over charred beams; the chimneys had fallen and lay in jutted curves like black spinal columns.

Most of the resorts had simply been abandoned. The main houses stood, but the stucco had peeled from beneath the windows and these looked out beyond the gates like haunted eyes. Handball backboards poked up from overgrown fields, warped plywood tombstones inscribed in flaking paint with the names of the dead.

As we drove past the backboard for Fein's Hillside Manor, I thought of my fight in first grade with Jeff Fein.

"The Eden's a shit house," Jeff hissed across our table in art class. "The pool's cracked. The food stinks!"

In my rage, I hammered Jeff again and again in his pudding-soft stomach until he recanted. Now, it seemed my blows had battered not Jeff, but his parents' hotel. Contrite, I admitted that Fein's Hillside indeed had been superior to the Eden, at least in regard to the cheesecake it served, the parquet floor in its lobby, and the slide by its pool – a white bow of steel that shone, iridescent, when the sun hit just so. I took no satisfaction that the Manor's pool was now gruesome with tree limbs, the lobby long gone.

Just past the Manor the road became a roller coaster. As a child I'd loved to ride in the back seat of our car, especially when my brother, Arthur, was driving. The car would fly over a rise, then drop. Giddy, I would scream out the names on each backboard while Arthur cursed the Eden in a voice that made me think of a radio turned so low you couldn't make out the words, you only knew the announcer was warning of catastrophes to come. Once, I asked Arthur why he drove so fast if he didn't want to get there. "If we have a crack-up," he said, "your mother might give me the afternoon off."

Today, with the roads coated in ice, my mother drove slowly, with great concentration. She was four-feet-eleven and seemed to be using the wheel to do chin-ups. The car barely moved, but she kept asking, Was she scaring me?

No, I was fine.

"But you keep sighing, sweetheart."

I pointed to the wreckage of the once-stately Queen Esther.

"The Esther's been closed for three years," my mother said. "You only noticed it now?"

The truth, we both knew, was that being away at college for only three months had given me the eyes to see my hometown as an outsider saw it – as something dying, or dead. The luckiest resorts had been sold and reincarnated as retreats for Zen Buddhists (the former Green Pastures now sprouted a garden of fat golden statues), rehabilitation centers for drug addicts, sleep-over camps for handicapped children. Not far from the Eden were a Bible school for slow-learning Christians and a retirement home for Jewish vaudevillians.

"These Hasids," I said, "what do they want to do with the Eden, anyway?"

"Sweetheart," my mother said, "we are not meeting this man so we can examine his credentials. We are showing him the Eden, in the best light possible, which probably means we should hope for an eclipse."

"I don't understand why you're so desperate to sell. After all these years, why now?"

"Because I'm old. After all these years, I'm old."

I had been staring at the rotting hotels for so long that when I turned and looked at my mother, the image persisted and she seemed to me as wasted as those ruins by the road. Not that she ever had been a beauty. Her hair was dull brown. The center of her mouth was a smear of red lipstick; frown lines descended half an inch from each end. For the tour, she had put on a skirt as shapeless and drab as a grocery bag, white anklets, loafers, a mangy camel coat. Still, she always had been plump, with the blush of a peach. Now, a dried fig.

"Did something happen?" I said. "Since I went away, I mean?"

"I appreciate the concern." She tightened her lips to demonstrate that she didn't value my concern in the least. "It's your father," she said. "He's not a young man."

In the three seasons of the year when the Eden was closed, my father taught cooking at the county voc-ed school, preparing his students to be chefs at hotels that no longer existed. They were tough kids, rambunctious. He used to come home at night exhausted, tug off his support-hose and fall straight into bed. Was he more tired these days? Did he doze as he lectured, head dipping forward into a soup pot?

A jeep with an upraised plow rounded the curve ahead of us and charged, furious at our red station wagon. My mother dropped the full force of her body onto the brake, then swiveled in her seat to make certain that the jeep wouldn't turn and charge again. I asked if she thought my grandmother would agree to sell the Eden.

"She can't run it herself. If we refuse, she has no choice."

"She could conjure her imps and demons to help her."

My mother frowned. "Your grandmother is a strong woman. Hasn't your generation made that a virtue?"

"You know you'll miss it," I said.

"*You'll* miss it. Not your father and myself. Remember last summer, when the stove blew up? I had to drive into town, fry enough *pirogen* for fifty-three people, then rush back to the hotel before they got cold. And dinner! A dozen pullets from that oven!"

"You're pretending. You really do love it."

"I did love it, at one time. When your grandfather was alive. I mean, when he was *living*. You have no idea what influence he had over people. They would be bickering, complaining. Then he would start to mingle, and before you knew it, they would be in tears, that's how hard they were laughing. As crazy as it was, with him it had spirit."

I would have reminded her that her father would sooner have sold his wife than his hotel, but just then we passed the handyman's cabin, white in the mist, and the argument turned to dust in my throat. In my months in New York, I had come to suspect that I had imagined my childhood trips to this shack. I had lived in a fairy tale, inventing a prince I could save from bewitchment so he could confirm I was nobility myself, as no one else would. A daydream. A lie. And yet here was the cabin, solid wood after all.

The station wagon pirouetted across the Eden's parking lot like an ungainly skater. It skidded to a stop and my mother got out and minced across the frozen mud to the gate. I followed her, then stopped in the middle of the rutted lot and looked up.

Seeing the Eden without its camouflage of leaves was like glimpsing a family friend in a doctor's office, naked beneath the harsh lights. More than ever I wished the Eden had been as successful as That Other Hotel – my grandmother wouldn't allow us to say its name in her presence – that splendid city on the hill, which started from beginnings as humble as ours but had only grown larger, more famous and more elaborate as the Eden decayed.

For fifty-nine years my grandmother had vetoed every improvement, living in the hope that her husband would sell the Eden and take her back to New York, to resume his position as foreman at a factory that made ladies' coats, as he was when she had met him, before he had been "bitten by the hotel bug," as Grandpa Abe put it. ("A bedbug!" she screamed. "That's all that bit you!") But after Abe's stroke, she realized that the Eden was all she would ever possess on this earth. She refused to consider selling it; the one time my parents dared to broach the subject of what they might do if they "got a good offer," my grandmother cursed and used the cleaver she'd been holding to hack a game hen in two.

I didn't want to think what or whom she might cleave if she looked out her window and noticed her son-in-law leading a Hasid around her hotel. My parents' plan was this: my mother and I would keep Nana diverted while my father took the Hasid on a lightning-quick tour. When all that remained was a matter of blackmail ("Here, sign this paper, or we'll let it sit idle and you won't get a cent"), they would hide Nana's knives and hope for the best.

My mother and I set off for the bungalow. The doorbell was useless. My grandmother was deaf, and, though my mother had the key, this still left the problem of how to make contact – if Nana were startled, she might assume a burglar had sneaked up behind her and roundhouse the culprit. The trick was to warn her by stomping your feet like an African hunter beating the bush.

We expected to find her in the stuffy back room where she passed the long winters like the miller's daughter, spinning straw into gold, or rather, converting a room full of garbage – milk bottles, flour sacks, bread wrappers, corn husks, wooden crates and dyed elbow-macaroni – into lamps, cushions, bath mats, night tables, vases, and items that seemed to have no other purpose than to keep the guests guessing as to what these might be. She'd also painted the artwork on the Eden's lobby walls: Queen Elizabeth on horseback, fox hunts, a chopping block in the Tower of London, various earls, dukes and knights, all of these copied from a book about England, as colorful as my grandmother's palette allowed. If she caught a guest staring at a painting, she would shout: "I used to live there!" and explain that her family spent a year in Liverpool on their way to New York. "The first day of school, naah, I can't say good morning in English. By the last day, Charles Dickens! The Round Table! Shakespeare! The teacher, she said I was a genius. In America, naah, I sew buttons on coats." She tapped the Queen Mother on her reddish-green nose. "She got nothing I don't!"

In the workshop we found a half-finished picture of Buckingham Palace made of dried split-peas and beans. But no Nana, anywhere.

"I don't think she went for groceries," my mother said. The cupboards were full of baby food, which, since my grandmother wouldn't pay for dentures, was all she could eat. "I'd better take the car and go find her. You stay here and warn your father."

I never had felt any great love or admiration for my grandmother. But, standing in her workshop that wintry afternoon, I experienced the unsettling sensation we were on the same side.

"Don't you feel guilty doing this?" I asked.

With a look that implied I was too smart to understand anything of consequence, my mother left me to contemplate the murky turpentine in a jar labeled STRAINED BEEF, the pile of dried peas, Nana's brushes and paints. The fumes burned my nostrils, and I finally escaped and skated down the path to wait for my father.

An iron arch spanned the walk, obscured by a chaos of warped wooden signs. The pictures showed primitive talent, though the artist since had turned to more regal subjects. At the center of the arch hung a painting of a couple in flesh-colored bathing suits. The tree in the background suggested these weren't ordinary guests, as did the red blob (a beach ball? some kind of fruit?) the woman was tossing toward the man. THE GARDEN OF EDEN it said below this couple, and, below that: YOUR HOSTS ABE AND JENNIE APPELBAUM, with APPEL much fatter so no one could miss the pun at the core of the owners' name. To the left of this sign hung a golfer in knickers, huge as Paul Bunyan compared to the forest and lake at his feet. EIGHTEEN-HOLE GOLF COURSE it said, though the sign didn't reveal that the golf course was public and twelve miles down the road. More truthful were the promises of SHUFFLEBOARD, BASEBALL, HEALTHFUL POOL, TV (honest enough in its singular number) and NITELY AMUSEMENT. At the far right, a chorus of cows, fish and hens raised their mouths and beaks to sing THREE MEALS A DAY, VERY STRICT KOSHER. And there, across the top: ALL THOSE WHO ENTER LEAVE YOUR CARES HERE. I reached up and stroked Adam's smooth chest, Eve's wavy hair, the apple tree, the apple, the pale lemon sun.

I always suspected I had been chosen by God for some special fate, but I didn't receive proof until I was nine. It was summer, mid June. Where could death hide on such a bright morning? Nowhere, I thought, and poked one bare foot out the bungalow door. How soft the grass looked! I longed to turn cartwheels, climb the old oak, perform a few miracles to take up the hour until the pool opened and I could show off my new lime-green two-piece.

"No," my mother told me. Her fingers closed around my suit straps.

"Why not?" I demanded.

"Put on your shoes first."

I wrinkled my nose.

"You heard me, Miss Piss."

In my mother's opinion, deadly microbes were breeding in every warm puddle. The germs of paralysis were tiny sharks teeming in each muddy drop.

"If you go around barefoot, you might pick up TB."

For years I had assumed she was saying Tee *Vee*. The current ran through the earth like a snake of hot sparks. If you stepped on the snake with bare feet, the pictures shot to your brain. One afternoon, when my mother wasn't looking, I took off my sneakers and searched for the spot. I planted my right foot, paused, saw no pictures, planted my left foot a few inches over, stepping and pausing until I had signed every patch of the Eden with my footprints. But I couldn't find the current. I even tried pressing my ear to the ground and listening for voices – Fred, Ethel, Rickie, and the red-headed Lucy for whom I had been named, or so my brother told me.

I kept doing this until Arthur discovered me down on all fours, ear to the ground. He jumped on my back and wouldn't let me up until I admitted what I was doing. Then he laughed so convulsively I could feel my body shake beneath his. He sputtered his last laugh and took pity on me, explaining the truth: that our family's hotel once had been a refuge for patients who coughed furiously and spat blood until they choked, eyes bulging, tongues black. Their mucus, Arthur told me, still wriggled with germs, which waited to crawl in the blisters on my feet. He thought this would scare me, but it excited me to think that the Eden was haunted with dead people's germs, and these lived on, unseen, awaiting a chance to make contact with me, inhabit my blood.

"Put your shoes on this minute," my mother ordered, "or no swimming for a month."

I didn't bother to tell her that I wasn't afraid of catching tuberculosis. What would that matter? TB was only one of a hundred virulent devils waiting to prey on a girl in bare feet.

"If you step on a rusted nail you'll get lockjaw."

I savored this tragedy. Arthur would be chasing me across the front lawn. I would step on a nail and stumble. He would catch me and threaten to pull down my bathing suit, as he often had done before, and when I tried to beg for mercy my jaw would lock shut. Slowly, he would realize what dreadful affliction had silenced his sister. He would beg my forgiveness, which of course I wouldn't grant.

Not that I believed I would die. How could such puny villains – a microbe, a nail – strike down a girl of rare visions and dreams? If anything, I sensed on that brilliant June morning not death but a challenge, an occasion to prove my powers at last.

I put on my flip-flops and dodged past my mother.

"Come back here!" she shouted. "Those things are so flimsy, a piece of glass could go through!"

But she didn't have time to run after me and tie real shoes on my feet. Flip-flops smacking against my heels, I ran to the camp house, an unpainted shack with a dozen old mattresses piled high inside. The raw wooden walls were inscribed with the signatures of campers now in their fifties: YUDEL LOVES EDITH; SHEL CLOBBERED MILTIE 8/10/32. Standing on my toes, I was just able to reach the top cubbyholes. Wasps dove from the eaves, but I wasn't afraid. I had given them instructions to strafe all intruders and leave me unstung. From the only cubbyhole with a door I withdrew a shabby book – a present from my Grandpa Abe the year before, on my eighth birthday. He had bought it for himself when he arrived in America; he wanted to own a copy of the Bible in English, and the bibles for adults were too hard to read. OLD TESTAMENT FOR CHILDREN, EDITED, ABRIDGED the title said in block letters. A smiling man and woman posed behind a tree; I recognized them as the couple tossing the beach ball on the Eden's main arch. In his soft stumbling voice, my grandfather started to read

aloud the story of Moses. I interrupted to ask why he pronounced the *w*'s as *v*'s.

"Vell," he said. A troubled look passed his face. He leaned
forward, the book slipping from his lap. He opened his mouth
to speak, and I sat waiting for an answer until my parents appeared in the doorway with a cake, which we didn't get to eat.
Though my grandfather lived on another eleven years, he
couldn't move or talk, so it seemed to me as if God bestowed
the Torah, not on Moses, but on me, Lucy Appelbaum, then He
lay down to sleep while I studied His gift, preparing for a test
I knew would come soon.

The more I read the Bible, the more I believed that Moses
and I were two of a kind. Hadn't a bush with flame-red leaves
ordered me to kneel beside the shuffleboard court because the
ground there was holy? And that same afternoon, hadn't a radio emitted a wail, after which the announcer, in his resonant
voice, commanded me to await instructions regarding the mission God had reserved especially for me? I heard God speaking
often, praising my deeds. In return, I asked Him favors: *Please,
God, let the sun stand still so I can swim one more hour.* My prayers
sometimes worked, but never when any witness was near.

And this was the puzzle that occupied my mind in the camp
house that morning: How could I prove how special I was if no
one required the knowledge I had gleaned from my book? I lay
on my back, studying the baffling words above the toilet,
preparing for the day I would be called upon to translate some
other warning God had written on a wall, as Daniel, my hero,
had been asked to explain MENE MENE TEKEL UPHARSIN to
wicked King Belshazzar.

"Attention, attention!" My mother's voice rang from loud-
speakers on poles all over the Eden's grounds. "Ladies and gentlemen, the pool is now open for your aquatic enjoyment."

I replaced my book in its cubbyhole and jumped down the
four steps. Slowed by my flip-flops, I left these behind, two

bright crimson footprints in the middle of the walk. Beside the pool, I paused on the hot concrete deck – good training, in case I was ever flung into a burning furnace, like Daniel. Then, with a cry, I raced to the edge and threw myself over.

Cold as perfection. I frog-kicked underwater. When I emerged I felt cleansed, though of what I wasn't sure. Maybe the chlorine would sterilize my skin so no ugly hair would sprout between my legs, as it did from the crotches of the women on the lounge chairs, black tendrils creeping down puckery thighs. I levered my body to the deck, exalting in the strength of my lean, freckled arms. I pinched my nose, rubbed it – if Arthur saw snot, he would blow his whistle and call out his findings to the busboys. The pool walls were painted turquoise, the water reflecting the sun like an enormous gem sunk in the pillowed acres of the Eden. The pool didn't have a lifeguard (SWIM AT OWN RISK warned a sign), but my brother had the job of keeping the water clean, and he cleared debris from the surface as obsessively as he scrubbed blackheads from his face. He dumped in chlorine until any moth or beetle fluttering too near dropped like a stone.

I breathed deeply, then dove. Emptying my lungs, I sank to the bottom, where I lay with the rough concrete scraping my belly. My blood throbbed loudly in my ears, the watery world pulsated with the question: *How long can you stay here, how long, how long . . .*

Forever, I answered. I could live without breathing, explore the world's oceans with no need for tanks. I flipped onto my back and floated there, between the bottom and the surface, the sunlight a spatter of gold drops above, the fir trees curved wings. I told myself that no one had seen the world *this* way.

When I grew bored with floating, I climbed from the pool and tossed a penny over my shoulder. "Arthur! Hey, Arthur! I bet I can find it in less than a minute!"

Not that my brother ever would time me. Not that he ever

paid attention. Like most children, I equated attention with love. But my brother thought the highest form of attention a brother could bestow was relentless correction. And because he did love me, he feared that I would become what he most hated: a woman who thought she was special. He classified people according to whether they demanded special treatment – "Waiter, make sure the fish has no bones!" "I want colder water!" "Artie, get me a fork whose tines aren't bent!" – or whether they sat quietly and ate what they were given. I knew I couldn't please him. From my orange hair to my feet, whose nails I painted red, I was too loud, too brash. But praise is most precious when given by those who dispense it most rarely. If my brother had commended me for finding that penny, I might have become a pearl diver. And when I rose from the depths and saw his turned head, I felt cheaper than the coppery coin in my fist. With no special talents, I must be the same as every other girl, as one drop of water is exactly like the other drops. This scared me so profoundly I had no other choice but to turn to the staff, who paid me attention because my last name was Appelbaum, a fact I tried hard to forget.

I climbed from the pool and shouted insults at the busboys until two of them grabbed me by the ankles and the wrists and – one, two, *three* – tossed me in the depths so water rose from the pool and flattened the hairdos of the women playing cards.

"Lucy! Don't splash!"

To protect their bouffants these women wore kerchiefs with hundreds of petals or tall hats whose filaments waved in the wind like the tentacles of spiny sea creatures. Some women played canasta, tapping spiky heels as they waited for their cards. (Their legs were shot blue, like the celery stalks my teacher had propped in an inkwell the year before, in third grade.) Other women played mahjongg – fast fingers, fast tongues, the ivory tiles clicking: "Two bam," "Red," "Two dot."

But if I drew too near their table, one of these women would grab me by the shoulders, exclaiming *zise mammele tayere* – sweet, dear little mother! – while the other women chimed:

"What bottle did that red hair come from!"

"Someone is going to wake up and find herself with a lovely little shape any day now!"

I was desperate to grow up, but the crêpe-papier skin hanging from their necks made me queasy, and I had to admit that growing up didn't stop at fifteen, or even at my parents' age, but kept on and on until you began to grow *down,* the women's spines curving until they were shorter than I was.

My only hope that old age needn't be frightening came from the Feidels. Each afternoon they appeared at the pool, Shirley in a trim maroon one-piece, Nathan in trunks neither baggy nor too tight. Shirley had the figure of a much younger woman, with smooth skin and long white hair, which she wore in a bun. Nathan had a thick square-cut silver mustache, a cleft chin and a nose that came straight from his brow. He and his wife would step down the ladders on opposite sides of the pool and, without hesitation, even on the chilliest day, slip into the water and swim toward one another, pass and keep swimming, twenty laps in counterpoint, strong rhythmic strokes, as the numbers on their wrists, written in an ink that never washed off, rose from the water again and again.

When they finished their swim, Nathan and Shirley climbed from the pool. Nathan draped his wife's shoulders with a thick purple towel they must have brought from home since the towels at the Eden were threadbare and white. Then Nat kissed his wife. No parts of their bodies touched except their lips, but I felt so unsettled that after they had gone I was attracted more strongly than ever to the waiters sunning on the deck.

An outsider might have thought the boys were sleeping, but I knew that they were actually using the sun's rays to recharge their batteries. How else could they find the energy to work seven days a week: out of bed at six to get ready for breakfast, clear the tables, serve lunch, set up for the next meal, a few hours' break before serving dinner, which took until eleven-thirty to clear? The steel trays they brandished might have been shields for an army of knights. Loaded with dishes, such a tray couldn't be lifted by two ordinary men. But a waiter could swing a tray to his shoulder and dart between the tables so the steaming soup flew above the heads of the indifferent diners. I didn't think it fair that the guests, who did no work, should lounge on cushioned chairs while the staff were forced to lie on the concrete deck. When I ran the Eden – and I never doubted that I would – things would be fair.

I stood above Herbie, the knight I loved best, Sir Herbie the Scrub-brush, bristling with black hairs. Beside him lay Larry, with a pink hairless chest and two tiny nipples like pink candy dots, and Steve, Michael, Bruce, all of them sleeping so soundly that I almost regretted what I had to do.

Almost. Not quite. The night before, the busboys had finished work early and decided to hitch-hike to town for ice cream. When I begged to go with them, Herbie said, "Loose, you won't miss much. The waitress at HoJo's will bring us our sundaes. We'll try to imagine what she looks like without that hair net, we'll pass out in our butterscotch syrup, and when the place closes, we'll get up and crawl home."

So why didn't they stay at the Eden, with me, and go to sleep early?

"We have to, that's all." He rubbed the bristles on his chin. "When guys get together, they do certain things. Maybe those things aren't so great. But it's worse for a person to be alone."

This I understood. When no one was watching me, I felt as if my life were a movie projected on thin air.

I scooped icy water from the pool, then uncupped my hands above Herbie's belly. Though he tightened his muscles, his eyes remained shut. I hated myself, but I had to keep going.

The third scoop of water made Herbie reach out and pass me on to Larry, who, in his sleep, passed me on to Steve, who passed me on to Michael, who passed me on to Bruce, whose arms closed around me, a carnivorous plant with a fly in its leaves. I squealed and squirmed with pleasure, flesh to hot flesh, until I heard a whistle.

"Stop that!" Arthur commanded from his lounge near the diving board. "Don't pester them, Lucy. Go and play with your dolls."

His voice stung as smartly as if he had squirted chlorine in my eyes. I told myself again that my brother didn't hate me, he hated the hotel. He was always complaining that the Eden was ruining his health and souring "his chances." He couldn't take time off to visit his roommate from his first year at Princeton, though this roommate's family owned a house at a place called Martha's Vineyard. No, Arthur was just too tired to let his love show. Seeing him now, twisting to massage his own knotted back, it came to me that he truly did need me.

I freed myself from Bruce, who immediately rolled over and dropped back to sleep. I took a few steps toward Arthur. I would rub his back and tell him the jokes that Maxxie Fox, the Eden's new comedian, had taught me the day before. *I was wrong*, he would say. *The minute you touched me, the pain disappeared.*

I had just reached the diving board when Linda Brush scooted past and settled on the lounge right next to Arthur. How could he stand to have her that near? Linda Brush was one of the middle-aged mothers who brought their children to the Eden for two or three months, leaving their husbands to work and sweat in New York. Her hair was a shiny black ball; a person could poke two fingers in those black-circled eyes, a thumb in that round mouth, and send that head rolling. She wore a two-piece bathing suit much like my own, except black. A scar crawled down her belly. I grew ill, thinking where that scar led and how the two Brush twins had lived in that stomach until the doctor slit it open and lifted them out.

The twins were identical. As a younger child I had thought this meant they were alike not only on the surface but the same through and through. I couldn't see them lying next to each other without feeling compelled to draw a blanket over one baby's face. Having a twin cheapened your worth; for all anyone could tell, your twin was the real you and you were the fake.

As the Brush twins grew older, I saw, to my relief, that they weren't the same. Samuel, the younger twin, followed Mitchell wherever he went, so dreamy and slow he seemed to be mocking Mitchell the way Arthur mocked me, repeating everything I said with a retarded child's slur. ("Stop doing that!" I would scream, and Arthur, thick tongued, would mimic "thtop doing that.") For as long as I knew him, Sam Brush retained an infant's blank face, whereas even by six Mitchell had hardened his features, sharpened his gaze, as though to help people tell them apart. Today, he was pressing a scalloped bottle cap into Sam's bare arm, as though cutting dough for cookies. Sam sat there and smiled.

Their mother didn't notice. She was squeezing white lotion across my brother's chest, teasing him about his dark skin and kinky hair. "Why, if Ah didn't know bet-tah, Ah'd think one of the Appelbahms had slept with they-ah dah-kies."

Why didn't my brother slap her? He just grunted, and I saw Linda slip her pink nails beneath the waistband of his trunks.

I jumped in the water and started swimming. I wouldn't touch the bottom or the sides. At four o'clock, my mother came to the pool for her one-hour break between managing the reception desk and managing the dining room. She stood beside the water in her rumpled yellow housedress.

"You're chattering like a skeleton," she said.

"Oh, Mom, how can a skeleton chatter? A skeleton is *dead*."

"And you will be, too, if you catch pneumonia."

I swam to the shallow end and climbed the steps as slowly as it is possible to climb steps.

"Quick! Go and change! If you stay in a damp suit you'll end up a cripple."

I rolled my eyes. "How could a damp suit – "

"Sylvia Siskind's daughter got polio from just a quick dip. Of course, that was a public pool. But we don't have to ask for trouble by walking around in damp suits."

I had no intention of changing to dry clothes. I would get a snack. By the time I returned to the pool, my mother would have left or forgotten her order. I hitched up my bottoms, marched across the lawn and right through the lobby, defying a sign that said NO WET SUITS, then I marched out the side door and up to a window in a ramshackle booth called The Concession.

"The usual," I said.

Mrs. Grieben, the concessionaire and sister of the cook, who was also Mrs. Grieben, since the sisters had married brothers, reached one flabby arm into the freezer and brought out a chocolate-covered marshmallow stick so frigid it hurt my teeth to bite it. Then she opened the cooler.

"Orange hair, orange soda," Mrs. Grieben said sagely, as if God had decreed that dark-haired children must drink Coke and blond ones cream soda.

The Orange Crush tasted like summer itself. I gulped half without stopping.

"Who gave you that *chazeray!*"

The voice made the bottle shake in my hand.

"Who gave you that pig food!" My grandmother raised a fist at Mrs. Grieben. "You want her to get fat as a pig, as a *chazer* like you?"

"You don't call me pig!"

"Pig! *Chazer!* Pig!" Nana whirled. "And you! Don't run around barefoot!" She said this in Yiddish – *gey nit arum borves* – and I wanted to laugh because this last word sounded like "boobas," but I knew what was coming.

"You go without shoes, your feet get stepped on!"

I jumped back in time to prevent Nana's heel from grinding my toes. As far as I could tell, this was the only real risk of not wearing shoes.

Nearly everyone I knew was terrified of Nana. As a toddler, Arthur had picked up a block and hurled it at her. He missed; she retrieved it and hurled it right back. Though the block split his scalp, Arthur was too stunned to cry, even when the doctor was stitching shut the wound.

My grandmother couldn't hear a word of bad news my parents shouted in her ear, but let an enemy whisper a disparaging word across the hotel and Nana would scream: "You should burn in Gehenna for such a lie!"

She didn't speak, she ranted, punctuating her sentences with goaty snorts – *naah, naah* – which made me believe this was how she had come to be called Nana in the first place.

"Don't run with that bottle in your mouth, you might trip, naah, naah, you'll knock your teeth out."

"I don't *have* any teeth."

But even when confronted with the gaping truth, my grandmother wouldn't relent. "Stay here until you're finished, naah. You don't walk, you can't fall."

I guzzled my soda and set the bottle on the counter. "I don't think you look like a pig," I assured Mrs. Grieben, then ran back to the pool.

What luck! My mother was playing canasta. I slipped quietly down the steps, but the waves spread like radar.

"Lucy, you'll get cramps!" She turned in her chair. "You need to wait an hour after eating, at least."

"But I only ate soda!"

"Then why is your face covered with chocolate?" She unrolled a tissue from her sleeve. "Here, spit."

I refused; she spit for me, scrubbing my cheeks and the skin under my nose until I could smell my mother's sour saliva. I squirmed free. Had Herbie and the other boys witnessed my shame? No, they had already left to set up for dinner.

"Come on, Mom," I pleaded. "Just a little while? Can I?" I was whining, I knew, but the sun already was touching the hill behind the Eden. "Now? Can I? Please?"

My mother's eyes strayed to the new hand of cards on the table. The other women's heels were tapping the deck. "Oh, all right. Just don't go into the deep end."

"I promise," I said. But even before she had played her first card I had ducked beneath the floats and was heading toward the marker that proclaimed 7 FEET.

The sunbathers were the first to pack up. The pinochle players stubbed out their stogies and hectored their wives into bidding their last hands. The canasta games ended. My mother stood and stretched. She saw me in the water. "Lucy, come out of there this instant!"

"Just one more lap."

"I can't stand here arguing."

Though Nana ruled the kitchen and my father served as her steward, my mother's job was hardest since she mixed with the guests, scurrying from table to table and enduring their complaints about cold soup and spoiled liver. They had paid a flat sum, which earned them the right to gobble all they could, three meals a day. Most of them tried to wolf down enough food to recoup their investment, and, if they could, accumulate interest.

"You're old enough to understand," my mother said. "Even with all our work . . . The prices these days! And how can we pay off our debts if we're only a quarter full? What will your father do, at his age . . . All I ask is, please, don't do so much to aggravate me."

The sadness in her voice made me want to comfort my mother. But before I could climb out, she said, "What's the use?" and hurried off.

Other than the Brush twins, their mother and Arthur, only my grandfather remained at the pool. He lay on a special wheeled lounge chair beneath an afghan his wife had crocheted, the yarn fuchsia, red and orange, a neon advertisement of his helplessness. I liked to sit beside him and tell him the events of my day. My grandfather never teased me. He never was called away to attend to a crisis. I would stretch out beside him and lie without moving to see what it felt like. Arthur, I knew, should already have rolled Grandpa Abe to the kitchen so someone could feed him dinner. Instead, my brother turned his recliner so he and Linda Brush could follow the last rays of the sun.

"I've got to go," he said blandly.

"Your busboy can do what needs doing. You work too hard, Artie. You don't want to die young."

I dove underwater. The surface squirmed with pink and red lines. *I'm a magic fish,* I thought, and swam up to eat the worms, closing my fish lips over every squiggle. When the worms disappeared, I decided to swim the length of the pool one more time and get out. I swam to the deep end, and on my way back was startled to find that someone had joined me. With the sunlight so weak and my eyesight so blurry from all that chlorine, all I could make out was the person's shape. He was smaller than I was, unless this was a trick of the way the bottom slanted.

Whoever it was, he could hold his breath longer than I could. I came up for air. My head and lungs ached, but I dove down again to see who could beat me at this skill that I had been practicing for so many years.

When I saw the boy's face, I was drained of jealousy. *Your lips are blue,* my mother said when I stayed in the pool too long, and I thought that she was lying, but this boy was so blue he blended with the water. I couldn't pull him up so I dragged him by his shorts. These began to come off, but my feet touched the bottom.

I burst to the surface. "Arthur!" I shouted.

I knew he would come running. I would get all the attention I had ever wanted, though even in that instant I was aware it wouldn't last.

He was there, beside me. He grabbed Sam from my arms – Arthur seemed to leap from the water without touching the wall, and when he laid the boy on the deck I could see that Sam was covered with angry red circles, as if a fish with teeth had sucked him all over. I remembered the bottle cap. "Mitchell," I said.

Their mother was shrieking. Arthur pushed me away and bent over Sam, one dark palm to the boy's thin blue chest, the hand rising each time Arthur blew in the boy's mouth, though whenever Arthur paused the hand would just lie there. "Get help!" he yelled. "An ambulance!"

If I thought anything at that moment, I thought I could help Sam more by staying than by going. Hadn't I found him and dragged him to safety? If no one else had been there, wouldn't I be the one blowing in his mouth? I tried to remember a prayer from my Old Testament, but all I could think of was, "Please, let Sam live."

"Goddamn it, Lucy!"

Arthur's voice set me moving, but it didn't stop my praying, and ten minutes later, when the ambulance pulled up, Linda Brush was still shrieking and I was still pleading, "God, let him live."

The volunteers carried Sam on a stretcher as Arthur walked beside them, lips pressed to Sam's. Linda Brush ran after them. She tripped on my flip-flops, cursed and got up. I saw blood on her knees. She and Arthur, half-naked, climbed into our Pontiac and followed the ambulance. Only when the siren had died in the distance was I able to stop praying. I saw my mother and Nana standing at the edge of the road, gesturing crazily at each other.

I walked to my grandfather's lounge. I had been told that he couldn't move, but one of his feet had poked free of the afghan. The ankle was bare, the foot itself covered by a brown backless slipper. I knew that he had a "problem with sugar" and somehow had lost two toes to this problem. I had always wanted to sneak a look at the stumps, but I tucked his leg beneath the afghan.

It came to me that my grandfather must have seen Sam fall into the pool. What did that feel like, straining so hard and not being able to do more than wiggle a foot? My grandfather seemed so helpless I climbed on his lounge and pulled the blanket over us both.

I heard my name. "Lucy!" Then, even more loudly: "Lucy, where are you?" A sharp whistle followed, and more notes, tu-tu-tu-tu.

My mother said, "No, Ma, leave the boy. No. Stop that."

I peeked from the blanket. Nana was holding Mitchell Brush high above the sidewalk, trying to shake the whistle from his clenched mouth.

"Tu-tu-tu-tu."

Nana shook him sharply and the whistle went flying. Mitchell's face was contorted, but he wouldn't cry.

"Stop, Ma, you'll snap something, you'll kill him."

I laid my head against my grandfather's chest. He murmured *there, there,* unless this was only the rumbling of his stomach, and I could feel his cold fingers tracing a message of love on my back.

My mother set the receiver in its cradle as tenderly as if this were Sam Brush himself, safe now in bed.

"He started to breathe in the ambulance," she told Mamie Goshgarian, the Eden's social director. The guests were occupied with dinner. Light broke through the trees surround-

ing the lobby windows; fragments glanced from brass ash-
trays and slid to the floor like panting gold birds. Most
evenings at this time I was gratefully calm, limp from my
hours swimming in the pool, lulled by the sense that I was
still floating on my back, rocked by small waves, and as
much as I begged to stay up for the show, I looked forward
to sleep.

But tonight I would sooner have climbed in my grave than
let the day end. When I noticed Mamie and my mother sneak-
ing from the dining room, I followed them to the small dusty
office behind the front desk. I stood in the doorway while my
mother called the hospital, hand cupped around the receiver in
case the news wasn't good.

But Sam was alive! He had been dead, then I saved him. I
imagined him sitting up in bed watching cartoons and smiling
the smile that reminded me of the M&M's face on a white-
frosted cupcake.

"Thank God!" Mamie sighed, swaying so hard the head of
her fox boa wagged too.

"Imagine the lawsuit that woman could have brought if the
boy had passed on!" My mother spit – *poo, poo, poo* – so the
Powers of Darkness wouldn't strike Sam dead even now.
"Arthur on the lounge chair with that *tayere tsatske*, not watching . . . Of course, *she* wasn't watching either, but she still would
have sued. As it is, I only hope our policy covers – "

"Don't worry, Ruthele. That insurance adjuster . . . the
Irisher who looks like Frank Sinatra? What's his name, Kilcoin?
He'll come out to see her." The fox seemed to wink. "He'll get
her to settle for *pishochs*, for his sake."

"Shush, Mamie, shush. *Kleyne kinder hobn groyse oyern.*" She
tilted her head in my direction.

How could she call me a child? How, when I had rescued
Sam? It occurred to me then that no one but my brother had
witnessed my miracle, unless Grandpa Abe counted.

"Mom? Did you know I was the one who found Sam in the pool?"

My mother regarded me as though I were making this up.

"It's true! First I pulled him out, and then I ran and got you to call the ambulance." I didn't add that my prayers convinced God to spare Sam, sensing this would throw my whole case in doubt.

"You did? Are you sure?"

"Ask Arthur!"

My mother jerked her head as if the truth slapped her. "You mean *he* didn't? I thought . . . Why, if that's true, I guess you did save him, honey."

A sense of completion came over me, so satisfying that even today, so many years later, it is the standard by which I judge what I lack. I had saved a boy's life. If it weren't for me, Sam Brush would be lying in a hole in the ground. Bringing him back to life was the sign I had been seeking. The Book of Lucy would take its place beside the Books of Esther and Ruth. I thought of the Purim play at the synagogue and how I had been given a non-speaking role as one of Vashti's harem-mates. In a rush of inspiration such as we're given only when we're young, I decided to act out The Rescue of Samuel for the talent show that night.

Until then I hadn't been allowed to take part. I couldn't tap dance or sing or play the piano. I only could repeat the dirty jokes I had learned from the comics. But even those jokes would have been more entertaining than Izzy Mornofsky's off-key rendition of the song he announced as "'Belly High,' the pregnant love story of a *sheyne meydel* from the South Pacific."

I began to ask my mother if I could go on after Mamie, but she took me around and kissed me and asked me to please promise that I wouldn't *ever* try to save anyone else.

I almost was too shocked to ask her why not.

"Honey, it's this way. A person in the water, he doesn't think clear. He might grab your throat and pull you down."

Why did my mother view any act of glory as a foolish mistake? So what if I *had* drowned? I imagined the mourners heaping praise on a girl who had sacrificed her life so another might live.

"You still haven't promised." She pressed my head between her hands.

"I won't!" I broke free. "I'm glad I saved Sam!"

"Of course you are, *bubele!*" This came from Mamie, in a singsong that welled from the depths of her bosom. "And I'm glad you saved him so quick. A brain-damaged child is *tsuris* I wouldn't wish on any mother. Not that my Lennie isn't also a blessing." .

Mamie's son, Lennie, had white skin, pink eyes, hair like spun glass and six toes on his left foot. Even so, I didn't pity him: his talents earned him the right to appear in the show. After his mother's act he would bounce from the wings and recite old routines from Marx Brothers movies. He knew every line, could mimic each brother. But he said their lines deadpan, like the children in my class who didn't understand the words they were reading. "You can't fool-a me," Lennie would intone in a flat Italian accent. "There ain't-a no sanity clause."

"He's a blessing," Mamie went on, "but, to be frank, he is also a heartache. Only this morning – "

The fur on Mamie's boa stood on end. A maelstrom of air blew into the office and with it came Nana, her apron as gory as if she had slaughtered an ox.

"*Nu, vos macht der narele?*" So, how's the little fool?

On the back of an envelope my mother printed: ALIVE. BRAIN OKAY.

"Naah, how could they tell?" My grandmother crumpled the envelope and threw it in the trash as disdainfully as if she were thereby discarding the entire Brush family.

I wasn't permitted to act out Sam's rescue but was forced to stand in the shadows at the back of the casino while my mother announced that Sam would be returning to the Eden next day, her tone reassuring, as if otherwise the guests might think that he had checked out because he didn't like the food. She gave no details. As she later told Mamie, "What they don't know can't hurt us." She forbade me to tell anyone anything, except for my father, who had praised me so extravagantly for so many years he seemed to have no superlatives left. "Haven't I always said you swim like a fish?" And since this was true – he *had* always said it – I couldn't take much pride in hearing it now.

As I lay in bed that night, I thought about how the Pharaoh hadn't believed Moses until he repeated his wonders ten times. I tried to recall the exact prayer I had uttered over Sam's corpse, but nothing came to mind. The magic, I decided, didn't lie in the words, but in my personal goodness and favor with God.

I awoke early the next morning and searched for a new corpse on which to test this hypothesis. I was helping Nana chop the heads from several dozen whitefish when I saw one head move. I watched as a rat dragged off its prize, the shiny golden fish-head bouncing across the floor. I touched Nana's wrist and pointed. She leapt from her stool and booted the rat so it flew through the gaping hole in the screen door. I ran out and stood over the rat's body. Concentrating mightily, I tried to revive the rat with the force of my soul. But its back remained twisted, its pointy-toothed grin a sarcastic jibe at my failure.

A few hours later I tried my powers again, on a more pleasant animal. Three kettles were boiling on the stove – two filled with *flanken,* one with a tongue. I sang to these pots. The ribs and the tongue would rise with the steam. I conjured the *kishke* Mrs. Grieben had stuffed with bread crumbs for dinner. The intestines would slither from the counter and float beside the ribs; the organs and bones would flesh themselves out, acquire skin, hooves, a tail. The cow would start mooing, then lick my hand with its grainy tongue.

When none of this happened, I decided that my powers

worked only on humans, and only on humans no more than half-dead. I found Grandpa Abe in his rocker. "God, let him move," I chanted. "God, let him speak."

My grandfather blinked. I stared at his hands until my vision blurred. Then I made myself see what I wanted to see: I saw his hands move.

That's when I fled, seized by the terror I would have felt if a mummy stretched out its hand. When I dared reclimb the porch, nothing moved except the squares of the afghan, which stretched with each breath.

All afternoon I moped around the camp house. What good was being chosen if no one believed you, if no one saw what you had done?

I jumped up. That was it. I would seek out my brother and make him apologize. I would make him say thanks. If it weren't for me, Arthur would have had Sam's death on his conscience.

I looked first in the dining room, where the busboys were setting up for dinner, juggling glassware and china and snapping white tablecloths like a troupe of magicians.

"Hey, Goosegirl." Herbie flicked a clean saucer on the table. "Want to help?"

"Oh, Herbie, I'd love to. But I've got to find Arthur."

"I think he's sick, Juicy. He didn't insult a single guest at lunch. Then he told me he wanted to be by himself." Herbie flipped his last fork, which landed in the middle of the last empty napkin. "Sure I couldn't tempt you into filling some sugar bowls?"

What wouldn't I have given on an ordinary night to be granted this task? "Do you think he's in the Horseshoe?"

Herbie considered a moment. "That seems a good guess." He hoisted a bus box and exited as gracefully as if he were carrying a ballerina offstage.

My brother, I was sure, wasn't really sick. He was sulking because I had proved myself to be a better lifeguard than he was. If only he conceded this, I wouldn't rub it in.

I skipped to the Horseshoe, an unpainted building named for its shape, though it might just as easily have been named for its smell. The roof leaked. The floor was bare cement. There was only one toilet for twenty-four boys. Arthur could have slept in the bungalow with us – I always had assumed he slept here because the Horseshoe was the only place at the Eden I didn't like to come, but now, stepping over the threshold, hand to my nose, I understood dimly that he slept here because to work beside Herbie and the other boys all day, then sleep in our bungalow, would have been wrong. I loved him for this. I would have slept here myself, but, since I couldn't, I was glad Arthur did. How could my parents make *anyone* sleep here – even Cyrus, the dish washer, who lay snoring on his cot, a square-bottomed bottle of Manischewitz cradled in one arm? I tiptoed around Cyrus, toward the one bed whose horsehair blanket was smooth.

Pinned to Arthur's pillow by a kitchen knife was a sheet of the Eden's letterhead, so brittle with age it gave me the sense that my brother's departure was already long past. I would never get to tell him I knew why he slept here.

"I hope this shit hole burns down," was all the note said. "Your loving heir, Arthur."

When my mother read the note, she feared that her only son had enlisted in the Army and would die at the hands of a Jew-hating sergeant. After a postcard informed her that Arthur was sunning himself on the shores of Martha's Vineyard, she denounced him for leaving the Eden without a headwaiter at the height of the season.

Knowing no Martha except Martha Washington and never having seen a vineyard except in my illustrated Old Testament,

I thought that my brother had gone to a place as noble and historical as America itself and even more holy than the wine groves of Noah. I was jealous, and lonely, and certain that he had left only to deny me the praise I deserved.

I wanted him back. Not that I longed for his insults. I was sure, from reading fairy tales, that if someone ran away he must return changed. I hadn't yet learned you could travel the earth and remain the same person you had been before you left, or you might remain at home and change into someone your mother didn't know.

The day after the accident the pool remained closed, the pump having choked on insects and leaves that my brother hadn't been there to skim. At another hotel, the handyman would have been ordered to fix it. At the Eden, Mr. Jefferson was politely requested to diagnose the pump's ailment and undertake its treatment. So much dignity and art did he bring to his work that no one dared to call him a bimmie – the word used for Cyrus and the other drunks and derelicts imported from the Bowery to staff the hotels – and only my grandmother dared to call Mr. Jefferson a *shvartzer,* a word that I had recently come to suspect meant worse things than "black."

How much worse I didn't know. Yiddish seemed less like a language than a code adults had devised to safeguard the secrets that made them adults. As soon as I thought I understood a word, its meaning would change. How could *shvartzer* mean a man who didn't like to work, and a man who worked hard at unpleasant tasks most white people were too lazy to do? How could it mean a man to be pitied because he lived in a slum, and a man to be spurned because he would dirty whatever apartment he set foot in; a man like a Jew in some way that made him more admirable than any white *goy,* yet a man who would never be like a Jew because he didn't enjoy reading?

Once something was named it should stay named, I thought. In English, a chair always was a chair. "Black" meant black. "Jew" meant Jew. (I later found out that English seemed pure only because I was young when I learned it. When I finally lost my innocence, English did too.) Above all, I believed that only one person should have any one name. I couldn't bear to think another Lucy Appelbaum might someday turn up. My father and mother were Julius and Ruth Appelbaum, the only ones on earth. And Mr. Jefferson was Mr. Jefferson, nothing more, nothing less than this man who stood before me in his white short-sleeved shirt, pressed khaki pants and black oxfords so shiny that when I looked down, two Lucy Appelbaums stared up from his toes.

He had been employed at the Eden since I was four. My parents often blessed the day he had stepped off the bus at the employment agency in Monticello. If the Eden looked no better for all his labors, this was only because my grandmother wouldn't pay for new materials but forced Mr. Jefferson to scavenge from the ruins of our competitors, or to sacrifice the less vital parts of the Eden.

Mr. Jefferson hitched up his trousers, got down on all fours and crawled into the pump house. When he backed out again he was shaking his head. "Can't do miracles," he told my mother. "I'm afraid, Mrs. A., we don't have another choice but to buy a new pump."

My mother kneaded her hands. "Mr. Jefferson, you know we can't afford to spend that kind of money."

He gave in so quickly it was clear that he had said this only for form. Maybe, he said, he could salvage the pump and filter with parts from an old vacuum cleaner.

"There's no other way?"

He assured her there wasn't. Head hanging low, my mother waddled off to get one.

Mr. Jefferson, meanwhile, opened his toolbox, which was so

large and filled with so many wonderful things that I wouldn't have been startled if he had brought out a helper – some genie, perhaps, or a young girl like me. But he removed only a handful of valves, which he popped in his mouth.

I gathered the courage to say his name.

"Mmm?" he replied, too courteous to talk with a mouth full of hardware.

I asked if he thought I could be his assistant.

"Mmm," he said. "Mmm-mm."

Mr. Jefferson never took the time from his work to listen to my jokes or my imitations of the guests. Everyone else seemed part of my audience; Mr. Jefferson I knew to be a performer himself. He didn't seem to care what anyone thought of his performance, least of all me, but sometimes he winked, or spoke to me so seriously it was clear that he didn't regard me as just any child. This was our bond: we each knew the other was not what the world took him or her to be. Oh, my parents conceded that Mr. Jefferson was extraordinary, but only as a handyman, while I suspected him to be extraordinary in some hidden way we couldn't guess.

My mother reappeared, tugging the Electrolux by its hose as a clown might lead an elephant. Mr. Jefferson met her halfway; in his long, knotted arms, the elephant shrank to a dachshund. He laid it in the grass, screwed off its head, then lifted out the various steel and mesh organs while my mother stood above him, clucking her tongue.

"Excuse me," she said, "I can't bear to watch. That poor machine is older than I am."

After she had gone, Mr. Jefferson again got down on all fours and went to work in the pump house. "Lucy, if you would please pass those pliers, if it's not an inconvenience? And perhaps hold that light?"

I grabbed the pliers and flashlight and crawled in beside him. The air was warm and stuffy. We were so close I smelled him – a spicy scent like the cinnamon coffee-cake the baker left overnight in the pantry to cool.

"Lucy? Could you keep that light steady?"

His fingers danced in the beam. At first I was confident. How could he fail? Then I slowly lost faith. "You don't think the pool will have to stay closed, do you?"

"Remember," he said, his mouth free of valves, "the race doesn't always go to the swift."

"It doesn't?"

"Not when it matters. Now, pass me that wrench."

A nudge here, some oil . . . The pump started humming.

"Not bad. Not bad." We backed into the sunlight. He rubbed the dirt from his palms, pink as smoked salmon. "I do believe, Lucy, we have brought the dead back to life."

Brought back the dead! Was this some sign that he knew?

He stood and stretched, whistling a flat tuneless song. His forehead was shaded by the visor of his cap, but his broad cheeks and chin caught the sunlight and glowed. His hair was so short it could have been painted, though only by someone as careful as he. I didn't like his nose – it was squashed, like my own – but I knew that he was handsome. (If only the guests wouldn't say this so often, their too-kindly voices hinting surprise.) I always had assumed Mr. Jefferson's age to be roughly my parents', but now, as he packed his tools in his toolbox, I saw that he wasn't much older than Arthur.

"Mr. Jefferson?" I said. "Do you ever go swimming?"

His whistling stopped. "I am afraid that I have never had the opportunity to receive instruction in that particular activity."

"I can swim," I told him. (*Goodie for you,* I heard my brother's voice mock.)

"I do believe I have seen evidence of your buoyancy," he said.

"Did you know I'm going to be the new lifeguard?" (*Sure you are,* Arthur chided. *Go away,* I told him, then realized with a pang that he already had.)

"Well, well." Mr. Jefferson's eyebrows climbed above the black rims of his glasses. "Such a young person . . . But I suppose that you do have impressive credentials."

I studied his face to make sure that he'd been serious, though the longer I stared the less certain I was. With the sun bright behind him, his face was so black it seemed more like a mask, the way Lennie Goshgarian's porcelain-white skin made him seem like a doll. But Lennie's mask seemed to have no one behind it, while the handyman's mask was more like the dark glasses a movie star might wear to disguise who he was.

I must have made him uncomfortable, staring that long. He gave me a look that implied *I* was the one who had done something wrong.

"Got to be going." He locked his toolbox. "Perhaps you'll assist me in some future endeavor. If you aren't preoccupied with your new responsibilities, that is."

"Endeavor"? Did he mean that he needed my help? I wanted to ask when this mission might start, but I was stopped by the idea that a man with a toolbox under his left arm and a butchered Electrolux under his right arm wouldn't want to stand talking, an observation that wouldn't have given me pause a few minutes earlier. Maybe he wouldn't be so busy that night. After work. In his shack.

No. I couldn't do that. Even to consider the possibility made me feel daring. As far as I knew, no one had ever visited Mr. Jefferson's home.

"See you later." He winked.

But then, maybe no one had ever been asked.

The cabin was white, with a border of zinnias. It had no mailbox or bell, nothing to indicate who might live inside. I am ashamed to remember I once was the girl who knocked on that door. Was I ever so callous? Was I truly that brave? I try to

imagine what my life would be like – what *his* life would be –
if I had turned and run away before the door opened.

"Yes?" he said. "Yes?"

I had gone there assuming he would say that he'd been
waiting and usher me in.

"You've come to – ?"

I moistened my mouth. "To visit," I said.

"To visit," he repeated. "And by 'visit' you mean to enter my
home at my behest. By 'visit' you do *not* mean to enter my quarters and foist your companionship upon your employee as
though he had no right to refuse?"

For the first time since I had learned how to speak, I could
not.

"And you do not think of me as your own Uncle Remus,
only too glad to entertain missy with a quaint bedtime tale? You
haven't been reading a popular novel about a man of my hue
who lives in a structure much like my own? You do not, in
other words, fancy yourself as my own Little Eva?"

It struck me, though dimly, that Mr. Jefferson was using
English as my parents used Yiddish, to guard against something too private for a child to get near. And what could have
made a child more determined to learn what it was?

"Long as *that's* understood." He stepped back. "Would you
care to come in?"

The other rooms at the Eden had dull, splintery floors, but
the floor in Mr. Jefferson's cabin was a smooth honey-brown.
In the center stood a table with two harp-backed chairs; beside
the table, a bed, its white sheets stretched taut (when I thought
of him sleeping, I saw him lying atop those sheets in his
starched khaki trousers, that white shirt, those black oxfords,
that flat, visored cap). One corner of the room was boxed in behind a red velvet swath from the curtain in the casino; the base
of a toilet showed beneath the hem like the feet of a comic waiting for his cue.

The rest of the cabin was lined with bookshelves. A book with gilt-edge pages lay open on the table, the ink like smashed ants. Beside the book stood a teapot and a cup of steaming tea.

Mr. Jefferson sat backwards on one chair and offered me the other. I perched on the edge. My spine, which had never obeyed Nana's jabs, snapped straight unbidden. I tucked my hands on my lap.

"As you are my visitor," he said, "it is my duty, nay, my pleasure, to offer refreshments. A cup of tea, hmm?"

"No thank you," I said, curious to taste a grown-up beverage like tea, but afraid to be a bother so he wouldn't ask me back.

"Well then, conversation?"

I nodded, but left the first word to him.

"Perhaps you would like to help me make sense of this book I was reading when you came in?" He pointed to the book. "Rabbi Chananya used to say that if two people sit at a table together and don't discuss the Bible, why, they're nothing more than scoffers. You wouldn't care to sit among scoffers, now would you?"

I saw my brother in a robe sitting cross-legged on the ground, listening to Moses. He jammed his thumbs in his ears and wiggled his fingers. *Nyah nyah,* Arthur taunted, until, with a roar, the ground opened, thunder rumbled and he slipped into the pit.

"Rabbi Chananya used to say, two people sit down together and talk about the Bible, the Divine Presence visits them. Now wouldn't that be something, if the Lord were to honor us with His presence, hmm, Lucy?"

I thought he meant *presents*. Not toys. Something serious. "You mean, like a book?"

I saw my mistake. Mr. Jefferson laughed, but he looked so young that I was glad I had said what I'd said.

"Well then, what should we talk about? Before you knocked I was reading about Abel and Cain. Is that a good story? Would you mind if we started with Abel and Cain?"

"Yes!" I said, as if I had been waiting my entire life for someone to mention those two.

"So you do know the story?"

To anyone else I would have bragged that I knew it by heart. "I know it a little," I said.

"Then you probably know the story's about a boy who murders his brother?"

That's all he said. Then Mr. Jefferson sat there and waited. The seed of a question germinated inside me. It sent up a shoot. Then a stem. Then a bud. I had to spit that question out or I would gag on the bloom.

"Everyone is pretending nothing bad happened! Mitchell tried to kill his brother and no one will do anything about it!"

He nodded and smiled as if this connection wouldn't have occurred to him unless I brought it to his notice. Then again, his smile hinted that he had told the story in the first place to make the connection clear to me.

"And what *should* they do, Lucy? Should they send a six-year-old boy to jail? Should his mother stop loving him? Would that help, do you think?"

It might help, I thought. How could a mother keep loving a child who tried to drown his twin? But I knew not to say this.

"That boy's going to feel his sin as long as he lives. Even Cain said his punishment – to wander the earth like an outcast, like a fugitive – was too harsh to bear. So God put this little smudge on Cain's brow. And not so other people would know to torment him. God hoped people would notice that mark and redeem Cain with their mercy. You understand what mercy means?"

I ventured that it meant people shouldn't beat up Cain.

Mr. Jefferson sucked on his lips. "Means you're supposed to be so good to someone, it overcomes the bad. Means you shouldn't want any credit for doing it, either." He took aim to hammer his next nail precisely. "Good deed doesn't count, you let people know."

I couldn't keep myself from raising a quiet objection. "But I saved him! Sam was dead and I saved him!"

"Nobody knows how to raise up the dead." He cocked his fingers like a gun. "Nobody, hear? It's a sin to believe so."

His finger was directed straight at my heart. I wanted to run and hide. And to stay and be judged.

His hand dropped. "Yes, sir. Good many people would have led different lives if they'd known how to raise up the dead. Your Grandpa Abe's daddy . . . You've heard what happened to *him*?"

I had. Arthur told me. Our grandfather's father had murdered the czar of Russia, chopped off his head, put it in a suitcase and carried it to America, where the head came to rest in a cardboard box in the cellar beneath the Main House. This scared me, of course – I went down to that cellar several times a week to fetch supplies for the busboys – but the story of the murder seemed much more exciting than the stories of how and why other Jews had come to live here.

Mr. Jefferson laughed. "Part about the head isn't true, I'm sorry to say. And it wasn't exactly the czar that got killed. What I heard, your great-grandpa saw some peasant beating his horse with a axe – the handle, not the sharp part – and he grabbed away that axe and whacked it at the peasant. Except he used the sharp part. Man gets angry, he does things he wouldn't ordinarily think to do. Not that the anger lets him off. Can't undo the harm just because the man did the deed in anger."

In anger? I brooded. "It happened to Moses," I said.

"To Moses? What happened to Moses?"

"He killed someone. He got angry and he hit him. That's why he left Egypt." Seeing Mr. Jefferson so clearly impressed, I ventured to add: "It was part of God's plan."

He whistled. "Got to admit you're ahead of me there." He tapped his book. "Still haven't reached the chapter on Moses."

I craned my head to see what was written in that book. It

was printed in columns, the margins so full of scribbled words I wouldn't have known where to start reading, even if the words hadn't been in Hebrew.

"Mr. Jefferson?" I said. "Can a Negro be Jewish?"

He looked at me strangely. Shook his head. Snorted. Then he took off his glasses, laid his face on his hand, and when he looked up again he had pulled off his mask. I saw how tired he was, the effort it had cost to spin all those long words, to perform for an audience.

"Oh, child," he said wearily, "that's the *only* thing the white folks ain't ever bothered to tell a Negro he couldn't be."

I kept going back. At first he seemed wary, as if I might poke into corners and snitch what I found. But there, in that shack, I was on my best behavior, didn't pry or show off. I sat quietly and listened, spoke only when asked. And, evening by evening, Mr. Jefferson relaxed.

When I got there the teapot would be waiting on the table, and two empty cups, lemon slices wedged like miniature suns on their rims. With great ceremony he would pour out the tea. The dark, steaming liquid made me think of potions offered by dwarves to help the heroine find a ring or decipher the secret language of birds; the bitterness of the tea seemed a small price to pay for gifts such as these.

Some evenings Mr. Jefferson would read aloud a story from one of his books, and I thought I understood the moral he was teaching. Other nights, he preached to a roomful of scholars who seemed to be sitting in rows behind my chair. Not that I minded. I drank in his voice along with the tea, and together these warmed me. My own family couldn't see past the next meal – how many briskets would we need? would the Mix-Master hold out? – while Mr. Jefferson's vision extended through eons.

"You know the Hasidim?" he said. He pronounced it *Ah seed 'em.*

Of course I did. The village swarmed with Hasids all summer. Still, in this room, I was never sure what I knew. I didn't want to seem proud. "The men in black coats? The women with that thick, shiny hair?"

He laughed. "Ah-seed-ism goes deeper than coats. Deeper than wigs. What sets the Ah-seed-em apart," he sipped his tea, "is believing you can't know God only by reading about Him in some book. You've got to pray to Him. Got to dance as hard as you can until you lift yourself up and stand right there beside Him. Imagine that, Lucy. Right beside God! Got to bring so much attention and joy to each little thing – eating and drinking, even washing your hands – you make that thing holy."

He poured two more cups of tea. "Way they tell the story, God made the world twice." He lifted the teapot toward the bulb dangling from the ceiling; its blue belly gleamed. "First time, He poured all His light and His love into that world He'd created." Mr. Jefferson raised the teapot's lid; light cascaded in from the bulb. "But that first world, it was too weak. Cracked. Fell to bits."

The teapot exploded. Hot molten gold rained down upon us.

"So, you see how it happened? Sparks of God's light swirled through that dark. They swirled and kept swirling, until, one day, God decided to give it one more try. Why He did that I couldn't tell you. He could have left it as it was. But He figured He ought to try it, give it one more chance, create us a *new* world. Stronger one. Better. And that's just what He did. And those sparks, they just sort of sifted here and there, took refuge where they could. Inside the stones. Inside the people. In the beasts of the field."

Gold flakes sifted into Mr. Jefferson's upturned nostrils, into the cuffs of his pants.

"Way the Ah-seed-em tell the story is this: God wants His

sparks back. Sent all His children on this mission. You did say you wanted a mission, hmm, Lucy? Mission is this: Got to look for those sparks. Everyone you meet, every little thing you see, got to pay attention, set the spark inside free so it can fly up and join those other sparks. And when God's got His sparks back, well, He'll let us stop looking. We can all come back home."

Mr. Jefferson put down the teapot. A miracle, I thought, the new world rebuilt from its scattered blue shards. I reached out to stroke it, but under my clumsy fingers the perfect new universe turned back into a pot. Some sparks must still be missing. How long until they were found? And please, God, could I be the one to finish the job?

For many days after, I wandered the Eden stooped as a monkey, paying close attention to rocks, pine cones, nuts. I cracked each nut open, but no spark flew out. When I saw some Hasids in town, I thought: *I know what you're doing.* But the black-coated men were too forbidding to approach, and the women shook their heads, disapproving of a girl who wore a bathing suit and flip-flops in the middle of the town, all bruises and scrapes, curls springing from my head like snakes from a can. Their own girls wore dresses that reached below their knees, white stockings, polished saddle-shoes, neatly brushed hair. Those mothers pitied me the way my mother pitied Lennie.

I was certain if only I wore the right clothes, I could pass for a Hasid. Meanwhile, I would let Mr. Jefferson teach me what the Hasids believed, how they prayed, what they ate, so that when the time came I could astonish them with my knowledge. That Mr. Jefferson had learned their secrets somehow made him seem smarter and more mysterious than the Hasids themselves.

He knew everything, didn't he? I'd never before known anyone who spoke a foreign language other than Yiddish – not that Yiddish seemed foreign for anyone except a black man to speak. One night I asked Mr. Jefferson if black people had their own secret language, and he coughed and said yes, but he hadn't learned it as a child and it was too late to learn it now. He knew Hebrew. Greek. And German. I loved to draw my finger across the exotic words imprinted on the spines of his books, a Braille for the lazy. I hated to read. Reading was lonely. Better to listen as Mr. Jefferson read aloud, his full pink-brown lips releasing each rounded vowel like a coin from a purse, his skin as inviting as the richest leather binding, though I would no more have touched him than I would have presumed to touch anything he owned.

I therefore was startled when my mother's first question upon being informed by Mamie Goshgarian that her daughter had been spotted leaving the handyman's cabin was: "Lucy, did he touch you?"

When I didn't – I couldn't – answer, my mother shook my shoulders so violently that my memories rattled in my head like the silvery beads in those puzzles you shake.

"Lucy! Did he touch you!"

A tiny bead of memory dropped into place. "Yes," I said. "Once."

"Where! Tell me this instant where he touched you!"

The memory grew clear. "On my fingers. I was moving my queen, but he tapped me on my hand and I moved a different piece."

My mother loosened her grip. I wriggled my shoulders to make sure they still worked.

"That's what you do there? You play games?"

Some nights we did.

"He didn't show you pictures? Of people. People with no clothes on?"

The answer, I was sure, would get someone in trouble.

"He did! Tell me, Lucy. What kind of pictures did he show you!"

One afternoon, he had taken out a book and shown me a drawing by someone whose name I took to be "Leonard Davinsky." I told this to my mother, hoping the artist's name might ease her fears. "The man had his arms and legs in a circle. Like this." I did a few jumping jacks, the way they had taught us in gym.

"It was a man? You're sure of that?"

I thought of the bundle between all those legs. "It was a man," I said firmly.

My mother said, "Tsk. So handsome, no wife . . . We should have guessed a long time ago." She shook her head sadly. "Okay, you can visit. But don't be a nuisance. After working a long day, a man deserves a little peace."

But the last thing I wanted was my mother's permission to visit Mr. Jefferson. I had won it, I felt, by hinting that Mr. Jefferson was a cripple in some way I didn't comprehend and he therefore couldn't have touched me even if he had wanted to. Why couldn't my mother, who was able to see the germs on a glass, see the much larger truth about Mr. Jefferson?

I began to hate anyone who couldn't – or wouldn't – see him as he actually was. Some people couldn't see Mr. Jefferson at all! He would be kneeling in the flower bed and a guest would toss a candy wrapper among the neat rows of plants. "Beg pardon!" he would boom in the stage-actor's voice he had stopped using with me. "I believe you have misplaced some detritus amongst the *Viola tricolor hortensis.*" Then he would stare at the offender, smiling a smile I knew to be false, until the guest bent slowly and retrieved whatever litter he had thrown.

Other guests scolded Mr. Jefferson as though he were younger than I was.

"Haven't I told you time and time again that the sink in my room fell off the wall?" Mrs. Heffer sunk her hands in the fleshy folds at her waist. "Haven't I told you I want it back up?"

Mr. Jefferson nodded. "You certainly have apprised me of that very information. On numerous occasions."

"Well then?"

"The problem is rather a daunting one, I fear." Not only had the sink in question "dropped" from the wall, the drainpipe had snapped. This had happened twice before in rooms Mrs. Heffer occupied. "The purveyor of hardware appurtenances in town informs me that he won't have that particular part in his establishment for another few days."

This seemed to appease Mrs. Heffer. But after she left I demanded to know why Mr. Jefferson hadn't said, "Mrs. Heffer, that sink fell off the wall in your room because you got tired of waiting for the toilet in the hall and you climbed up and sat on that sink to do your business."

"I am a gentleman, Lucy. And a gentleman is nothing if he isn't discreet."

Not bound by the rules of gentility, I waited until Mrs. Heffer began filling the tub in the bathroom she shared with the other guests. While she collected her towel from her room, I dropped a spider and a centipede among the bubbles to keep her company.

But those guests who tipped their hats to Mr. Jefferson and inquired about his health, who asked his opinion about the weather or how to make their zinnias bloom as nicely as his, these guests I rewarded with fresh rolls from the bakery, extra towels for the pool, a blanket for their picnics. I bestowed most of these favors on Shirley and Nat Feidel, until the day I heard Nat trying to lure my friend to New York to manage his repair shop.

"Wake up, Jefferson! The Mountains are dying. Another few years – " Nat made a noise with his lips like the Mountains deflating. "Besides, a man with your talents ought to be his own boss. Come to the City. After I'm gone, who knows but you'll own the business."

"I'm a country boy," he said.

"So? I'll give you the key to Central Park!"

The strategy failed. But the thought that he *might* go, that nothing within my powers could keep Mr. Jefferson at the Eden if he didn't want to stay, gave me no rest. I regarded him as a treasure whose value I wanted others to appreciate but feared they might steal. As the only other people who recognized his worth, Shirley and Nat were the most likely thieves. Whenever I caught them anywhere near Mr. Jefferson, I made sure to interrupt, though Shirley and Nat ignored me as they would have ignored an ill-trained puppy at their feet. My mother said the Feidels hadn't had children because of "what happened" at the camp they had been sent to. Perhaps they acted stiffly in my presence because the sight of children brought them grief. But I don't think that likely. War or not, Shirley would have expected a girl my age to sit quietly while her elders were speaking, to play piano, read a book. If she and Nat could have chosen any child they wished, they would have chosen Mr. Jefferson. I was certain that my friend would move to New York and run Nat's repair shop. Once, I went so far as to crush some red berries and pour this elixir into Nat's tomato juice. He never got sick, but when I'm forced to remember how he finally did die, it's as if he had switched the glasses and *I'd* drunk that poison. This many years later, it still works in my blood.

Late that summer I came upon Mr. Jefferson chatting with Shirley Feidel under the old oak behind the Ranch. The chairs in which they sat were common to every Catskills hotel; with their high backs and low rear legs, the chairs resembled dogs squatting on their haunches. The oak tree stretched its limbs above their heads the way Grandpa Abe used to hold his quivering hands above my own head as he mumbled a prayer he seemed embarrassed to say: "May the Lord bless and keep you, may the Lord cause his face to shine down upon you . . ."

They were speaking a language like Yiddish, but rougher.

Shirley chanted a poem. Mr. Jefferson joined her. Shirley patted his knee; seeing her hand on his leg made me jump. Then she reached in her straw bag. "*Ein Geschenk,*" she said.

He took the book. "*Danke,*" he said, and this made me furious. Why couldn't he say "thanks" like any normal person?

That evening in his cabin I spilled tea on the book. "I'm sorry," I said.

"No. I don't think you are."

I didn't know the name of the feeling that made me shout: "I hate her! I hate both of them!"

But he knew the name. "Can you really be jealous of what little I have?"

I felt ugly and small, and I couldn't find the words to explain that I wasn't jealous of his gift as much as I envied Shirley for having something that he wanted. Already I had guessed I would probably disappoint him. He was trying to teach me some feat I would never be agile enough to perform. How could he think that other Lucy Appelbaum – wiser, more generous, more humble and kind – could truly be me if I needed to struggle so hard to be her?

As I grew older, I started to wonder how he endured the life of a recluse. In winter, when my family moved back to town, my parents paid Mr. Jefferson to keep the Eden's pipes from freezing and chase out the vagrants who broke into rooms and fell asleep with their cigarettes lit. A few times a month he walked to town for groceries, but his only other diversion was crossing the street to my grandparents' bungalow to make sure they didn't need an ambulance or a hearse. Since Nana was deaf and Grandpa Abe stony in the arms of his stroke, Mr. Jefferson was forced to stand outside the bungalow until Nana happened to see him.

"Go away!" she would yell. "We're not dead yet, naah!"

Even if she had needed his help, Nana wouldn't have allowed Mr. Jefferson beyond the front gate. *Der ganeyvisher shvartzer,* she called him – the thieving black man. Or *der klaper* – the nail banger. Or *reb kolboynik* – Mr. Know-It-All. Or, inexplicably, *der intershtipper,* a phrase that roughly translates as "the one who's horning in." What did she think he would steal? Why did she hate him even more than she hated everyone else? Because he didn't hate *her?* Because he refused to pay her the compliment of acting afraid?

Not until later did I come to understand that my grandmother was suspicious of a man who owned nothing and wanted still less. More than this, I think, she resented his studies. After Nana's death I found in her trunk *The Legends of King Arthur* inscribed "To Miss Jennifer Gottlieb, for her achievements, this eighth day of May 1908." She had moved with her father from Russia to Liverpool in 1907, when she was ten; a year later, Jennie Gottlieb was sitting on a bench in a Manhattan sweatshop sewing buttons on ladies' coats. If not for her tyrant of a father and her no-goodnik of a husband, she could have been anything. And what did they make her? A button sewer! A floor scrubber! A pot washer! A cook! How did anyone expect her to find time to read? That someone else in her position accomplished this feat belied her excuse. She hated Mr. Jefferson because he hadn't given in to the resentment that soured her own life. Did she hate him even more because he was black? I think the hatred came first. Whatever color he had been, she would have searched for the weapon that wounded him most.

And perhaps she did wound him, but he wouldn't let this show. Each time my grandmother hurled an epithet, Mr. Jefferson repeated it aloud, first in Yiddish, then in English, moving his lips in an exaggerated way to prove he knew what it meant. And then he would smile, flattered that anyone would go to all the trouble to invent a curse for his benefit. Nana invented more curses, but when Mr. Jefferson smiled, those curses seemed to turn to blessings mid-air.

Even if he had found these battles amusing, they didn't take much time. How did he get through those slow afternoons, the long quiet nights? Such solitude and silence would have driven me mad. I barely could stand the few days before the season's end at the Eden and the first day of school, where I entertained my classmates with stories about the waiters I had startled in the woods with middle-aged guests.

"Lucy, you're lying. They weren't. *You didn't.*"

But that was the most attention I got from anyone all term. "Attention! Attention!" I wanted to cry from the school's P.A. system. But what would I say once I had gained this attention? I imagined running for class president, but I couldn't think of any plan for reform. I wasn't the type to spray paint my name across the gym floor, as a kid from the trailer park beyond the village had done, but I knew what he had felt standing on the bleachers inspecting his work.

I wasn't unattractive – I was lanky and tall, with curly orange hair that fell in rings to my waist – but I wasn't pretty either, my face too wide and flat, cheeks spattered with freckles like seeds on a dinner roll. Men I passed on the street tended to scowl, as if I had gotten up their hopes just to disappoint them. (*You're not so bad-looking*, my brother once said, though to me this implied *You're not so good-looking either.*) I wasn't stupid, or smart. I might have been the class clown, but the only jokes I knew were the vulgar routines I had learned from the Eden's comics, and whenever I recited these my classmates would groan. I couldn't draw, cook or sing. And I could not sit still.

"Lucy, be quiet," my history teacher said. "You might be a princess at your family's hotel, but to us you're just spoiled."

Maybe I *was* spoiled. Sometimes I think so, and I hate to look back on the self-centered child I was then. More often, I think my spirit merely cried out for greatness, as any soul should.

For a while, in ninth grade, I considered becoming a doctor. I would bring back the dead – not with my prayers but with my skills as a healer, the new hearts and lungs I would invent from rubber bags, motors and gears, the way Mr. Jefferson built new pumps from spare parts. But I didn't have the patience to sit alone and memorize the phyla of frogs, and I hated to believe that Darwin was right and millions of generations of who-knew-what species had moldered away without leaving a trace, that a creature's mutations – what made it different from its predecessors, more special, unique – led more often to its death than a new, advanced race. I earned a B— in biology, while Marv Lipsett, whose parents owned the chicken farm near the Eden, earned an A+. Marv consoled me by promising that I could be his surgical assistant when he fixed people's hearts. But I didn't want to be anyone's assistant. If I couldn't lead a club, I wouldn't join. I had one or two friends – most kids in Paradise had known each other since birth and were friends with the kids who sat near them in class – but how could I tell Sylvia Alpert or Marianne Auclair that I had been chosen by God? (Years later, at a reunion, Marianne confided that she had also felt chosen – *she'd* been elected to save the world's poor – and I felt a pang to admit that I hadn't been unique even in this.)

I didn't dare confide my ambitions and doubts to anyone except Mr. Jefferson.

"Why, Lucy!" he'd exclaim. "A girl of your talents!," though he never seemed to specify what these talents might be. He believed I would find a calling simply because I wanted to find one. "A child asks for bread, God doesn't give her stones. No telling how far you might go." He waved toward the cabin's window, which was propped open with a book.

"But *where* might I go, exactly? After I graduate, I mean."

"Hmm." He sucked his lips. "Have you ever thought of New York? That's where *most* people go."

I had been to Manhattan several times with my father to buy fresh fish wholesale, and once on a field trip to the Museum of Natural History. But the skyscrapers and crowds, even the dinosaurs and whales in the museum, made me feel small. If I couldn't prove myself special in a tiny town like Paradise, how could I prove I was special in New York?

"It's not very far away. What is it, a hundred or so miles down the road?" He began pacing the cabin as if to test this hypothesis. "So many things. Such people out there."

I expected a dose of encouragement.

"Such wonderful things and such god-awful people." He smacked the wall beneath the window, dislodging the book so the window smacked shut. "Life is . . . Well, life . . ."

"Yes?" I said. "Life?," hoping as only a sixteen-year-old can hope for a clue about life.

"Never mind," he said. "It's harder than you think. You can start out with big plans. The very *grandest* of plans. But they might not work out."

I felt that I had toppled from a very great height. If Mr. Jefferson of all people thought I would fail . . . Then I glanced at his face and saw that he had been speaking of his own life, not mine. I was startled to discover this made me feel worse.

"I don't want to scare you. Your mother's done enough of that already. But maybe she's got . . . Maybe there is some sort of force, some Evil Eye or something, whatever it is, hates to see ambition. In some folks, leastwise."

Surely not in me!

"Oh, I know what you're thinking. I once thought that too. Thought I could go wherever I wanted. Do anything. Be anything."

He paced and kept pacing – the cabin seemed smaller with each step he took – until, in his travels, he bumped against my chair and regarded me as if I might be an acquaintance he knew from back home. He reached for my cheek. I thought he would pinch it, as guests had been pinching my cheek since I could remember, and I drew back, from reflex. He let his hand fall.

"Never mind," he said. "You'll get along fine." He tried to sound convincing. "You won't mess up like I did."

I must have known that he hadn't become a handyman by choice. I must have known that Mr. Jefferson would have been elsewhere if he hadn't *messed up*. In a muddled way, I thought he had failed a big test or broken some important rule; because he was black, the test had been harder than it would have been for whites, the rule somehow unfair. But I never had imagined what that failure must cost. Sitting in his cabin, I was astonished by feelings I guessed must be his: jealousy that I was starting my life as a grown-up when his own life was ruined; remorse for this jealousy; pain that no one else would ever hear the lessons he wanted to teach. I had never felt anyone's pain but my own. "Oh!" I said. "Oh!," as if I suddenly had discovered the talent for which I had been searching so long, like throwing my voice or reading someone's mind. His anger squeezed out my breath, and I turned away abruptly, which broke the connection between us as effectively as if I had yanked out some wire linking my heart to his.

Two years later, on prom night, I put on a silky green dress bought with money I had earned working at the Eden the summer before. I took a gift-wrapped box from my closet and a bottle of cheap champagne from the windowsill. Then I tried to sneak out without my mother asking *Where do you think you're going?*, a plausible question since I didn't have a date.

She was sitting at the kitchen table with the Eden's big black ledger and a shoe box stuffed with bills. She would add, then subtract, then erase an entire column, fretful as a woman dividing half a loaf so each of her children would go to bed hungry but none would starve to death. My father was washing the dishes, arms submerged in water so hot the steam fogged his head.

"Oh, honey!" he cried. "Let me get the camera."

What did my father care if no boy had rung the doorbell and pinned a corsage to my gown? He took such pride in my existence, his heart would have burst from anything more. How angry this made me! I thought that his loving me solely because I was his daughter denied that I had qualities a stranger might love.

"I'm not going to the prom," I said. "Nobody asked me."

His hands were so thickly callused no pot could scorch them, no knife pierce his skin. I had seen him chop onions half an afternoon without shedding a single tear. My grandmother's worst insults couldn't make my father flinch. And so, when I saw the hurt in his eyes, sunken as they were in those leathery cheeks, I felt as if I had stuck a pin in a mannequin and heard it cry out.

My mother looked up. "All right," she said. "You want me to ask? I'll ask. Why so dressed up?" She pressed her palms to the ledger, sitting there like God with the Book of Life open to the page with my name. "Nothing comes of nothing," she said. By which she meant: *Look what you get for spending so much time with the handyman instead of boys your own age like Jeffrey Fein or Marvin Lipsett.* She pulled another bill from the shoe box. "You're not a child anymore."

"We could go to a movie," my father said. Soapy water dripped from the plate. "Would that help?"

"No thank you," I said, scornful as a tourist in a country so poor it has nothing worth buying. "I have other plans tonight."

"Plans!" my mother said.

"Plans. With a friend."

"Friends are fine." She waved a bill to remind me what I owed her. "But friends won't warm your bones in old age. Friends won't give you children."

"Children!" I said. "I'm only eighteen. I have more important things to do than have children."

"Such as? Your generation keeps saying it has more important things to do than raise a family, but they never say what's so important. So now, I ask you, what's more important than finding someone to marry? Than bringing a child into the world?"

They waited for an answer – my father at the sink, my mother with her shoe box full of bills – and because I didn't have one, I turned and walked out.

It was the third week in April. I had forgotten to wear my coat, and my dress was so thin I might as well have been naked. Driving up the hill in my parents' ancient Pontiac, whose heater didn't work, I began to go numb.

Friends won't warm your bones.

"I am not cold!" I said aloud, in the same tone of denial I had used all those times she'd said my lips had gone blue.

What's more important than someone to marry?

I pulled off the road and sat staring at the dark cloud above the valley, imagining the ritual going on even now, the procession down Main Street – every year on prom night the senior class marched from Paradise High through the center of town while parents lined the street calling names and snapping photos. The students walked two by two, the wind tousling their ruffled shirt-fronts, the filmy sleeves of gowns, the towers of curls twined with colored ribbons, the gaudy red petals of carnations and boutonnières. I could smell cologne, sweat, corsages. I saw the bursts of flashbulbs, the glitter of jewels that mothers had allowed their daughters to wear for the first time that night.

Every couple matched. For seven years my classmates had

been allowed to date whomever they pleased. Allan Kravitz, whose family ran the kosher fish store, was never seen without Elizabeth Coke, whose father was the minister at the Methodist church. Boo Richards, the star of the basketball team, a willowy boy with a chiseled face and mica-smooth skin, went out with a different white girl each week, while Bathsheba, his sister and the smartest girl at school, secretly dated Mr. McBride, who taught senior math and was white as the chalk dust on the argyle sweater he always wore. But now, as my classmates marched along Main Street, Allan Kravitz was paired with Wendy Shapiro, and Betsy Coke with Dirk Hamlin, who was Baptist at least. Boo Richards, in tails, walked beside Pamela Love, a beautiful black girl who sang soprano in the chorus and who might have gone to Julliard if she hadn't gotten pregnant with Boo's daughter that spring, while Bathsheba was paired with a dull, quiet black boy who hated to read.

I got out of the car and stood on the crest of the hill, as if watching Boo and Pamela in their foil-covered crowns lead the other couples to the south end of Main, then double back toward school, where they would all file inside. The heavens might burst, the parents of Paradise might drown in the flood, but when the waters receded those steel doors would swing open and the procession would file out, like paired with like, so life in our town could go on as before.

Wet now, and shaking, I climbed back in the car. If I hadn't longed for hot tea I might have gone home.

You're not a child anymore.

I drove farther up the hill, rubbing fog from the windshield. I parked by the cabin – the rain was falling so hard my dress clung to my skin. I knocked. No one answered. How thoughtless I had been! I hadn't even asked. I presumed he'd be pleased.

When the door finally swung open I could tell that Mr. Jefferson had been taking a nap. He seemed bleary-eyed, dazed. His shirt-tail hung out. He squinted as if he wasn't sure who I was. Then his eyes focused. One brow shot above his glasses. "Lucy," he said.

I stepped inside the threshold and held out my gift. He took it and unwrapped it.

"A radio!" he said. And I winced when I saw that to plug in that radio he would have to unplug the only lamp in the room.

"Never mind," he said. "I've been wanting a radio exactly like this one for, oh, the past hundred years." He found a candle in a drawer; by its flickering light he fiddled with the dial, tuning it past the shrill rock 'n roll and the news of that day to the faintest station beyond the others, pulling in the voices through decades of static:

Don't sit under the apple tree with anyone else but me, no, no, no . . .

"The Andrews Sisters!" he said, happy as if he suddenly had discovered his own long-lost siblings. "Exactly the song for a girl who'll be leaving soon for college."

Don't go walkin' down Lovers' Lane with anyone else but me, no, no, no . . .

He threw back his head and waggled one finger. His shadow swayed on the wall, and his voice soared up to join those of his sisters. I always had suspected he might have a fine voice, but I never dreamed he someday might be singing to me, a song just for me down to its wordplay – "Appelbaum," I knew, meant "apple tree" in German.

Now, don't you go walkin' down Lovers' Lane, no, no, no . . . not until you see me come marchin' home, home, home sweet home.

The trumpets raced faster but he didn't miss a syllable, faster and faster until at last it was done. He rocked his head in his hands, catching his breath. Then he looked up and smiled the sort of smile I might have called sloppy if anyone but Mr. Jefferson had smiled it.

"Lucy," he said, "you sure look a *sight.*"

Arthur had taunted me so many times with "Pop-Eye!" and "Bozo!" I barely could believe this might be a compliment. When I realized that it was, I felt myself blush. What must he think, a girl of eighteen showing up at his door in a clinging-wet dress with champagne . . .

So why *had* I come?

Only to prove I'd grown up. And to hear his assurance that the men I would meet in New York would be superior to . . . whom? Jeff Fein and Marv Lipsett?

"May I have the next dance?" He extended his arms. "The Mills Brothers! Mmmm." It was a slow misty song and when he started to croon it, voice throaty and sad, I imagined a family of all the world's musical brothers and sisters – Mills, Andrews, Lennon, Ames, Everly, Righteous – singing this song.

Once in a while
will you try to give
one little thought to me,
though someone else may be
nearer your heart?

He never had touched me. Not since that chess game. Not since my mother had asked *Did he touch you?* nine years before.

Once in a while
will you dream of the moments
I shared with you,
moments before we two
drifted apart?

I never had believed my mother's accusation that Mr. Jefferson was gay. Then why hadn't I wondered why a handsome young man would live so alone? Why hadn't I imagined myself in his arms? Because he was a handyman and black? Because he was fifteen years older than I was? Because he was smarter? Yes, all those reasons. But mostly I wanted to keep believing he was perfect, he would be here forever, whenever I needed him.

"You don't doubt my intentions, do you, Lucy?"

His arms were still raised. I thought he looked hurt.

"You must know by now, I'm a gentleman. And a gentleman is nothing if he isn't discreet." His smile held the memory of everything that had gone on between us, a nine-year-old secret.

His hand touched my back. Our palms met. I lifted my wrist to his shoulder. I felt his hot skin. We moved our feet in a box.

In love's smoldering ember
one spark may remain.
If love still can remember
the spark may burn again.

He stepped on my sandal. "Sorry." He staggered, kicking my shin. He tripped. Missed the beat. But he never stopped laughing. "Fooled you! Ah-ha! A colored boy who can't dance!"

Suddenly, I felt witty. "Ah-ha, I fooled *you*. A Jew with no money!"

He uncorked the champagne, which sprayed toward the ceiling then rained down upon us in a shower of gold.

"To your future!" he said. We drank one cup, then another, toasting my future until my eyesight grew blurred and I thought I saw something – a hag's face, an eye . . .

I shuddered. It couldn't be. Nana was asleep by seven most evenings, and it now was past one.

But something was out there.

Naah, naah, naah, naah . . .

At first it was benign. Then sharper, more emphatic: Naah! Naah! Naah! Naah!

Just crickets. Or frogs. I was drunk, I thought. *I'm drunk.*

"Mr. Jefferson," I said, "what's your first name?"

He seemed as sober as, well, as sober as Mr. Jefferson under normal conditions. "Seeing as how I got no other gift for the graduate." He burped. "Call me Thomas."

"Thomas Jefferson?"

"My great-great-great-somethin'."

"The president? You and he . . ."

"Said it before, world's a mighty strange place."

"But why do you hide it? If I were related to a president – "

He shook his head. "Being an old-fashion Negro gentleman named Tom is just asking to get your self-respect trompled on. Other hand, 'Mr. Jefferson' is asking for 'bout as much respect as a handyman can hope."

"So it's all right if I call you – "

"If you use your discretion."

But he needn't have worried. I was so used to calling him "Mr. Jefferson" that I couldn't call him "Thomas" and so called him nothing for the rest of that night. Only at two, when he had brewed me strong tea to sober me up and was escorting me to my car, only then was I able to say, "Thank you . . . Thomas."

He ran one finger down my forehead, down my nose to my throat. "No need to thank *me*." He leaned down a little.

Naah, naah, naah, NAAH!

I turned and saw no one, but the moment had passed. I stumbled to the Pontiac, waved and drove off. When I glanced in the mirror, the cabin had already melted away.

I went to New York. And as soon as I got there I longed to go home. Like many young girls, I assumed that I was destined to grow up a queen. But I grieved more than most when I learned I was wrong.

I couldn't endure being average, one of three thousand freshmen in the N.Y.U. dorms (*N.Y. Jew,* Arthur called it). Already I could see that whatever field I chose – philosophy, art, the history of medieval France – someone would always be smarter than I was. Even my brother, who surprised me one night by showing up at my door (he had been sent by his firm on business, he said), seemed at a loss to suggest what I might do with my life.

"Don't worry," he said. "I'm sure you'll find something."

But what should I become – a lawyer, like him? An accountant? A nurse? All those occupations seemed . . . small. On the day I turned nineteen I received a postcard of the Eden from Nana that urged: "LEARN TO RUN A BUSINESS SO YOU WON'T NEED A MAN." But what did I care for selling ladies' coats, or light bulbs, or cars? My mother suggested I get an education degree and return to Paradise to teach, but I hated to think that I would have as my audience children who would ignore me the way I had ignored the women and men who tried to teach me.

For a while I considered a life on the stage. I memorized Desdemona's lines and tried out for *Othello,* but I overacted so badly everyone smirked. I nearly got the part of Toto the Little Imperialist Dog in a feminist production of *The Wizard of Oz,* but then the director asked me to sing.

Among my thousands of classmates, my only distinction was where I had grown up. "The Catskills?" they said. "You mean they're still there?," as if a whole range of mountains might have picked up and moved. Another student told me that her parents had met and married at a Borscht Belt hotel. "I always wondered what it was like there, but I figured all those places died a long time ago," so I felt I had been born in Pompeii or Atlantis, some romantic doomed world, and everything I loved soon would be buried beneath ashes and salt.

Oh, I knew at some level the Borscht Belt was crude. The Eden was shabby, its glory long past. But this was 1978. Everyone was searching for distinctions to claim. The freedom we had acquired to go anywhere, be anything, frightened us, I think. To be like everyone was to be no one.

One Friday in October every club on campus set up booths

to attract younger members like me. Beneath a banner on which an Afro-headed silhouette raised its clenched fist, the black students clustered. The Pan-Asian Society offered booths for Korean, Chinese and Japanese students, though most of the Asian students in my class had grown up on Long Island and preferred cole slaw to *kim chee* and lox to raw fish. There were societies for students of Italian-American descent, for Native Americans, Latinos, Arabs. The Lubavitcher Hasidim tried to lure their co-religionists into their Mitzvah Mobile, while a group of Jewish militants whipped up support for Meir Kahane. The children of survivors tolled out a list of Holocaust victims, while a Zionist group attempted to persuade whoever stopped by to make *aliyah*. There were advertisements for classes in which to study Torah, Jewish history, philosophy, Yiddish, Hebrew, Aramaic. There were fliers advertising a kosher vegetarian dining hall and services for Orthodox, Reform and Conservative Jews. There was even, I learned later, a nongroup for Jews too sophisticated to think of joining a group for Jews – these were mostly the offspring of wealthy German families who had lived for generations on Central Park West.

There were so many clubs for Jews it was hard to feel distinction for being a Jew. Yet, standing at that fair, it occurred to me that I was the only student whose family owned an authentic Borscht Belt hotel. I would be nothing without the Eden. If my parents really sold it, as they had been threatening to do, I would have no kingdom to reign.

One evening that first term, the other girls in my dorm started talking about their boyfriends. "Go around the circle and tell about the first boy you had sex with," ordered Genevieve, a poet who smoked thin brown cigars.

One by one, the girls giggled and sighed about the boys they'd met at camp, on debate trips, in Israel, backstage between acts of some play they put on. A few of the more daring admitted to affairs with their father's best friend, the vice-principal at their high school or the boss at the restaurant where they waited tables to earn tuition. My turn would come soon. Should I pass? Tell the truth? I feared what they would say: to keep from being fired, our handyman pretended to like the boss's daughter; I was gauche to admit that my family employed a black person in a menial job; black men befriended white girls for only one thing; blacks who dated whites were traitors to their race. I considered regaling my circle mates with the story of my flirtation with the insurance adjuster, how I had been foolish enough to give in to Jimmy Kilcoin's flattery and promises the summer before, when I worked as the receptionist behind the Eden's desk. I might have been able to make Jimmy seem more attractive and respectable than he was. But my shame was too fresh. And I wasn't good at lying: to make Jimmy seem respectable I would have needed to invent an entirely new man.

The girl to my right finally stopped talking. All eyes turned my way.

"There's this guy Herbie," I said. "He works at our hotel. And, well, he's kind of liked me ever since I was a kid."

Genevieve tapped her ashes in another girl's Coke can, then exhaled smoke through her nose. "Like, *how* young?" she said. "When he started liking you, I mean."

"Nine," I said.

"Nine!"

"Well," I explained hastily, "there were all these waiters and busboys, and there weren't many girls, so all of them, well, they paid attention to me . . ."

"Paid attention?" Genevieve said. "What kind of attention?"

The other girls leaned toward me. I considered what to say. And that's when the phone rang – the public phone down the hall – and the R.A. shouted out my name because the call was for me.

"We're selling it," my mother said. "Some Hasid wants to

buy it. He's coming up this weekend, and if everything goes well, we'll have a check Sunday night."

"You can't do that," I said.

"Can't?" she said. "Why not?"

I didn't know what to answer. My heart panicked as if she'd told me that they were putting a beloved pet to sleep, though the Eden wasn't mine and I hadn't ever done much to care for its needs. I wasn't sure what I would do, how I could protest if my parents were as tired of running the hotel as my mother claimed they were. But I had to try. I had to be there.

And so, two mornings later, I took the Shortline bus to Paradise. Against her will, my mother picked me up at the station and drove me to the hotel. She went to find my grandmother while I waited for my father and the Hasid beneath the Eden's arch.

At last I saw the Pontiac burst over the hill. The tires screamed on the ice; it dove into the parking lot and spun about-face. My father leapt from the passenger's seat. Why had he let this strange man take the wheel? Everyone knew the Hasids were the worst drivers on the planet.

My father hurried toward me.

"What took you so long?" I asked.

He rarely uttered two words at once. Now he couldn't stop. "The man said he wanted to ask me a question. I thought he would ask me why I don't wear a yarmulke or go to *shul* more often, but he asked me the oddest . . . He wanted to know, Is there joy in my life? And personal things. Very personal things, about your mother and me." His heavy head wagged. "He asked if I would let him drive, because he never gets the chance to. I should have said no, but I didn't want to make the man angry."

The Hasid stepped from the Pontiac – surprisingly handsome, ruddy face alight with the thrill of the drive. A huge black fur hat perched atop his head like a panther. He couldn't have been forty, square shouldered, wrists poking from his sleeves. His trousers were short, and, oddly enough on this cold rainy day, his ankles were bare. Every time his shoes sank into the slush, a chill ran up my neck.

"Nana's missing," I told my father.

He whirled. Was she there, behind that tree? Spying from that window? It embarrassed me, how much my father feared my grandmother. If he hadn't been so timid, she wouldn't have despised him. She might have given him the Eden when my grandfather died.

The Hasid came close, the wings of his coat flapping behind. He passed beneath the arch; I could have knocked off his hat.

"I grew up here," I said loudly, not certain what I meant, or why I had even bothered, since he already had climbed the steps and left me outside.

An Art Deco monument to misplaced optimism, the lobby was the only part of the Eden that had been designed by an architect instead of Grandpa Abe. The check-in desk rippled with onyx and ivory. On either side grew palms; from the beaks of two herons flying above the desk trailed the word RESERVA-TIONS. To enter the office, you released a latch among the palm fronds and swung up a secret panel. As a child, when I had done this, I tingled with the privilege of access to places others weren't allowed to go. I flicked on the microphone and brayed the announcement Grandpa Abe had printed on a card: "Good morning, good morning, it's a lovely new day. The herring are jumping, the sour cream is flowing, and breakfast is now being served in the dining room, eat in good health."

The Hasid rapped the wall, searching for a way to enter the office. My father had disappeared, and, rather than ask a woman for advice, the Hasid hitched up his coat and hoisted himself up and over the desk.

I tiptoed across the carpet to the other end of the lobby (at the close of every season Nana strewed camphor; seven months later, like a mad Spring incarnate, she swept up the mothballs, though the scent lingered on) and peered out the window at the Eden's casino, a squat wooden building my grandmother had painted the red of dried blood. Soon a rabbi would lecture from the stage on which comics once had *sh-pritz*ed their monologues; in the folding chairs that shook beneath the weight of laughing guests, Hasids soon would *daven*, jerking this way and that.

A board creaked. Nana's ambush? No, the Hasid must be exploring the rooms above the lobby, where the wallpaper bloomed purple and green with fungus and the floor was so warped the beds rocked like cradles. No one went up there except the Feidels, who insisted on renting Room 12 every year, to re-enact the honeymoon they had spent at the Eden in 1945, and the chambermaids, who climbed the steps to fetch sheets from the enormous linen closet, the same closet in which I had lost my virginity to the insurance adjuster a few months before.

The Hasid came down the stairs. "The kitchen," he told my father, who had reappeared from his hiding place. "I must see the kitchen."

My father pointed the way and the Hasid rushed ahead. By the time I caught up, the Hasid was ransacking the drawers, testing my grandmother's knives on a curly hair from his beard, and my father was hiding in the pantry, inspecting the memorabilia he'd tacked on the walls – Arthur's various diplomas, my first-grade report card (*Lucy might have potential, but she lacks self-control . . .*), a snapshot of Arthur blowing out the candles on a seven-tiered cake.

"You do think we're doing the right thing, don't you, sweetheart?"

He looked even more exhausted than my mother had warned. What else could I do but shake my head yes?

As my father and the Hasid continued their tour – the Eden's outlying cottages were grouped around the meadow like sway-backed old horses – I followed them along the path. Every year, at least a few of our guests tripped on the macadam, bumpy as the veins on an old woman's hand; this past summer alone there had been two broken hips and innumerable sprains, bruises and lacerations, so that every few days Jimmy Kilcoin would appear and ask my opinion as to whether "the claimant" had been wobbling on high heels or wearing his glasses at the "time of occurrence." Between questions, Jimmy reached across the desk and played with my hair. If no guests were present, he nuzzled my ear, whispered *sexpot* and *princess*. Who had ever paid me such compliments? Surely not my parents, who believed that praising a child would provoke the Evil Eye. My brother had announced so many times that I was loud and obnoxious, I had come to accept this, though I understood later he meant only that I looked and acted too Jewish.

Jimmy Kilcoin, being Catholic, thought a Jew was exotic, as I thought a Catholic who had grown up in the coal mines of Scranton, Pennsylvania, who had joined the Navy and been injured on a ship off Korea, who had slept with so many women that he had come to be called the Don Juan of the Catskills, was an uncommon prize. I hated to think I would leave for school a virgin, and I didn't want to sleep with a boy my own age. I went up to that linen closet with Jimmy Kilcoin because I thought this would prove how exceptional I was, though as soon as we finished and I found myself lying on a pile of stale sheets with Jimmy beside me, his hand on my hip, I saw that I was only one of the many women he had slept with, and I tried to keep my distance until the Eden closed for the year and I left for New York.

"Excuse me," my father said to the Hasid, "there's more land, back there." My father waved toward the mountain. "Would you care to go see it?"

The Eden's rear fifty acres were rich in berries and plums, with a small pond for swimming, if you didn't mind the algae. Every August, Herbie and the other boys raided the kitchen for pails, which they never filled since they preferred to eat from the bushes until their tongues were bright blue. They pelted one another with overripe plums, or played softball in the meadow – they wore nothing but cut-offs, using their T-shirts to swab their sweaty armpits and chests.

"Hey, Loose Goose, bring me some water!"

"Fetch my glove, Lucy!"

The Hasid cared nothing for meadows or fruit trees but insisted on inspecting every single room, each like the others, musty and dark (the rooms weren't heated and so never lost their dampness all year). He tested each mattress – filthy and striped, like prisoners of war too emaciated to rise. "Too soft," he pronounced. "Too lumpy." "Too hard." On through the Ranch House, the Chalet, the Palace, Rose Cottage . . . "Too thin," the Hasid said as he stretched on one bed (like Goldilocks, I thought, or the princess who refused to sleep on the pea). "This one isn't bad," he said finally, "but I wish your hotel had more double beds," which surprised me, since I knew that a Hasidic husband wasn't allowed to sleep with his wife for two weeks each month.

"Too short," he admonished one bed. "What do you expect, I should chop off my feet?"

It galled me that he would speak to a mattress but not a woman. Offended and bored, I started to bait him, trailing him so closely I trod on his heels.

"It's warm in here," I said, and took off my coat. I was wearing a dress I had bought in New York to impress everyone in Paradise with how stylish I had become, though my mother's frown confirmed that I looked like a tart. The Hasid twisted his beard, but still he ignored me.

I waited until he was testing the last mattress, then sat down beside him.

He turned to face me. His eye twitched. He glared at me so hotly that *I* became flustered.

"I'm tired," I said.

He lifted one hand. I thought that he might slap me, but he reached for my breast and pinched it, once, hard, then left the room so quickly I wouldn't have believed any of this had happened, if my breast hadn't hurt.

Well, I had provoked him. The pinch, like a slap, was meant to punish my immodesty. But something about the way the Hasid's eye twitched made me think that he had enjoyed the punishment he'd inflicted.

I stood on the porch and watched as my father showed the Hasid our pool, hoping, as I knew, that he wouldn't raise the tarp and notice the crack that ran its whole length. But the Hasid was too busy surveying the wire fence. He would cover the fence with canvas and convert the pool to a *mikve,* a ritual bath. No one would ever swim there. No Hasidic woman would appear half naked in public.

I touched my breast. Hypocrite.

The Hasid strode from the pool. He was coming back to get me! But he veered from the path and headed toward the Horseshoe – he must have seen its crumbling roof from the road. No, he turned again. He was going to inspect the handyman's cabin. I ought to catch up; its occupant deserved better than to learn of the sale of his home from the buyer.

I ran down the road, but I still was too late to do more than watch as the Hasid flung open the door and discovered a black man enthroned on his toilet, reading a book.

The Hasid stood a moment, shocked, then backed off the porch. My father stammered an apology, then loped in pursuit. With dignity, Thomas drew the curtain about him.

"Lucy," he said. "Wasn't expecting to see you. Thought you might have written to let me know how you're getting on. Everything's fine in New York, I presume?"

I would have lied and said "Fine!," as I had lied to my parents, but something about that disembodied voice, secret and near as my own beating heart, made me confess.

"I hate it," I said. And, what I couldn't say, that I hated him too, hated him for thinking I was better than I was. If I stayed, he would ask what I had been learning at school, what subjects I would study the following term. I would need to explain why I was doing poorly, why no courses seemed to interest me, why I was wasting the opportunity to accomplish what he hadn't been allowed to accomplish, what he had tried and messed up.

The toilet flushed. A hand reached out to part the drape, but I ran from the shack before the rest of him could emerge. I ran, and kept running, and so I arrived at the parking lot before my father and the Hasid, before my mother drove up (*I couldn't find your grandmother anywhere*), and I saw before anyone else that two of the Pontiac's tires had been slashed, the rear fender dented and both headlights cracked.

When the Hasid told my father that, despite the Eden's faults, he would buy our hotel, Arthur took the day off and drove from Boston to Paradise to handle the sale. They agreed on the terms, shook hands, signed the papers. The Hasid gave Arthur a check.

A week later, when he called me, I was back in New York, studying for a test.

"Worthless!" Arthur shouted. "The damn check was worthless! I wanted to sic the cops on the guys, but your parents wouldn't let me. 'What would the town think, arresting a Hasid.' 'Never mind a Hasid, he's a con man! He's a crook! And you're letting him off just because he wears *tsitsit!*'"

I was holding the phone at arm's length; the other girls on the hall were looking up to see whose voice was so loud.

"Well, I'll tell you what *I've* got. I've got a signed Purchase and Sale. I've got a check I took in good faith as a down payment on the Eden. And I've got an overwhelming desire to unload that old deathtrap before it collapses on somebody's head."

It tried my best to calm him, but my brother kept ranting.

"I've called every synagogue in Crown Heights, and I tell you, they've heard of this clown. I just had to mention his name and they said *oy* and hung up. But one of these guys gave me the address of, I don't know, the Hasid who's allowed to talk to the public."

"They've got a P.R. man? He said he would talk to you?"

"Yeah. When I told him I intended to sue his pants off."

"Oh Arthur, you didn't!" Why was I protecting this Hasid? I should have told my brother that the con artist was a masher as well.

"Now don't get self-righteous. Open or closed, the Eden pays property taxes. And a mortgage. Two mortgages, in fact. And the damn insurance company just sent a notice they're doubling the rates. Mom and Dad could never afford the premiums. They can't even afford to close the place and retire. So maybe it's worth my while to come down and see if I can get a check that won't bounce."

The night before, I had dreamed I was taking inventory of everything at the Eden – every piece of china, every pillowcase and blanket, every Ping-Pong ball, lounge chair, even the trees. I went through boxes in the cellar – odd garter belts and shoes left by absentminded guests decades before, chipped goblets, cracked mirrors, the skull of the man my great-grandfather had killed. I sorted this bric-a-brac as intently as if I were sorting pieces of a puzzle. Why did I think that if even one piece were missing, I would never be whole?

"Well, what about it? If I drive down tomorrow night, can I sleep in your dorm?"

"Sure," I told Arthur. "If you let me go with you."

"Look. I promise I won't punch this yambo. I'm just going there to talk."

"I trust you," I lied. "I only want . . . I just think I ought to be there. It's my hotel, too."

"Okay, okay." He was saving his wrath for the Hasid. "I'll be there at six-thirty. Don't make me wait."

I never had considered my body to be an invitation to sin. But as I pulled on the dowdy black woolen dress my mother had given me when I left for New York, my breasts seemed to swell to a strip queen's proportions. I heard Nana's voice: *Vi a nafke* – like a prostitute. I covered my calves with black socks. This looked nicely frumpy, but when I sat down, my kneecaps popped out, freckled and lewd as extra breasts.

It would just have to do. Arthur would honk his horn any minute.

Oh, but my *hair*. True, Hasidic women didn't shave their heads until after they were married. But most Hasidic women didn't look like the Medusa. I smothered the snakes beneath a scarf and raced down to meet my brother before they writhed free.

"You look awful," Arthur said when I climbed in his car.

"I'm just showing respect."

"Maybe you think I should have worn a false beard? Tacked *peyes* to my sideburns?"

My brother trimmed his hair so close to his scalp it barely had room to curl. He shaved twice a day – once I had even caught him shaving his back. But he couldn't hide his bumpy nose, his dark olive skin. I imagined him in clothing stores, taking hours to decide if a particular tie was tasteful, if an overcoat was the sort a wealthy gentile would wear – or a show-offy Jew. It seemed to require as much self-control to avoid acting like a Jew as to observe the commandments and actually be one.

"You put on a suit. That's all I expected." Though it might not have killed you to wear a yarmulke, I thought.

"Okay, okay," as if long years of fighting had given us each the powers to guess the other's objections. "Open the glove box."

The command would have seemed natural if we had been riding in our parents' Pontiac, its glove box stuffed full with black nylon yarmulkes, the mementos of funerals of great-aunts and great-uncles, my parents' friends in Paradise and guests who spent their summers at the Eden as loyally as they would now spend them in their coffins, presumably with fewer complaints. At the graveside the rabbi would distribute a black yarmulke to every male mourner. Distracted by grief, my father would forget to take his skullcap off until he and my mother were back in their car. "Honey, it's over," she would say, and my father would nod as sadly as if "it" meant their lives and slip the yarmulke in the glove box.

But this was Arthur's Camaro, and therefore I was startled when the glove box fell open and a flurry of white yarmulkes burst forth like doves. What were they from? Not funerals, surely. I peered at one dove's belly: *Souvenir of the wedding of Joy and Mark Dibble, October 16, 1977.* And another: *Sharon Kahn and Myles Kay, joined in matrimony 6/22/75.*

I had met Sharon and Myles. Like most of Arthur's friends, they were Jews who had attended Exeter and Princeton. Worldly. Refined. "See?" he could say. "I have Jewish friends, but they're Jews who have taste." I could picture all these weddings: a clean-shaven rabbi, Pachelbel or jazz, lobster soufflé, the only Jewish touch the presence of these yarmulkes along with the usual napkins and matchbooks since the bride's parents relished seeing their name embossed on as many objects as possible.

Cynthia and William, wedded this 4th day of May . . .
Abigail Moore and Byron Whitley Katz 1-11-76.

Always an usher and never the groom. Well, that was his fault. Plenty of women wanted to date a good-looking lawyer, but few of these women fit my brother's criteria of beauty and wealth. No matter how attractive a Jewish girl might be, Arthur saw premonitions of the matrons by the pool. No matter how soft her voice, he heard: "Artie! More fish!" He selected his women for their pale hair and soft voices, their narrow hips and flat chests. But those rich Christian beauties – his class-mates at Princeton, the daughters of the partners at Treadwell, Mead, Hoar – were so finely made they found Arthur coarse. His kinky hair scraped their skin, his bitter voice stung. And what could be coarser than a Borscht Belt hotel?

I floated a white yarmulke on my brother's dark curls. "Arthur, if they don't want to buy it, you can't force them."

"Yeah. Guess I can't." His anger had melted into dejection. "But I sure as hell can try."

Though we knew were close to the Hasidic neighborhood, everyone we passed was black. The houses drooped. Crumpled papers lay sodden on the lawns.

"Look. Over there!" I pointed to a man with a bushy blond beard. He wore a fedora and spectacles. "Follow him," I said, and Arthur drove behind the man, who was walking at a clip, swinging his briefcase.

The man turned down a street crowded with a kosher butcher shop, a kosher bakery, a kosher pizzeria. The side-walks became lively with Hasidic men on their way home from work; in their Burberry raincoats, they could have passed as salesmen or computer engineers, which I learned later they were. The women pushed two or three babies at a time in extra-wide strollers, pausing now and then to let their tod-dlers catch up.

The man turned again, and we found ourselves driving down a wide cheerful avenue. I had pictured Crown Heights to be a medieval ghetto, but the houses here had ruddy brick faces with white doors and white trim. On one door a sign proclaimed: THE MESSIAH IS COMING! A bumper sticker on a blue Continental said: THIS CAR RUNS ON GAS, NOT ON SHABBAT.

We parked and got out. In the twilight, amid all those dark hats, Arthur's white yarmulke bobbed like the ball in a sing-along cartoon. I followed it as he searched for the right house. Climbed the stoop. Waited.

The woman who answered the door seemed so accustomed to hugging all her visitors that she reached out for me and only drew back when she saw she didn't know me. Her bosom was lumpy, as if too many people had clutched it too hard and the stuffing had shifted. Her black wig seemed askew.

"Your husband," Arthur said. "He's expecting us."

The woman clearly had heard as much about Arthur as she had heard about a possible invasion from Mars. But she knew the word husband. "Yes, yes!" she cried, "my husband!" and she ran off to get him.

"See?" I hissed. "He won't tell you anything."

"Oh yeah?" Arthur said, cocky as a lawyer who each day makes gangsters confess.

But the man who emerged from his study seemed less like a gangster than the Almighty Judge. His beard alone seemed to take up half the foyer.

"So!" he bellowed. "So!"

"I have a few questions." Arthur's voice cracked.

"Questions!" The Hasid clearly thought questions were in order, as long as he asked them. "Come!" He thrust my brother through his study door.

The man's wife wiped her floury hands on her apron.

"Please," I said, "don't let me get in your way."

"Oh, no trouble!" she said. "It's only . . . the soup . . ."

I followed her to the kitchen, which was surprisingly modern, each item in its place, though with so many items in so many places, so many pots on so many burners, so many ingredients in so many bowls, it seemed to be the kitchen that nourished every Jew in the Diaspora.

"Ah," the woman said. "You have come with . . . your husband . . . who needs to see *my* husband?," relieved to have found this link between worlds.

"Well, yes, but you see, he's actually my brother."

"Your brother!" All right. She understood brothers as well as she understood husbands. "And you and your brother have come to us from – ?"

"The Catskills? The Mountains?"

"The Mountains!" she marveled. "You come from the Mountains?"

"You've been there?"

"Oh, no. But other people, they tell me the Mountains are a wonderful place."

I still sensed discomfort. She spoke English the way she would handle her best china.

"*Darf ich red yiddish?*" I asked.

Her stout arms flew up. "You speak Yiddish!"

"*Ich red nor a bissel.*"

"*Du redst yiddish! Vunderlich! Un dayn tatte oych?*"

Yes, I said, my father speaks Yiddish.

She clapped her floury hands. "*Vunderlich! Un dayn mamme oych?*"

Yes, yes, I said, my mother does, too.

Happily, she sprinkled sugar on a tray of raw cookies. "*Un dayn bruder redt yiddish?*"

"*A bissel.*" That was, if "putz" and "shmuck" counted.

When she ran out of relatives I started to squirm, fearing the next question might be: *Do you honor Shabbat?* But my examiner had only gotten as far as summarizing my preceding answers – *So, your family speaks Yiddish!* – when an invasion began. Midgets in plaid dresses down to their ankles piled their schoolbooks on the table and skipped to their mother, whose apron they tugged as they reached up for a kiss. Without being told, each girl pulled a chair to the counter and began to peel the vegetables, peeping at me shyly and giggling to her sisters between in-turned hands. Then came three little boys in white button-down shirts and hand-crocheted yarmulkes, and two teenage boys, arguing hotly – though they greeted their mother, they stonily avoided glancing my way. The younger boys ran out in the yard while the older boys picked up their argument where they had left it and went to wait for their meal.

The girls, who by now had finished the potatoes, grabbed handfuls of silverware and skipped out to set the table. From another part of the house, my brother's voice rose – shouted down by the Hasid.

"Oh," the woman said, reaching up distractedly to tug her wig, "my husband will never tell him the truth. Never. Your brother must have come to . . . That crazy man! That *meshuggener*! I shouldn't say another word, but I hate the idea that you will go away thinking we all are so dishonest. Worse, that we lie to cover our own." She tugged the wig so hard it covered one ear. "Not that the man who came to your hotel is one of ours. You noticed his *shtraymel*? His fur hat? Our men wear cloth."

So much meaning in a hat! Worlds within worlds . . .

"This man you met, he is like a child! He couldn't stand that we insisted on following our *rebbe* instead of following him." The potatoes bubbled over. Barehanded, the woman readjusted the lid. "Already this man has attracted a few disciples – mostly foolish *goyim* who don't know any better. To them, a Hasid, even a crazy Hasid, is some kind of – what is their word, guru? And a Hasid who sees – " she blushed and fiddled with the wig – "who sees . . . sees pleasure as a way to gain redemption!" She suddenly looked horrified. "You won't tell my husband what I've told you? He already thinks I'm not to be trusted."

I promised I wouldn't tell her husband what I knew, though I never said I wouldn't tell my brother.

"Good! So that's settled. Come, I need to see how the table's getting on." She led me to the dining room, where her daughters stood giggling as she studied what they'd done. She counted settings half-aloud: one, two . . . thirteen. Then she looked at me and clapped her hands to her chest. "Surely you'll stay for dinner!"

"I would love to," I said. "But I don't think my brother – "

"Oh," she said, "you must! We'll have to convince him!"

Arthur appeared a few minutes later, glum and subdued. The smell of meat and cookies helped persuade him to stay. And maybe he hoped to wheedle information from his host as we ate.

Everyone filed in and took a place around the table. A photo of a man I assumed to be the *rebbe* smiled down from the wall; he had a square-cut white beard and eyes like the scrolls on a violin's face. The Chief Justice entered and took his seat between his two eldest sons. At the opposite end his wife presided, flanked by the two tiniest girls, who pinched her and poked her: "*Mamme*, are there cookies?" "When my meat comes, will you cut it?"

One by one we marched to the kitchen to wash our hands, then marched back to the dining room to hear the Chief Justice bless the food. He didn't direct these blessings to the light bulb, as my own father did (when he said the blessings at all), but rather to a Being with the power to bring forth bread from the earth and fruit from the vine, or, in His anger, withhold these. I was lulled by the sonorous, all-knowing voice, the comforting ritual, the warmth emanating from the girls and their mother, who chattered in Yiddish, every sentence containing the word *khasene* – marriage – or *eyfele* – baby. This was their world. They would marry by twenty, bear a baby each year. No man but their husband would ever look in their eyes. (The eldest girl, who couldn't have been more than fifteen, kept stealing glances at Arthur. When he stared openly back, she spilled a spoonful of soup on the cloth.) And yet they seemed happy. Their duties were strict, but this freed them from making difficult decisions or striving for anything other than God.

Without question, the men were certain that their place in the universe was here, in this house, at this table, arguing about precisely this topic – whatever that was. Yiddish burst from their lips; their words darted and swooped about the table like swallows. For all I could tell, they were arguing about whether a flea has a navel, but I chose to believe they were debating a point on which the very salvation of humankind teetered. I wanted desperately to join them, but how could I, when I understood every fifth word? Mine was the Yiddish of foul-mouthed comics. My few phrases lay on my tongue like dead crows. A Hasid at heart? My Judaism was no more than nostalgia, a warm toasty marshmallow stuck in my throat.

But it was better than nothing. Who cared if the Eden was a faint, distorted echo of life in Crown Heights? Wasn't an echo better than silence? If my classmates wished to see what the Borscht Belt was like, well, I could show them. If the place smelled of mothballs, I could open all the windows and let in the fresh air. *Come in,* I would say. *Taste the food. Look around.*

The Hasid's wife and daughters cleared the dirty table, then returned to the dining room with sparkling platters of sugar cookies. I wanted to laugh, throw my arms around each girl, even the two taciturn sons. Wasn't this euphoria, this love for all things, the way God let you know your vision was true?

The Chief Justice stood. He and his family recited the grace after meals, which I began to sing too, to show I knew the Hebrew. Even Arthur joined in, though he said the words a split-second late: "Lord, sustain all of us, do good to all, provide food for all. Blessed are You, O Lord our God, who sustaineth all the living creatures on Earth."

I made it through the rest of my second term at school. I even took finals, though I'd done so poorly in my classes I didn't see the point. What I wanted most from life was to run a hotel, and by luck my family owned one. I would manage the Eden that summer, then transfer to a small public college Upstate that had a school of hotel science. I would ask my parents for the money that I'd saved by attending a cheaper university and invest it in my scheme to run the Eden full-time.

I kept these plans to myself, but when Arthur drove me home at the end of spring term, he sensed something was up.

"Come on, Lucy, tell me. I'm sure I can help." He tempted me the way he had done years before: *Come on, Lucy, jump, I won't let you fall*, stretching his arms so invitingly I ignored my better judgment and jumped from the oak . . . only to land – *slurp* – in the mud when Arthur stepped back.

"Look, I can see you've got something on your mind. Is it someone you met and you think Mom won't like him? Or maybe you want to go to Europe but you're afraid Mom will say no? Or there's something else you decided to do, and you think Mom and Dad won't approve? I won't make fun of you, I promise. Whatever it is, you can tell me."

He kept coaxing me, pleading. We drove through the Lincoln Tunnel, then on through New Jersey. The signs of Paramus flashed through the sleet: CARPET WORLD, SHOE WORLD, and my favorite store, CHRISTMAS WORLD, its enormous Santa poised like a diver on the roof, appropriate since CHRISTMAS WORLD would soon undergo its annual transformation to POOL WORLD. My brother coaxed; I resisted – until we passed the sign that said EXIT TO CATSKILLS REGION, ONE MILE. I felt my heart leap. How wonderful it was to have grown up in a REGION, a world that existed solely to provide, not carpets or shoes, but good food and peaceful sleep, a day or a whole summer of nourishing life. Who cared what Arthur thought?

"I want to take over the Eden and run it."

The Camaro braked to a stop not far from the toll booths. My brother looked across the seat. When I said that I was serious he got out and opened the trunk.

Wearily, I followed. The gravel was wet and my sneakers soaked through.

"If you want to bury yourself alive, be my guest." He wrestled one of my boxes from the trunk and let it drop. "If you want to commit spiritual suicide, fine." He deposited a second box beside the first. "I don't have to help."

He hauled out the rest of my possessions. The bottoms of the boxes turned to pulp, but I didn't try to stop him.

"I'm not suicidal," I said. "And I don't want your help."

"No, you don't want anyone's help. And you know why? Because you're trying to fail. You and everyone else in this family. What is it, anyway? Is success evil? What are you all afraid of? You know what your mother thinks? She thinks the *goyim* will see me in this car and they'll say, 'Look at that damn Jew-lawyer in his sports car. Let's beat him up. Let's send him to the ovens.' This is America! They don't love you for being a loser. They love you for being rich. They love you for being successful."

A ragged ridge of snow ran along the highway. Embedded in the ice were a tailpipe and some carpet like the remains of a woolly mammoth. Cars whooshed past – *thwump, thwump, thwump* – sucking at me as if I had something they wanted.

Arthur gestured toward Paramus. "Half those stores and factories are owned by Jews. We're just doing well, that's all, and that makes you feel guilty. You and your kind, you pine for the *shtetls*." He kicked a box, which sighed and caved in. "You know what the *shtetls* were? Open sewers. Hovels. Children dying of horrible diseases. Is that what you want to do with the

Eden, turn it into a *shtetl?*" He slapped his forehead. "Sure! What a gimmick! You can make the guests wear rags, wash their clothes on rocks in the pond, work hard all day for a few rotten potatoes. And once in a while you can hire some of the *goyim* from town to dress up like Cossacks and ride into the Eden on horseback, pluck a few beards, threaten to impale a few babies. I can see the ads now: 'Do you feel guilty about having it so good? Have trouble feeling like a *real* Jew? Come to the Catskills! Experience a good old-fashioned pogrom!' "

"I have no intention of turning the Eden into a *shtetl.*" I intended to run it as it had always been run, but I saw suddenly that to do this would assure I would fail. And, despite what Arthur thought, I did not want to fail. I wanted the Eden to be famous. I wanted my guests to find the same joy I had known as a child. But it wouldn't be enough to organize games of Who Can Stay Underwater the Longest.

Arthur fingered the knot of the tie he wasn't wearing. "You're not Abe, you know. Even Abe wasn't Abe. I mean, was it really so saintly of him to make Nana sweat in the kitchen while he was out flirting with the guests? Your own parents, he sacrificed them too. Because he loved playing God. Granting favors. Arranging marriages. He thought one lousy week in the country could change a person's whole miserable life. He thought he could work miracles." Arthur snorted. "Maybe you are like him. You think you can save the Eden the way you saved Sam Brush. Well, I'll let you in on a secret." He leaned close. "Without me, and without the ambulance, Sam Brush would have been dead meat. And it wouldn't have been such a tragedy, now would it."

"Arthur!" All right, so Sam had become addicted to pot, liquor, glue. But he had joined Jews for Jesus and given up his vices, and now, two years later, he was back in eighth grade. "He might do some good yet," I told Arthur. "It's like some little snail or lizard or something. No one knows what it's good for, but if it died out, the whole Sahara Desert would get thrown out of whack."

"Things die out because they don't serve any use. And if one or two of them manage to survive, they get put in a zoo so people can gawk at them. Is that what you want, to run a freak show? 'Step right up, folks! Come see the last small hotel in the Borscht Belt!'"

I turned away to shield my idea from his sarcasm, which was all the more pointed since I feared it was true. It *was* a cheap gimmick to show off the Eden as a freak, to make money selling kitsch. But I couldn't accept the truth from a brother who said it in such a sharp tone. I told myself that preserving the Eden would be a service to history, like restoring a castle or a mansion.

"Look," Arthur said. "Do you really think Jews are so different from anyone else? On Sunday mornings the Christians eat bagels with their bacon and eggs, and we eat bacon and eggs with our bagels. Maybe the Christians conduct themselves with a bit more dignity, but that's about it. Don't you know? The only anti-Semitism left in America comes from guys like Jefferson, who say 'Yes ma'am' and 'No ma'am,' then shuffle home and dream about knifing their kindly Jew-bosses in the back."

I slammed down the trunk. "Go ahead. Leave me here. I'll flag down the bus when it stops at the toll."

He seemed more defensive. "All right, I shouldn't have said that." He thought I was angry because of what he said about Christians and Jews. "Come on, get back in the car."

I shook my head no. But just then a bottle smashed the pavement near our feet. A fountain of glass shot up; beer spattered Arthur's trousers. Some teenage boys hooted and Arthur gave them the finger. The van raced through the toll booth without paying and a siren went off.

"I said I was sorry. If you want to flush your life down the toilet, I can't stop you. At any rate, I can't leave you here."

I looked toward the mountains, beyond which rain clouds were gathering. I had so much to carry. And the bus driver might not agree to take me on.

I got back in the car. Arthur loaded my boxes in the trunk. We drove to the toll booth.

"Just promise me one thing." He fumbled in his pocket for change. "If I find a new buyer, you won't make a fuss. You'll just let me sell the place." He tossed the coins in the basket and reached for my arm. "Promise me, Lucy?"

I once would have promised whatever he asked, in return for so little. But he asked for too much now. If I gave up the Eden, what would I have left? If the answer was nothing, I would rather not know. All the way to Paradise I sat pressed against my door. Arthur gave up imploring, just cursed the other drivers until he pulled up in front of our parents' house in town.

"*You* break the news. I have a brief to prepare for tomorrow, I don't have time for your foolishness."

I knew that my parents would be disappointed if Arthur didn't stay, but telling them my plans would be easier if he wasn't there to mock them.

He tried one last time. "If you're tired of New York, come up to live in Boston. My place is too big for one person. Anyway, I wouldn't mind . . . It wouldn't be so bad having company. I'll help you find a job. If you want to go to school, I'll help out."

In my two terms at college the only book I had finished was a novel in which an unmarried sister kept house for her older brother and tried to prevent him from going astray. Could a brother really be so close to his sister? Maybe in England. Even there, I suspected, the custom had died out in Victorian times. Yet here was my brother making such an offer. He was willing to include his uncouth younger sister in the life he had been laboring so hard to create. He would prove that it was possible to teach a crude Jewess to behave like a debutante and sweetly discuss the rain on Cape Cod.

"Arthur, I swear I'm not doing this to embarrass you. I don't intend to throw away my life. I *want* to run the Eden. I want to make it successful. It's the only thing I can do."

He pounded the Camaro's fender. "You're not stupid! There are a million things you could do, if you would just get it out of your head that it's boring to work a normal job."

My mother came to the door – and froze when she saw her daughter's possessions piled in the street, her daughter slumped against those boxes as if she had been evicted.

"She's all yours!" Arthur shouted, and he drove off before my mother or I could ask who was whose.

I had hoped that my parents would be more grateful than my brother.

"Grateful?" my mother said. "The Eden is like a person who all his life has asked for a little work to do. Nobody listens, they let him starve. Then he gets old, he wants to retire, and somebody tells him, 'Okay, now you must go to work.'"

"You don't think I can do it."

"Maybe you can, maybe you can't. But for what? A big nothing."

"It won't be for nothing. I have my ideas." And I told them these ideas as they popped in my head – new decor in the rooms, a new chef and baker, the right kind of publicity, and, someday, I hoped, heat in the rooms so we could keep the Eden open all year, with skating on the pond and skiing on the mountain.

And my parents gave in, not because they believed these plans would succeed, but because they couldn't bear to be the ones to pull the plug if there still were some hope the Eden might live.

I handed a scrap of paper to Nana. YOU CAN KEEP THE HOTEL. I'LL HELP YOU RUN IT.

She threw the paper back. "Wipe your *tuches* with your help, naah!"

I had found her in her workshop, painting a trash can – it had once been an industrial-size container of pot cheese, but Nana had adorned it with ladies in plumed hats and extravagant bustles, copying their figures from her book about England, though the ladies in the book had quieter taste.

I picked up the scrap of paper. BUT I WANT TO, I wrote.

"'Want'! You're just like your grandfather. The others have no choice, your mother and that good-for-nothing husband of hers. What else can they do, naah?" She lifted the trash can. "At your age I was married three years already. 'College?' he says. 'You want to use your brains, use them to help run this hotel.' Brains? I need my brains to pluck a chicken? But you! You could run a big business! Be rich! Even a teacher, naah, it isn't worth much, but a woman has a job, she doesn't have to take crap from a man. You have the chance I didn't have!"

She hurled the trash can. I ducked. The can rolled into a corner, as if the fancy ladies were trying to hide.

I DON'T CARE WHAT YOU THINK.

"If you don't care, naah, then why did you come?"

I walked to the door.

"You could be something! You have the chance I didn't have!"

Standing on the lawn, I could still hear her shouting. I might have felt sympathy for the life that my grandmother hadn't been allowed to live, but I needed to believe she was my enemy. How else could I justify stealing the only thing she had left?

It was the very end of April. An inch of late snow covered the shingled roofs and the tarp on the swimming pool. The Eden seemed peaceful, with the dignity and composure of an elderly man who's passed on in his sleep. It reminded me of the way my grandfather had looked lying in the bungalow the September before – he had waited until Labor Day, as if he didn't want to inconvenience his family by dying until the guests had gone home. I'd had a foreboding the day before his death, but I thought I was just dreading my departure for school. When my mother found her father, he was lying on the floor beside his wheelchair. Somehow, she hoisted his body to the mattress, then covered it with the sheet (PROPERTY OF GARDEN OF EDEN HOTEL was stamped on the cotton). My mother went to tell Nana and my father; unsuspecting, I came in to find some pillows I would need to take to school. I lifted the sheet. Death had relaxed what the stroke had contorted. I kissed his dumpling cheek, as I hadn't been able to bring myself to do since he'd suffered the stroke. And I cried as I hadn't cried my whole life, great shaking sobs, until my mother came back and saw me and nodded, she finally approved of something I had done.

Now, as I stood on Nana's lawn, hearing her curse me, I wondered if I had loved Grandpa Abe so much because I hadn't been old enough to see him the way my brother had seen him – as someone human, and flawed. And, just for that moment, I wondered if I shouldn't let the Eden lie peacefully beneath its white sheet.

But a breeze blew just then. The earth stirred beneath my feet, a sleeper rolling over. As I crossed the front lawn I whispered each building's name – the Chalet, the Pagoda, Rose Cottage, the Ranch – and each building seemed to rouse itself, groaning and creaking. I knelt beside the flower beds and flattened my hands to the cold soil – I could almost feel the crocuses nuzzling my palms.

Run a hotel? I was only nineteen. My parents had agreed to spend a few days helping me get ready, but after June first I would be on my own.

You flunked most of your courses. You'll fail at this too.

And the next thing I knew I was standing on the porch of the handyman's cabin. I wanted him to tell me that I had done the right thing. *Run the Eden? Nothing to it. Not for a girl with talents like yours.*

"Hello? Someone out there?"

His voice squeezed my heart. I lifted my hand to knock. And I held it there, thinking. It was one thing to knock on a door as a child, get a lonely young man accustomed to your presence, then leave him as you made your way in the world. But to knock a second time, to knock as a grown-up . . .

"Hello?" he called. "Hello?"

According to my brother, any Jew who thought a black person liked her was deluded or blind. I didn't believe this exactly. But maybe I should.

"That you out there, Lucy?"

The quiver in his voice convinced me that he actually hoped it was me. I opened the door. He looked smaller somehow. More ordinary, like any man reading his paper at the table, a napkin across his lap, a bowl of soup at his hand, the empty can beside the sink. Also near the sink lay a sponge, a bar of soap, a large metal tub and a towel. The way these were placed, and the way his skin and hair still gave off a damp sheen, made me understand that he had just taken a sponge bath and shampooed his hair. I hadn't wondered how he washed. I must have thought he found an empty tub across the street. But the boilers were shut now. I imagined him stripping to his underwear, sponging an arm, then a leg, soaping his hair, and this filled me with such tenderness I wanted to tell him, *I know how you bathe.*

He looked a bit drawn, with a half-moon of coal smudged beneath each eye. But he smiled, and I realized that I still found him handsome. This made me nervous, that I now found him both ordinary and handsome. He was thirty-three, or thirty-four. It seemed old, and it didn't.

He got up from the table and I saw with a start that he wasn't wearing shoes. One sock was darned. I thought that he might hug me, but he folded his paper – or rather, he tried to, but he couldn't find the creases – and laid it on the table.

"Missed you," he said. "Missed you quite a bit."

My heart burst wide open. "I should have written you. I shouldn't – "

He shushed me. "You were busy with classes. Meeting new people. That's just how it should be."

I told him how badly I had done, how lonely I had been. I watched his face to see if he would lose his temper and accuse me, as my grandmother had accused me, of wasting the only thing he had wanted in his own life.

If he did feel resentful, Thomas didn't let this show. He sucked on his lips and listened until I was done. Then he said that he believed each human heart needed to be free to go after the things it loved. If my heart led me to the Eden, it was right that I come back.

"Just remember," he said, "you haven't messed up. If things here don't work out, you can always go back to school. You can let them sell the Eden. You can try something else. I know you don't believe that. That's not the way a person thinks at your age. But someday you'll be glad someone said this to you. Hear me? You've still got lots of chances."

I wanted to ask why *he* hadn't gotten more chances. Because he wasn't white? Because he had messed up in a way that was worse than most people messed up?

He set the table for tea. Then, as we sat drinking, I told him my plans – everything from reviving Yiddish theater and klezmer music to proving to the world that kosher cuisine needn't be bland. "In a few years," I told him, "the Eden will be the only place left where someone can see what the Catskills were like."

I meant what I said. Then why did the words sound so artificial?

He kneaded his eyes with his thumbs. Tugged the visor on his cap. Stood and paced, sat back down. I thought he would raise objections. Arthur had tried and failed to shoot down my dream, but if Thomas took aim I would have nothing left.

"Got to admit, when I heard your parents intended on selling, I was sort of relieved."

His eyes strayed to the crumpled newspaper, which was open to the want ads. Was he studying the classifieds to find where the need for handymen was greatest, where cabins came cheap?

"I was all set to leave. Then I saw you that day, with your father and that rabbi. And I knew what would happen. Knew this place was too . . . Well, it's a whole way of life." He poured me more tea. "Think you ought to do it?"

My stomach knotted. I drooped.

"I just mean, well, maybe the old forms won't work. Maybe you've got to let the Eden . . . *evolve*. Into something, well, something more . . . Sure you want to keep it only for Jews? That always seemed, well, sort of *limited* to me."

I tried to imagine the Eden crowded with a convention of Mormons from Utah, Catholics from Pittsburgh, black Baptists from Mississippi. What would they eat? Wasn't brisket just pot roast? Would a Mormon like *kugel*? If we served steak and mashed potatoes, if the comics told their jokes in English, if everyone were welcome, what would make the Eden more special than a Holiday Inn?

"Never mind," he said. "Guess I'm just talking to hear myself talk." He slapped his knees. "Have to let me know how all these plans of yours turn out."

I felt the anger and despair that overcomes you when a man you've taken for granted hints that he might leave.

"But you can't go," I said. "I can't do any of this without you."

"Sure you can. Lots of guys can use a hammer. And it's better if it's not . . . Better if a person . . ."

"I thought we'd be partners," I said, though I hadn't really thought this until a moment before. "Not technically. I won't own the Eden." Until Nana died. "But I thought we could be . . . If I ever make a profit, I'll be glad to give half . . ."

"Not partners. No." He held out his palms and wagged them. "Never had much inclination for the business end of things. Wasn't cut out to run anything, least of all a hotel. A Jewish hotel at that! There's my books, and my . . . privacy. I'm too old a Negro to change his tricks now."

Too old? Was he expecting to work as a handyman until he dropped dead? Was that his ambition? I was holding out half my life – who was he to refuse it? I pounded the table. My tea cup tipped, soaking a corner of his paper.

I was suddenly ashamed. How could I be angry at him for wanting to live in peace without having to humor the likes of Mrs. Heffer? I was sure that he would go, and this made me so desolate I buried my face on my arms. I felt his hand on my head. Or I thought I felt his hand. Or maybe I just wished this.

"I'm sorry," I said. "I'll hire someone else. But you shouldn't . . . you don't have to leave."

I had said the right thing.

"You can keep living here. I'll still pay you."

He winced. "I won't take your money. You have to understand that, I can't take your money, Lucy. If you need me that badly, all right. I'll stay. I'll help out. I'll do what I can do."

I could tell that he was acting against his better judgment, which, for a man who prides himself on always doing what's right, ought to be a warning.

"That's crazy. You have to let me pay you. What will you live on?"

"That's my business. My part of the bargain is staying here and helping, for a little while at least. Your part is not treating me . . . not talking about money. That understood? Do we have ourselves a deal here?"

He held out his hand. I lifted my own to shake it, but our hands never met, as if we both understood that making contact now would cause some shock to surge through us. We had touched before, on prom night. But that had been the end of something, and this would be the start.

All of this scared me – how desolate I felt when he said he might leave, the way we now stood, the tension so great an arc of electricity might leap between our hands. Now, looking back, knowing all I know that followed, would I insist Thomas stay? No. But I'm glad I can't have that choice.

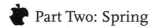 Part Two: Spring

A fly-speckled door led in from the street. I had twisted my ankle, falling through the rotted porch of Rose Cottage, and the stairs loomed before me, so crooked and steep I would have turned back if the Eden's fate hadn't hung on what I had come here to do. I hopped on my good foot, one step at a time. The railing pulled away from the wall, as macabre as if I had shaken hands with an old man and his arm had come off. I paused on the landing, looking up, looking down. How many foolish things do we finish simply because the effort expended in climbing halfway seems too precious to waste?

The second-floor hall was so dimly lit I navigated by touch, heading toward the faint illumination of a door marked COLONIAL CONNECTICUT INSURANCE.

Four powdery women worked in the anteroom. Each wore a white sweater clasped around her neck, sleeves hanging limp as moth wings. Each wore a headset. Their fingers brushed the keys of their typewriters daintily. They shifted their heads – left to right, right to left.

"Please," I said loudly. "May I see Mr. Kilcoin?"

They lifted their chins and blinked.

"I want Mr. Kilcoin," I repeated.

"Oh. She wants Mr. Kilcoin." They smiled slowly at one another. With the bandage on my leg, I must be a claimant; being female besides, I must be Mr. Kilcoin's mistress.

"And who . . . might we . . . ask . . . *wants* Mr. Kilcoin?," as if to imply that any one of a million feminine names might be the answer.

I wasn't ashamed. I knew why I had gone up to the linen closet with Jimmy Kilcoin that day. He had seemed wicked. Forbidden. And he gave the last lie to the lesson that my brother tried so hard to teach me: that all Christian men were ethereal beings who never would see beauty in a rude girl like me.

"Never mind," I said. "I'll find him myself." And that's just what I did.

I hadn't come with a plan. I only knew this: I had already given Jimmy something of worth, and now I would ask that he give something back. I thought that because *he* wanted *me*, because I was young and he was middle-aged, I had more power than he did. If he demanded more than I had given him already, I would say no and walk out.

Seven steel desks lined the back room in which the adjusters did their paperwork. All seven bore nameplates: Kilcoin, Birney, Noble, Corrigan, O'Dowd, McGillicuddy, Blake. Six desks were bare, but the one that said "Kilcoin" had a small stack of files and a smoldering cigarette-butt in the foil ashtray.

"Hey!" He came in, slicking down a tuft of reddish-gray hair. He smiled an uneven smile — like most unmarried men his age he seemed only half-tame, like a squirrel or a fox you're tempted to pet. And it came to me then that understanding why you had slept with such a man had nothing to do with whether you would give in and sleep with him again.

"Lucy Appelbaum," he marveled, and, in saying my name, made me feel something no one else did: that I was a woman who deserved the attention of every man I met. What did it matter if my nose was too flat, cheeks freckled, hair frizzed? Eyes, freckles, hair — these were nothing but a way to tell women apart.

"So, how long's it been? Ten months? That's all? Seems a hell of a lot longer, just sitting here wondering if I'd ever see you again."

I mustn't believe what I knew couldn't be true. He couldn't have been thinking of no one but me since the summer before. I told myself again I didn't want to be one of the countless women he had slept with. What I forgot was that so many women slept with Jimmy Kilcoin because he persuaded each of them that she was the only woman he cared for.

He wheeled the chair from Corrigan's desk to his own – this seemed wrong to me, like stealing from the dead. "Sit, sit." He gestured toward the cracked leather seat.

My ankle throbbed, and standing made me feel exposed. Against my better judgment, I did what he said.

He perched on his desk, crossed his legs and leaned down with a tender look on his face. "I'm sorry, kid. Truly sorry. What can I do? Just say the word."

Did he mean he was sorry that Colonial Conn had doubled the Eden's premium? Then I saw that Jimmy's eyes were fixed on my leg.

"It's a crime. A dirty crime. Tell me who did it and I'll be all over the bastard."

"Nobody did it."

"When I find out which client – "

"It wasn't anyone, Jimmy. That isn't why I'm here."

"It's not?" He leaned closer. "Whatever the reason, I'm glad you came. Old Jimmy gets mighty lonely these days."

I thought he was saying this for sympathy. Then I noticed the dust hanging in the air, settling on the desks, covering the last traces of Messers Birney, Noble, Corrigan, O'Dowd, McGillicuddy, Blake.

"What happened?" I asked.

He waved toward the filing cabinets. DECEASED, the drawers were labeled. CASE CLOSED. EXPIRED. "One more big claim and . . ." He guillotined his neck. "Where would I go, kid?" He peered out the grimy window. "That's my favorite view. I look out on that and I know where I am. A man needs an anchor. I got my fill of drifting in the Navy."

He told me the story I had heard twice before: how the Kilcoins before him all had been drifters; how his mother lost her moorings and floated out of his life when Jimmy was fifteen; how he ran off and joined the Navy and within a few months his mail to his father was being returned ADDRESSEE UNKNOWN;

and how, at age twenty, he found himself wandering the streets of Manhattan with no guide except a fellow ex-sailor who said the place to get laid was the Catskills. *You see? It's all Jews there.* But Jimmy did not see, so his companion took pity and explained that Jewish girls didn't believe in hell. Nothing in their bible said they couldn't take precautions. And these Jewish girls, see, when they went looking for action, they went looking in the Catskills. If they met a Jewish guy with plenty of bucks, fine. If not, well, they didn't mind passing time with fellas like them. And Jimmy didn't have to worry they'd start talking marriage, because he wasn't their kind, see?

This time he saw. Though modesty prevented him from saying it, the women in the Catskills responded so warmly to a red-headed ringer for Frank Sinatra that Jimmy decided to live out his life there. He became an adjuster – the ad specified that no experience was needed, although Jimmy was confident that his knowledge of poker – odds, bluffing, risks – would make him invaluable in insurance. And his boss, it turned out, liked to hire gentiles since a Jewish adjuster might be too generous to an injured claimant of his faith.

Jimmy didn't say so, but he must have soon realized what leverage the job gave him over his claimants, especially the women. He tried not to use it, preferring to rely on his good looks and humor, his ability to make a woman cry "Thank you!" to acknowledge the receipt not of money, but pleasure. He encouraged these women to whisper their desires. He remembered what they said; if memory failed, he could turn to these files – I imagined him jotting a shorthand of passion on the jacket of each.

If not for these files, this nameplate, this desk, if not for the thousands of Jews whose claims he'd adjusted . . . Oh, it was clear! Colonial Conn needed gentiles like Jimmy, and Jimmy needed Jewish women like me so he would know who he was – a Catholic, a man.

Flush with the notion that *I* could use *him,* I announced why I had come. "The premium," I said. "We can't pay it."

He didn't seem upset that I had switched topics. In Jimmy's mind, pleasure and business were as near to one another as his pockets to his genitals.

"I know, kid. It's rough. But I heard your folks were selling. Always did like your folks. Time they got some enjoyment from life."

"They will. Listen, Jimmy. I'm going to run it."

"Run the Eden? Come on. A chance to go to college and you'd come back to this?"

Would I spend the rest of my life listening to people regret that I had wasted the chance they didn't have? I told myself that Jimmy could have gone to college on the G.I. Bill. He could have worked his way through. Even if he had gone, what would he have studied – picking up girls?

I struggled to my feet. "Never mind my reasons. We can't pay. What good will it do the company to make us shut down?"

He thumped his breast pocket. Did I think it was his fault? If he'd had his way, he would have cut the premiums. But no one ever asked him. A few owners had come crawling to his boss. Hell, that didn't do much good. Eicher was hoping if the Catskills operation closed down, he'd finally get a shot at an office in Hartford, though in Jimmy's opinion the hotshots in Hartford would be only too glad to find an excuse to put this old Yid out to pasture. He put his arm around my shoulder. "Not many people remember old Jimmy. I'm touched you came, kid."

I shook off his arm. "I came to find out if you'd help. That's the *only* reason I came."

"Why shouldn't I help?" He cracked his knuckles. "Guy's gotta admire the way you won't just lie down and roll over. You did what I would do. You decided to fight. But hey, you know my theory. The minute I saw that red hair, those freckles, that button nose, I knew you hadda have some Irish blood in those veins." He nudged me. "Come on, kid. You must have felt something or you wouldn't have gone up to that closet with so little persuading."

So little? I'd resisted most of July! Then I understood. When a woman gave in, Jimmy felt disappointed. He enjoyed the pursuit for its own sake. I could string him along for a few months, at least. And then it wouldn't matter. The Eden's season would be enough of a success that I could pay the damn premium, or else we would have to close. In the back of my mind I probably believed that if worse came to worst and I had to sleep with Jimmy, it wouldn't cost that much. He wasn't married, was he? Who would be hurt? I thought I could live like that goddess who spent her summers above ground without being corrupted by her winters in Hell.

"I'll do what I can, kid – pull a few strings, get my pal Miller to fudge some inspections. We'll say your pool is out of commission, you closed the casino . . . Fewer hazards, lower rates. It won't be easy, but what the heck, for a friend . . ."

I had won? That was all? I had given up nothing. Elated, I thanked him.

"It's worth it to see you so happy. Anyone told you how gorgeous you look when you turn on that smile?"

I stepped back, out of range of his flattery.

"Hey kid, one condition."

What if he demanded that I sleep with him now? What if Jimmy cared less for the game than results?

"What kind of condition?"

"Hey! Don't worry!" He lifted one hand like a witness swearing to tell the truth. "I'm an old man! I'm harmless! It's just that you never can tell when you might need a favor. If the time comes, I feel safer knowing I have some chips I can call in."

I should have said no. But just then I felt I had so many chips, I could spare any number. I didn't understand that once you started saying such words to yourself – "favors" and "chips" – you'd already lost whatever you were hoping to win.

I tore down the curtains – and started an avalanche of dried wasps and dead bats. Over the decades Nana had papered the rooms with remnants she had wheedled from Doodie's Hotel Supplies. When a piece was too short to cover all four walls, she finished the room with other patterns: Dutch boys on two sides, shamrocks on the third, and the final wall papered a velvety red that must have been designed for bordellos.

We steamed it and scraped it, layer by layer, until we unearthed the bare plaster. Then we swooshed on fresh paint in thick creamy strokes. We sanded the floors and slathered on varnish until the wood glowed and the air was pungent with hope.

One afternoon, as we worked back-to-back in a tiny room in Rose Cottage, Thomas started to whistle a Mills Brothers tune, the slap of his brush a snare-drum percussion. I felt lightheaded, a reaction I blamed on the paint fumes. I wore overalls and sneakers, every inch spattered, and a rag on my head, though I had managed to get paint in my ears. Thomas, as always, wore a white shirt and khaki trousers with a perfect crease down the front, not a smear of paint anywhere, though the hair on his arms was misted white. He seemed restless, withdrawn. When I asked his advice – should I buy nicer curtains, or just wash the old ones? – he said you couldn't turn a whore – he pronounced it "a hoor" – into a lady just by putting her into a clean dress, now could you.

I stiffened as if *I* had been insulted.

"I wouldn't pay so much mind to those curtains," he said. "What about all the repairs I need to get to? You're young, you mend fast. One of those old folks falls through a porch . . ."

I swatted the wall with my brush. "If you're going to be such a pessimist, why don't you leave?" I said this impulsively, the way a child shouts at a parent *I wish you were dead*, only to be seized by the terror that he would go.

"I might just do that," he said. "Stranger things have happened."

The fear that he might leave kept raising the question of where he had lived before he'd come to the Eden. Despite his bad humor, I couldn't help but ask.

"Never been curious about such things before now." He pried open a new can and stirred it with a stick, dredging up the thicker paint from the bottom.

"I was curious," I said. "I was just too scared to ask."

He dipped his brush in the bucket. "And now?"

"Now, I guess . . . I just care, okay? Isn't that enough reason?"

He applied the brush to the wall with deliberate strokes. "And that entitles you to an explanation?"

"Forget it. You're right. Your life's a big mystery. I wouldn't understand."

Up and down went the bristles. "You could order me to tell you. Boss has that right."

I threw the brush. It smacked his neck, painted a stripe down his shirt, white on white, then continued down his trousers, with a final dab at one shoe. He rubbed the paint on his neck. He deserved it, I thought. What crime had I committed? What right did he have to remain so aloof?

He held the brush to his face. "Sure you don't want to finish the job?"

"I said I care about you. Is that so terrible? Would it be so terrible to admit you care about me?"

He held my brush by the bristles. Reluctantly, I took it. He turned back to the wall, as if to write his reply. "Well, girl," he said. He was laughing by now, but he still sounded angry. "I sure as hell ain't working here because I like borscht."

I awoke the next morning and started to sing, almost in tune: "Don't sit under the apple tree with anyone else but me, no, no, no . . ." He'd said he loved me, hadn't he? He'd at least said he cared. With Thomas Jefferson beside me, what couldn't I accomplish?

I whisked room to room, yanking orange doilies from the bureaus and fuchsia cushions from the chairs. The furniture dated back to the time when the Eden had been Dr. Gerhardt's Sanitarium for Consumptives and Neurasthenics; stripped of camouflage and polished, most of the pieces had the charm of antiques. In a frenzy I gathered up the milk-bottle vases, the bath mats of woven bread-wrappers, the triptych of Henry the Eighth (who took up two panels) and his daughter Bloody Mary, and carted them to the cellar. Even on my last trip, when I ran into Nana, I kept dumping lamp shades (of melon rinds, lacquered) along with the rest. Because my grandmother's handiwork was ugly, it seemed evil. While Thomas rescued machines from premature death, my grandmother condemned pieces of junk to remain in her service past their time. She tried to create beautiful things but produced trash.

I tossed the last painting in the cellar and snapped the lock shut.

"You'll be sorry!" Nana shouted, as if I had captured an army of zombies who would awaken in the night and obey her commands.

Sure enough, when I passed the cellar next day, I saw the lock broken. The zombies had escaped, though a trail of bottle caps and painted lima beans led in a jagged trail to her door.

In those innocent years before World War II, a fad for pagodas swept across the Catskills. But my grandfather's attempt to copy the style turned out more like a wedding cake than a Japanese shrine. I was on my knees, shingling the bottommost tier. Thomas was shingling the peaked roof on top, silhouetted against a sky the radiant blue of a seltzer bottle.

"Be careful!" I shouted.

He looked down, amused. "You speaking to me, girl? I was *born* on a rooftop. Storks in Virginia didn't waste time aiming for chimneys when they had a delivery of colored to make."

The boasting seemed forced; he still looked so vulnerable, perched on that roof.

"You want me to find another helper? Go on now, get working." He climbed across the peak to shingle the other side.

I got to my feet. The height made me dizzy, but I couldn't resist stealing one more aerial view of our – *my* – hotel. The air was cool and fresh; it smelled of survival – mud and damp wood, sweet fresh-cut grass. The lawn glittered with the rain that had fallen that dawn. I could hear the faint squeak of the oak trees exercising their arthritic limbs, the new maples growing, the ground sucking moisture with insatiable thirst. By the end of June, lush foliage would hide the buildings' worst flaws. The vines on the trellis beside the Main House were sprouting nipple-pink buds. Curlicue tendrils would unwind from the branches and grow grapes like green buckshot; the peeling trellis would disappear beneath the huge spreading leaves, and the grapes would turn purple, fragrant as jam.

Why wouldn't young Jews want to come here – if not for the season, then a week, a few days? The Eden was cheap, less than two hours' drive from that desert, Manhattan. Who had decreed that Jewish resorts must be tasteless? Why not homey, unpretentious . . . The Eden was . . . nice. Not breathtaking, true. But tranquil, and secluded, now that the nearby resorts had burned down. Only Pospissil's Playland still was visible from here, its bungalows like crumpled cardboard boxes that would soon rot and vanish.

"You practicing to be a weathervane?" Thomas asked. "I need some more shingles, if you aren't too busy."

I felt that I had been caught admiring my own image in a mirror. I hurried down the ladder. Thomas unfurled a rope; I knotted a bundle of shingles to the end and watched it ascend, up past the first floor, past the second . . .

"Doesn't this strike you as kind of futile?"

Star bursts of light blinded me, but I knew my brother's voice. I turned and saw Arthur. "If you don't approve, why did you bother coming? I don't need your heckling." Since I had taken over the hotel, he had grown even more abusive than before.

"I was on my way to the City. I just thought . . . I stopped off to see Mom and Dad."

"They're home. I've told you a hundred times, they're only going to help out a few days before we open."

He loosened his tie. "I was curious. I didn't intend to heckle. I just couldn't help it once I got here."

"You mentioned an appointment?"

"Not an appointment, exactly. I don't have to be there until dinnertime." He slipped off his sports coat. For a moment I thought my brother intended to help us shingle the roof.

"Don't let me stand in the way of your social life," I said.

"At least I have a social life. In case you haven't noticed, you're a little too old to spend your evenings in Jefferson's shack. It's not so cute anymore."

"Then aren't I too old to be told what to do?" I glanced up at the roof. Thomas hadn't moved from his place beside the ladder.

Arthur followed my gaze. He squinted up at Thomas. Then he squinted down at me. "What are you saying?"

It came to me that the most hurtful thing I could do then was smile.

"You idiot," Arthur said. He looked up at Thomas. "You're both idiots!" he shouted. Not knowing what else to do, he threw his tie on the ground. I expected it to turn to a snake, as Aaron's rod had changed to a snake in front of Pharaoh. But it lay there, a tie. Arthur must have felt foolish – he bent and picked it up on his way to the car.

I looked up at the roof. Thomas was climbing to the other

side – too quickly. I stood listening as if I knew what I would hear. And it came, a second later, like thunder after lightning, the clash of – what? shingles? – as they clattered to the walk.

A hoarse voice – my name. Then a second crash, the explosion of metal on macadam.

I ran around the back of the Pagoda, trying to make sense of what I saw. Thomas lay dangling from the roof, arms raised above his head, clutching a hammer whose claw was hooked beneath the last shingle he had nailed. His legs were suspended in the air. The gutter lay below, on the path. He looked so precarious I was afraid to make a move.

"Hold on," I said finally, though of course I didn't need to. I wrenched away my gaze and ran to get the ladder, which was so rickety that when I tried to pull it along the edge of the roof, it bounced, began to vibrate, then writhed from my arms.

I swore. Then I listened. In a very low voice he was saying *shit, shit, shit, shit.*

I dragged the ladder through the grass. It was heavier than I had believed a wooden ladder could be. I leaned it against the building and kept pushing it up until the top rung brushed his oxfords.

Why didn't he move? All he had to do was wriggle to one side and let himself down. Should I climb up and get him? But no, there he came, left foot, then right foot.

He stood before me, shaken, glasses bent and awry. He had lost his cap, exposing a bald patch on top. I had never seen him bareheaded.

He collapsed on the lawn. I stretched out beside him and we lay shaking in the sun, like a woman and a man exhausted by love.

"I don't know . . ." He threw his arm across his eyes. "I don't even know how to begin to say it."

I imagined him thanking me and was startled to find how distasteful this was.

"Your brother is right. You are getting too old to hang around my place. People are going to think . . . Hell, *I'm* too old for this. I been here too long."

"You told me you would stay."

"I did. And I'll try to. I'll help as much as I can."

He didn't sound convincing.

"I don't get it," I said. "I don't understand anything about you."

"Not much to understand." He tore grass from the lawn. "Always been strange." He stopped. That was all.

"Yes?" I said. "You were strange?"

He considered the boy he had been. "Leastwise, strange for where I was. For who I was supposed to be."

The presence of his younger self was so strong I could see him. He wore a white shirt and black pants. His hair was shaved so short I could see his knobby skull. I lifted my arm, but the boy flinched and shied away.

Sometimes, Thomas said, his only memory of childhood was of having a book ripped from his hands – by his siblings, or his schoolmates, the older boys hanging out on the corner. By high school he was spending most of his days at the colored library in Charlottesville. He thought if he read all the philosophy books and encyclopedias, he could somehow go to college. Not the little school for black kids. The big one. The university his namesake had built.

"Wasn't any of this self-hatred nonsense. Too *vain* to hate myself. Just seemed, well, kind of limited, going to school with nobody but poor black folks. Too *vain* to be limited. Did Leonardo da Vinci limit himself? Did Benjamin Franklin?"

"Or Thomas Jefferson?"

He laughed like a person who is pleased that an intricate joke has been discovered by someone who can appreciate the wit required to play it. "Thought it didn't matter they'd never let a colored boy through the door before me. Didn't matter about the money. I thought, How can they keep out the great-grandkid of the guy who built that damn school?"

"So you really are related? To Thomas Jefferson? The real one?"

"Hell, I thought I *was* the real one. Every chance I got, I'd run off to Monticello. Used to stick around until closing . . . everyone was gone, I'd pretend I owned the place. Those were *my* books, *my* garden, the inventions *I* invented." He laughed again. "Never occurred to me if the university let in all the colored kids around Charlottesville thought they were descended from the president, they wouldn't have room for the white kids. I just figured I belonged there, and somehow they'd know. I'd go up there and they'd realize I was part of the family. I'd go up there, I'd talk to them a while, I'd amaze them with the breadth and depth of my self-acquired learning, throw in some Shakespeare, quote that old Bible – 'Yea, verily! I have understanding as well as you do! I am not inferior to you! Yea, who knoweth not such things as these?' They would hear that old Bible and they'd throw open their arms: 'You're the one we been waiting for! Forget about that money! We love the colored!'"

He shook his head. "I went up there. Sometimes I can't believe anyone . . . But I did! I actually knocked at those doors! I said why I'd come! And they listened. Oh, they were *gentlemen.* Those nice tweed suits. All those books. Those little metal things they used to tamp down their pipes. I held the door for one of them. I remember it, I did hold a door. I might even have held a coat sleeve!"

He looked at me as if I surely would agree that holding a sleeve was absurd.

"In just that one morning I talked to, oh, I don't know, six secretaries? One dean? Seven full professors? And who knows how many less-than-full professors. Quite a morning's work. Had to rest. Had to take some refreshment. Had to get up my strength to knock on some more doors, hold some more sleeves."

He closed his eyes and grimaced, or maybe it was a grin.

"Found a nice sunny spot on top of some stairs. Loosened my shoes. Just a little, mind you. Didn't want the white folks to think I was the kind of Negro take his shoes off right there, in public. You didn't take off your shoes in public. And you didn't eat in public. Not if you knew who you were. Not if your mother made *sure* you knew who you were. I had this candy bar, and I just kind of broke off pieces – you know, I kept it in my pocket, sneaked the pieces to my mouth, tried not to chew. And I took out a book. Way in the back of my mind, I guess I hoped some professor would happen by and notice this neatly attired colored boy with his shoes on and this shabby but impressive edition of *Faust* open on his lap, and, well, the rest would follow."

As he had told me himself, sometimes we get what we never should have wished for. A professor walked by. Nicely dressed. Decent. He did indeed seem glad that a colored boy should be reading such a difficult book. He said that he was curious whether Thomas thought the Devil had a legal claim on Faust's soul.

"Now, you got to understand," Thomas explained, "he didn't present this like a question two men might discuss. He said it like a test. Like the test I'd been waiting my whole life to take. Shouldn't have answered, I know that now. But I didn't know it then. I was still at that age when a boy thinks he's got to answer every question anyone asks. Felt I'd been chosen of all the colored boys in the Commonwealth of Virginia to argue for . . . Well, I felt like every man, woman and child in the country, black, white or otherwise, was watching us up there, at the top of those steps.

"And so I said: 'No, sir, the Devil did not have a claim on Faust's soul, because the Devil didn't give Faust what he promised. Faust never did get his moment of peace.'

"'But boy!'" Thomas threw his voice in a cranky falsetto.

"'Boy, you take a closer look at their contract! What do you make of the terms of their contract!'

"I remember it annoyed me, that he used that word, 'contract,' like we were discussing the bill of sale for a mule. I told him God didn't care about whether Faust violated that contract or not. That contract belonged to the Devil. Only thing mattered to God was whether old Faust kept striving for the right way to live.

"'Striving for power, you mean! Faust just wants power! That's a sin, isn't it, boy, to want more power than God gives you!'

"And I said no, it wasn't a sin, and we argued about that for a while. And I must have been winning, because he switched questions on me. The man asked, What did I think Faust meant by the words 'the Eternal Feminine.' The force, or whatever it is, that draws us all upward. Most of us, leastwise. And that's when I saw. In *his* mind, the Eternal Feminine was this beautiful white lady perched on that law school behind us, and I was too close to that Eternal Feminine already, on top of those stairs.

"I should have stopped then. I know that now. But then? Hell, it was like some sort of chess match old Mephistopheles himself had cooked up. I couldn't back down. And this gentleman professor couldn't back down. And we argued in the sun there, argued and kept on arguing. And maybe I was winning. And maybe he was sorry he'd made the first move. Or maybe he just got tired and wanted to end the discussion the only way he knew how."

I wished he would stop the story. I didn't want to know how much he must have lost, because how could I replace it? How could a man who had come to me from such an alien world, who had lived so much life I hadn't lived, see me as any more than a child?

But Thomas kept talking. He seemed to speak a language whose words I didn't know. I remember only these facts: how the professor took away the book and tossed it down the steps; how Thomas asked the man to please pick it up, and, when he wouldn't, gave the professor a shove to get him started.

The man stumbled and fell down two or three steps. He ended up sitting there, leg bent to one side. Thomas said that he was surprised the professor's socks didn't match, and he looked up to tell someone, but he saw some students approaching and decided that he ought not say a thing. He excused himself, as if he had a class he was late for, and a few hours later he was on a bus for New York.

"But it was an accident," I said.

"Yes, it was that. It surely was an accident."

"I don't get it. You broke a man's leg? You ruined your life for that?"

He shook his head. "Didn't run off just because I was scared of what they'd do to me, breaking that man's leg. That man . . . I didn't just want to shove him. Lucy, I wanted to . . . Over a lousy book! I wanted to kill that man. I wanted to push him down and kick his head and kill him."

"Okay, you were angry. But I don't see why – "

"Lucy, you've got to stop seeing me the way you did when . . . You think, just because I can keep it all inside, it must be, well, easy to keep there."

I noticed my hands were bleeding, and I was glad for the blood, for the slivers in my palm, glad for this penance for the ease of my life. He was right, I hadn't really seen him before. And I was losing him, bit by bit, before I even had him.

When he got to New York, he said, he needed money. He met a man in a lunchroom who ran an employment agency right there, from his booth. Next thing Thomas knew, he was on a bus to the Catskills.

"To Paradise!" he said. "Seemed they needed a fix-it man at some hotel called the Garden of Eden. The Garden of Eden! In Paradise, New York!"

The more he laughed, the more I could see how enormous his pain was. Crying was small. He had cried himself out a long time before, then he'd had to move on, the way a person counts on his fingers and toes until he reaches twenty, then needs to find another system to use. I started crying with him, as if that somehow might help.

"Lucy? It's nothing. I'm all right now. It hasn't been so bad. I stayed here because I wanted to stay. Where else could I work three months a year and get paid for twelve? Free room and board. All that time to read and think. Time to be by myself. Your family's been decent. Your grandfather, he used to come down to my place a lot, to get away from your grandmother. And the Feidels – fine folks, the Feidels – they used to bring me books. Nat taught me some Talmud, to pass the time. Then he stopped. Said I knew everything he had to teach me, but I think it just hurt too much, how he'd given up his studies for fixing toasters. And Shirley, she still brings me books now and again. One summer, she brought me that nice leather *Faust*. You remember, hmm, Lucy? Had quite a lot of time to examine the terms of that contract." His laugh had the sound of nails scraping steel. "Decided I was right. Decided old Mr. Mephistopheles was only bluffing, trying to win Faust's soul on a bluff."

What did I care who got whose soul? I stared at the bald spot. "Can I ask you something else?"

He shrugged. "Depends what."

"Why do you wear that cap?"

"My cap?"

"Is it because you . . . You wear it all the time, even inside."

He looked puzzled. "You think it's like some sort of yarmulke?" He pronounced the word yar-mul-kee, the way it was written, instead of slurring it – *yom-i-ka* – the way the rest of us did. "You think I turned Jewish? You think that's why I wear that old thing?" He ducked his head and laughed. "Guess I considered it, once upon a time. I liked the way those old rab-bis worked a trade so they could do their studying for pleasure. I thought being Jewish was the appropriate religion for a fugi-tive. For an exile."

"You don't now?"

He hesitated, as if the answer might offend me. "Too much I couldn't swallow. Doubt I ever could accept any one way of thinking. You know me, I'm a scavenger. Keep what's useful, get rid of what isn't."

"And the hat?"

"Very useful. That old shack sure gets chilly, especially at night."

And me? Had I been useful? I couldn't say this, of course, any more than I could have asked what it felt like to live as the only non-Jew among Jews, the only black among whites. I couldn't admit that the place I felt most at home was so foreign to the person with whom I wanted to share it. Instead, what I said was, "You must have been lonely. For the company of adults, I mean."

"Adults? Why would . . . Oh. You mean *adults*. You mean, was I *lonely* for the *company* of *adults*. Well, no. No, I wasn't. Appreciate your concern, but I can't say I was. Always lots of *adults* to keep a man *company*, if that's what he wants."

"But you never left the cabin!"

He grinned. "Sure I did. Went to town most days, didn't I? Lots of adults to keep me company in town. Besides, I didn't need to go anywhere if what I wanted was company. Linda Brush and the rest, on tip-ee-toe at midnight . . . 'Knock-knock, Mr. Jefferson, you in there?' "

"You're lying! They didn't. *You* didn't." I felt ill.

"Afraid they did. As for me, well, I'm just flesh and blood. I'm a human being, Lucy. Not that I answered every knock. Not that turning away some of those ladies required much effort."

I swallowed. "What about me?"

"You were nine years old!"

"Later."

"How much later?"

"Well, now."

He got to his feet, narrowing his eyes toward the horizon, as if some message were scribbled across the treetops and, without his glasses, he couldn't make it out. "Now. Well, now I'm just rusty. And afraid of starting something I can't stick around to finish." He started walking in a circle, and he must have decided that he ought to have a purpose, because he began looking for his cap. He spotted it, finally, and snatched it from the ground, put it back on his head, and this seemed to compose him.

"I said I would stay, and I will. Just don't ask me how long."

I promised that I wouldn't. Though this was exactly what I most wanted to know.

I kicked free of my overalls, yanked the rag from my hair.

A crow cackled overhead.

"Scram!" I said. "Go away! This is my meadow!"

Though only May twentieth, it was ninety-two degrees. I had been hard at work since six, helping Thomas rebuild the porch of Rose Cottage. I was itchy, I stank, but Thomas had tarred the crack in the swimming pool and it hadn't yet dried. I could have made do with a shower, but what better way to establish my ownership over the land than treat this pond as my tub?

Three weeks of labor had hardened my body. Freckles bloomed on my arms. I did a little dance, loving the feel of warm dirt beneath my feet.

The best way to enter the pond was by sliding down a rock mottled with liverwort. Though I doubted that the moss could truly cause warts, as Arthur once told me, it did feel like liver.

I endured the goose bumps it gave because the water here was deep; I wouldn't touch the bottom, which I still half-believed was tangled with the skeletons of stoolies and thugs whose bodies had been dumped here by Murder Inc. during Prohibition.

The water was cold, but it was still clear of algae. I swam to the lily pads and forced myself to pat one. Arthur used to tell me that blood-sucking leeches clung to the stems. Only when Herbie persuaded me the leeches were fiction by swimming through the stalks, plucking a lemony flower and bringing it back in his teeth would I swim here again.

For a while, in the early seventies, I had gotten a postcard from Herbie every few months. ("Hey, Goose, I'm in college. The other guys say the food stinks, but it's sure better than that slop your grandmother fed us.") Then the postcards stopped coming. He was living in Sweden, someone said, or maybe it was India, in a temple for Buddhist monks. This latter was the story I chose to believe – I thought Herbie would be content in such peaceful surroundings, with the other monks as brothers and higher laws to obey. Then word trickled back that he had run away to Israel, joined the army and deserted.

Of all people, Arthur went to Israel to retrieve him. I remember my father asking what "the Holy Land" was like, and Arthur saying that the Holy Land was the kind of place crazies like Herbie thought was heaven because if you managed to get in, you would be happy and whole, the way you were as a kid. And they had to let you in – Jewish crazies, at least. But once you got in you had to act sane; things were crazy enough in Israel without real crazies, he said.

My father turned away, unable to hear my brother slander Israel, not to mention poor Herbie, who, *nebbech,* couldn't help his affliction. When Herbie returned to the Eden, face twitching like a rabbit's from whatever pills he was on, my father gave him a job. At first, Herbie couldn't remember an order long enough to fill it. But the longer he worked the more his memory improved. Though he wouldn't discuss the army, he would talk to me for hours about his summers as a busboy, in such intricate detail he might have been Lennie reciting a Marx Brothers routine (not that I made this connection until later, that living in the past is a symptom you're too weak to live in the here-and-now).

The bushes on the shore beyond the pond began to rattle. A squirrel flew up a tree.

"Thomas?" I called, though I doubted it was him – he had gone to town to buy bricks and carry out some business he declined to describe. But who else could it be – Arthur? or my parents? Who else might be out here this time of year?

It came to me then that it might have been the Hasid. When he couldn't afford the Eden, he settled on the empty chicken farm at Lipsett's. I grew chilled with the possibility; the pond turned to ice. I squinted at the path that led across the hill – I had taken it thousands of times to play with Marv, stealing the rejects from the egg candler's baskets, dissecting dead chicks. Hens were as finicky as hotel guests, but, according to Marv, his parents were smarter than mine since eggs weren't luxuries – even if people couldn't afford vacations, they needed to eat.

Despite the Lipsetts' wisdom, egg prices fell. The Lipsetts hung on longer than most, but Marv's father passed away – they found him one morning, two unbroken pee-wees still warm in his hands – and Marv's mother now was anxious to move to California and live near her son, Marv having become "an obstetrician to the stars," as my own mother put it. The Hasid could have bought the Lipsetts' farm for the lint in his pocket. Did he and his followers hold their orgies in the chicken coop where Marv once had shown me a two-headed hen? I tried to call *Who is it!,* but the words froze in my throat.

"Lucy? Is that you?" Thomas stepped into the clearing and stood shading his eyes. "Lucy? You in there?"

Beneath the murky water my breasts floated like dirty mushrooms; my feet, limpid fish, flashed this way and that. My clothes lay on shore, near a small red-striped towel. As icy as I had felt a moment before, I might now have been swimming in a pit of molten lava. I hoped Thomas would leave without seeing me. I prayed he might stay.

He climbed the rock, teetered. I saw a smile cross his face. "Thought you might be here."

"Why?" I said. "Is something wrong? What happened? What's the matter?"

"Who says anything's the matter? I finished up in town sooner than I expected. You weren't exactly subtle dropping hints about coming here."

The way he looked at me then made me realize I was floating naked in front of a man I had known all my life. Shame would set in soon. I never would be able to face him again.

I waited for this to happen. He wasn't staring, exactly. But he hadn't turned away.

"Do you want to come in?" I asked.

"You know I can't swim."

I was still in the water but I was sweating. "Well, it's time you learned, isn't it?"

He averted his gaze. "That was sort of my intention. But . . . I didn't expect to find you in quite such . . . To find you . . ."

Why did he have to be so considerate! All right, if he wanted me dressed, I would dress. His head was still turned so I climbed out on shore and buttoned on my blouse. I looked at my overalls, still soggy with sweat, the rag for my hair. I slipped back in the water.

"You can look now," I said.

He turned back to face me. Stroked his jaw. Tugged his collar. "It *is* kind of hot. Yes, it surely is hot." He removed his cap, and once again I was startled by the bare patch. He hung his shirt on a bush, stepped out of his trousers and folded them, so. He tugged off each sock and turned one inside the other. Then he waded in the water as far as his knees. A vein on each arm snaked from his armpit to his wrist. Tight black curls nestled in the ridge along his chest. His nipples stood out like the tips of two acorns.

I loved him that morning. I loved everything about him – the turtlish way he stuck out his head, half blind without his glasses; the way his white cotton shorts ballooned around his hips as he kept taking steps, arms raised above his head like a prisoner surrendering.

"I'm too heavy," he said. "I tell you, I'll sink." And he didn't only mean he would sink through the water, but through the muck below that. The Powers of Darkness, like whatever rough beast haunted Loch Ness, would grab his ankles and pull.

"Relax," I kept telling him. I cradled his waist. "I won't let you drown. Lean back. Just let go."

He bent back at such an angle I thought his spine might snap. The back of his head touched the water, but his feet wouldn't leave the bottom. They were heavy as stumps. I imagined the toes digging in, like roots.

Then I had an idea.

"Smile," I commanded.

He didn't smile, exactly, but he did close his eyes.

"All right then," I whispered. "Pretend the world's a nice place."

His lips puckered, like a purse keeping in coins. And then, finally, he laughed. His feet rose, and kept rising. He floated free of my hands. His fingers unclenched and he let down his arms, then he raised them again, slowly, tracing two arcs. His legs opened, then closed, so he looked like the drawing he had shown me that day, the man by Leonardo, all those outstretched arms and legs like the rays on a compass, pointing out every direction on Earth.

I was better than I am. For a month. A few weeks. I sat at his table, addressing brochures or juggling accounts, and Thomas would read me bits of Spinoza, Egyptian mythology, the more obscure verses of Job, the Song of Songs. Our knees brushed beneath the table. Once, I felt his socked toes rub my calf. He would touch my elbow and recite a psalm he had just finished translating from the Hebrew, or he would fix me a tuna sandwich while whistling "Sweet Georgia Brown." And I listened. I *heard*. I had become so sure of who I was and where I belonged that I could leave my self behind, like clothes on a shore, and be anyone, go anywhere, at least for a while.

What couldn't I accomplish? I replaced long-dead bulbs in a chandelier that hung so high above the dining room it belonged to a universe light-years away. I wiped the dust from each prism, flicked the switch and watched a galaxy of crystal stars burst into being above Table 3. Beneath the lobby rug I unearthed a Bird of Paradise mosaic even my parents had forgotten was there. I polished the round-bellied pitchers until they shone on their shelf like twenty silver moons. Crystal door knobs, chrome faucets, cut-glass ash stands and lamps . . . no one had paid attention to these objects in years. I scrubbed and I cleaned until everything glowed – chairs, foot stools, banisters (I planted a kiss on the newel post, on its shiny brown head). I bought two dozen almost-new mattresses from Doodie's; bent double, I carried each to its bed. I wouldn't ask for help, afraid Thomas might mistake my request for an order. I didn't ask for his help once that whole month. When he found out that I had used my college savings to buy the mattresses, I thought he might scold me. But he repeated his maxim – that each human heart needed to be free to pursue what it wanted, and if my heart wanted mattresses, he was happy that I had found some at such a reasonable price.

Never had I found myself wishing for so much to give some-one else. While I worked, he could study, if not this first sum-mer then maybe the next. He would never again have to pump out a cesspool, haul trash, ream a drain. I would hire another handyman, and only if that employee couldn't accomplish a re-pair would Thomas step in. I saw us living together – not in the handyman's shack, but the bungalow my parents and grandparents had shared while they ran the Eden. If I didn't let myself imagine making love to Thomas, it was partly because I didn't want what we did to remind me in any way of what I had done with Jimmy. Would I have allowed myself more dreams – a wedding night, a child – if he hadn't been black? If he hadn't been a handyman? If I hadn't known my family would so disapprove? Yes, I suppose. But there also was the fact that I had called him Mr. Jefferson for so many years be-fore I called him Thomas; he was so many years older, so dis-tant and fastidious; and he didn't take the first step across all that distance toward me.

Even the tiniest improvements that I made frightened my mother. When I showed her the chandelier, she gasped: "So much light!" as if enemy bombers might launch an attack. The new paint, the new curtains . . . *Vi a teyten bankes,* she mut-tered, it's like cupping a corpse.

Still, she had promised to help me set up. Two days before Memorial Weekend we stood behind the desk, preparing for chaos. I had gone through the mail and was struggling to read a note scrawled on a scrap of brown paper bag.

"The Communists are coming after all," I said finally. "Most of them, at any rate."

"Shh," my mother said. "You're not supposed to call them that."

As a child I believed that if anyone knew who our guests re-ally were – not members of the Brooklyn Yiddish Literature

Society, but Communists, *Reds* – they would immediately be shot. How romantic this seemed! Like the Hasids, the Communists had a mission, I thought. They didn't sit around the pool playing cards all day. They plotted, they marched, they did calisthenics, all in the name of helping bring about a new heaven on Earth.

My loyalty to their cause was shaken when I learned that in this new heaven my family wouldn't own the Eden, but rather the State would (I took this to mean the State of New York). My loyalty was shaken even more when I heard their leader, Gus Beck, declaiming in the dining room that the individual was nothing. It was selfish to insist you were worth more than your Brother. In China, he said, the peasants didn't mind being faceless, as long as they were given enough rice to eat.

Faceless – the very word made me wince. If Chinese peasants didn't mind giving up their faces, it was only because they looked so much alike. How could Florence Steinburt, Lew Sussman, Archie Krupnik, Mel Gold and Gus Beck, their faces distinct and fantastic as those of the characters in *The Wizard of Oz*, relinquish their identities for a few bags of rice?

I decided they were lying. They would give up their faces for a while, so they couldn't be identified. Off would come those eyebrows, those crooked noses, enormous earlobes and moles, until nothing remained but the bare Potato Heads beneath. After they had won this revolution they were fighting, they would stick their noses back on and resume their identities as Florence Steinburt, Lew Sussman, Archie Krupnik, Mel Gold.

My mother studied the note, the corners of her mouth working like a hawk's wings. "Poor Mr. Beck!" She applied a palm to each cheek. "A furniture-maker with a broken right arm!"

Besides making chairs, Comrade Beck was the Corresponding Secretary of the cell to which he belonged. He had slipped on the ice; while he suffered in traction, no one else had remembered to make reservations.

> Only now, when I am again in my home and learning to write with my Left Hand does it lie in my Power to Correct the Wrongs of the Past. I trust you will not let Profit take precedence over Loyalty and so give our rooms to Rich Guests who pay more.
>
> Yours in Solidarity, Gustaf V. Beck.

Beneath his left-leaning signature ran a postscript that read: "Please do not trouble to make reservations for those whose names follow . . ."

I flipped through the Eden's guest list, crossing out the names of the Communists who had died in the preceding nine months.

"I don't mean to interfere," my mother said, "but maybe you shouldn't charge him anything this summer. At least until he's mended. How can he pay if he can't work?"

Even with two good arms, Comrade Beck paid only twelve-fifty a week for his stay at the Eden, a rate guaranteed in perpetuity to the Communists by Grandpa Abe because he once had been in charge of the sweatshop at which they led a failed strike. As my mother went on making her case, I added, subtracted and multiplied with an ease I had never shown in math class. When I saw the amount I would lose if the Communists stayed another summer, I felt as if I were staggering beneath those twelve men and women and my mother was trying to load an anvil on top.

"Comrade Beck is ninety-one," I said. "I'm sure he qualifies for Social Security."

"Oh, he never would accept it. A man of his views! He thinks it's a crumb thrown to the workers to keep them from demanding the rest of the cake. Besides, a Communist doesn't send the government his address."

"Mother. I hardly think the government is interested in deporting a broken-down furniture-maker. And if they're so proud of these views of theirs, why do they still call themselves a Yiddish Literature Society? It just gives them a thrill, pretending they're at risk."

"Excuse me, Miss J. Edgar Hoover. You think only the movie stars lost their positions from that *petzel* McCarthy?" She pretended to spit. "Mrs. Seiken, a teacher, she wouldn't take the oath, they threw her out. Jake Slapikoff's boy had a wonderful job, engineer for a plant that built ships, they took back his clearance. That's why they changed to a Yiddish Society, for protecting the children. What these people have been through . . . The Czar, Hitler, Stalin . . . You think even in America it's so safe to say you're a Communist? To fight for a union?"

How had I come to be arguing against Mrs. Seiken and unions? Maybe I didn't long for the day when all human beings would be faceless comrades, but that day wouldn't be brought any nearer by the activities of the Brooklyn Yiddish Literature Society. And how had my mother come to defend them? She hated the way Comrade Beck left his complaints on the desk, demands as formal as the conditions of a treaty. "Petitions?" she would say. "If they want us to fix a faucet, they can't ask us face to face? They can't treat us as if we're human beings too?"

It came to me that my mother's new sympathy for the Communists stemmed from her knowledge that while I would be here reading their petitions, she would be at home in Paradise, sipping iced tea.

I busied myself with the guest list. "Who did he say won't be coming this year?," as if life were a party and these two invitees had expressed their regrets.

"I can barely make out . . . Okay, it's a W, it must be Mr. Wexler. No loss there, is it." She covered her mouth. "And poor Mrs. Krindler!"

I drew my pen through WEXLER, YEHUDAH, and KRINDLER, MRS. PERRY.

"Not that I mean to interfere, but you shouldn't cross anyone off the list until you've sent a condolence card, it might slip your mind."

So many guests died each winter that my mother had mimeographed our family's regrets. When she sent condolences to a guest's survivors, she slipped in a reminder to make reservations for the upcoming year. Sometimes this worked, but usually the spouse faded too quickly to send back the form. I had vowed I would write personal notes to the families of this winter's deceased, but dozens had died. I had very little time, and what could I say to the Wexlers and the Krindlers – *Your loved one was certainly a credit to the Kremlin?* I rummaged beneath the counter for copies of the letter that hadn't yet faded to lilac ghosts.

"About the payroll," my mother said above my head. "Cyrus gets paid at the end of the summer. He'll swear he's on the wagon, but if you give in, you'll have to wash pots until he sobers up. The busboys and waiters can live on tips – if you give them their wages too early, they'll run off."

"When I have a few waiters, I'll worry what to pay them."

"I don't understand why boys today won't – "

"Because waiting tables is hard work and their parents can send them to college without it. All you get are the dregs, like the Brush twins."

My mother's forehead bunched in rows. "You're not really considering . . ."

"Do I have a choice? Even with Herbie I'm four waiters short."

"I suppose you know best, dear." Which meant: *It's your headache.* "Now, let me see . . . I always give the boy" – Lennie was my age – "a few extra dollars so he can go to a picture show. The rest to his mother, twice a month."

What could I do? My mother had signed a five-year contract

with Mamie. Instead of using her salary to hire young comics from New York, I would have to pay Mamie for bullying guests into Grandmothers' Pageants by the pool.

The door squeaked – *oy vey.* I rose from beneath the desk in time to see Thomas cross the lobby with a plunger.

"Mr. Jefferson," my mother said.

He stopped by the exit. Water dripped from the plunger to the rug.

"Those drains in Rose Cottage, I hope you managed to get them unclogged."

"Mother!" I said.

"What? I shouldn't remind him . . . Oh, yes, all right. I suppose it's your job to tell him now, isn't it."

He lifted an eyebrow as if to inquire if I had any orders to deliver. I turned away. He left the lobby – the hinges of that door cried *ai-ai-ai-ai.*

"Sweetheart?" My mother ran a finger across the room chart. "McDonald? Sandor? Newkirk? Who are these people? You know the Communists always stay in Rose Cottage. Who else would put up with those *chaloshes* red walls?"

"The Cottage is white now, remember? I gave them the Palace."

"Oh, but the Palace isn't fit for – "

"A Communist? They shouldn't mind about the lack of luxuries, should they." I printed their names on the room chart, two to a box, then hung the chart on its nail.

"No, no," my mother said, erasing the names I had written. "They should each get a single. Otherwise they'll spend the whole summer complaining about their roommates."

I couldn't bear to see my mother touching that room chart. Why wouldn't she leave? With a twinge, I remembered how she used to bridle under Nana's control, Nana refusing to give up her place behind the desk until she could no longer hear the phones. "You enjoy licking asses? So go ahead, lick, naah." She retreated to the kitchen, where at least she could lord it over the cook. For the rest of that summer a halo of peace floated over the desk with the palm trees and herons. My mother beamed like a lighthouse: *This way! All questions answered! All problems solved!* Now, she gave off as much light as a jar of dead fireflies.

Gently, I pried the room chart from her hands. "They're Communists," I said. "They believe in Free Love."

"Don't get fresh. I still have a say in what goes on around here. After I'm dead you can do what you want."

"That's ridiculous," I told her, as if her death were a bogey she had invented just to scare me.

She took back the chart. "So you really got some young people to make reservations? I have to admit, I thought you were wasting stamps to send out those flyers." She said this as if confessing her doubt for the first time; in fact, she had been clucking her disapproval since I had shown her the new brochures. The old ones had bragged of such pitiful offerings ("A sink in each room! Late-night snack once a week!") it was like being told your blind date was a catch because he had two ears and one nose. Even the photos gave the lie to their boast – the wide-angle lens caused the bedrooms to leer like funhouse reflections. To replace them, I pilfered photos from our attic – a jitterbug contest; Nat and Shirley waltzing (how odd, I thought, that Nana figured in the background of every photo of Nat); a youthful Abe Appelbaum swinging by his heels from the arm of the oak; the wedding of Mamie and Cecil Goshgarian, apparently as lively as their fights came to be after Lennie was born. I laid out the photos so the brochure looked like an album. "MEMORIES OF THE MOUNTAINS. FIND OUT WHAT YOUR GRANDPARENTS SAW IN THE CATSKILLS." Then I mailed the brochures to synagogues and social groups across the Northeast.

"So how many people wrote back they were coming?"

"Forty-two."

"It couldn't be!"

I showed her the letters. A Yiddish class had pounced on the chance to engage native speakers in conversation. A couple named Smith from Tucson, Arizona, had written to say they wanted their children to "taste Jewish culture." And a team of anthropologists from Columbia University had decided to study the Borscht Belt "before it's too late."

"Study? You mean, like we're a tribe of wild Indians?" She peered across the lobby, trying to see the Eden as a scientist might. "Just tell me one more thing. This television producer you mentioned? Why would he think we're worth . . ." She pulled down my chin so our eyes met. "Did you sleep with this man? Is that why he's coming?"

She had made this same accusation after I came back from seeing Jimmy Kilcoin. In that case, my guilt over previous sins kept me from showing as much indignation as I ought to. "I shouldn't even answer. But, as it so happens, the producer is a woman. It's only a local station in New York. She saw the brochure at her temple and the idea just came to her."

"All that attention, millions of eyes . . ."

"The Evil Eye, you mean."

"Yes. Yes, I do."

I brought down my fist, which set the tinny bell on the desk vibrating. "Don't you want guests? All these years you've been running a hotel, you hoped no one came?"

"I don't expect you should understand. It's like when a mother wants that her children should be happy and healthy, but she tries not to push them."

"Don't worry about that. Every other Jewish mother in America pushes her kids to be the brightest, the best. But you – Arthur's right. Everything is a danger. You want us to fail."

"The dangers are real! In those TV shows, the Jewish mothers are always crazy with worry, but nobody gets hurt, because it's only TV, so the mothers look silly. In real life, people get hurt."

"Excuse me for saying the Evil Eye isn't what hurts them."

The lines on her face were an abstract expression of disgust. "Call it what you want, but too much ambition, too much beauty or wealth are curses in themselves." The loose skin at her neck swelled like a frog's. "Night after night I listened to my mother goading my father, he should go back to the textile business, forget the hotel. But he hated that business. All the times he had to take some girl aside and scold her, she was coming in late for God-knows-what problems . . . He didn't want more money. He didn't want position. All he wanted was that people should like him."

She swelled even more; I took a step back, in case she burst.

"She wouldn't let him be! Always belittling . . . A man like my father! I would find him out in the field, crying, she'd accused him of being too selfish to care for his family – his wife had to work, his little girl Ruthie didn't have nice dresses." She grabbed a fistful of her shift. "Tell me, have I ever been one to care about dresses? I didn't care as a child, I cared even less when I got older and she started in on me. 'Go to college. Run a business. Be a doctor, a lawyer. Don't let a helpless man drag you down.'"

So many years obeying the commandment Thou Shalt Honor Thy Parents, but she couldn't hold back now.

"I wasn't that kind. I wasn't smart, wasn't cut-throat. I wanted a family. 'So marry,' she said, 'but marry a man who has some ambition!'" My mother shuddered beneath her now-deflated skin. "As if I could have been one of those awful gold-diggers who kept her claws sharp for the first rich business-man who came within reach, never mind he's a *zhlob*." She swaggered like an ape, a gorilla accountant copping a feel. "During the war, she let up a little. The only men were rejects. But afterwards, she lost all restraint. 'This one's a specialist. The father of that one owns every liquor store in the Bronx.' Who knows but I might have given in, but your father came home – my own good-for-nothing cousin Julie Appelbaum – and I said, 'He's the one!' Such a beating she gave me! I was twenty-three years old and she beat me with a hairbrush!"

That my parents had been cousins before they became husband and wife struck me as less brave than lazy. My father's father, Buddy, had been raised as a sort of adopted kid-brother to my mother's father, Abe. Buddy and his wife, Lucille, worked at the Eden most of their lives. Julius, their son, served in the kitchen as his father's assistant until he was drafted, then spent the war cooking for the troops. After his discharge, he took a train from Fort Dix to Paradise without even stopping in Manhattan to celebrate. He arrived at the Eden after midnight (this was the only story about his life I could convince him to tell), "And I saw little Ruthie asleep in that big chair next to the desk, curled up like a kitten. I didn't want to wake her, she was smiling so peacefully." He stood there half an hour, duffel bag at his feet. "But she finally stirred a little. She looked up at me. Such a smile! I knew I was home."

Such wonder in his voice. Such pride in a wife who could have complied with her mother's demands and managed a larger, more lucrative business, or at least been the helpmate of a more prosperous man.

"Not that I expect someone of your generation to see what I'm saying." She unrolled a tissue from her sleeve and jabbed it at her nose. "But if you ask me, too much ambition turns a person to gall. Look at your grandmother, and your brother . . . Arthur may hate her, but that's because he's so much like her. It's my fault, letting her name him for that *goyishe* king, it gave him ideas."

I always had assumed Arthur was named for a long-dead relation, like most Jewish kids. What ideas had it given him to learn that he had been named for the founder of Camelot? None, that I could see.

"Nana wanted to name *you* Guinevere," my mother informed

me. "A *shiksa* queen who's famous for fooling around! You have me to thank you were named for your sweet grandmother Lucille instead."

Named for a woman whose most famous trait was a silence so thorough no one could quote a single thing she ever said . . . I preferred to believe my namesake had been Lucy Ricardo.

"She's furious you're back." She sideswiped her nose and rolled the tissue in her cuff.

"Aren't you tired of placating her? Nothing makes her happy. And why should I try to make *you* happy? What do you want? Should I get married and raise kids who have no dreams except to raise their own kids?"

"Nothing is more important than family. I have always believed that. It's how I've always lived."

"And was it worth it? Did it make anyone happy? You? Or your mother?"

"It made my father happy. And that's what I wanted. I made my father happy."

The last week in May my grandmother emerged from her bungalow like a figure from a clock. She flailed at dusty carpets, rattled soup tureens and pots. I had fooled myself to think she was keeping her distance because she approved of what I had done. Now I saw she had been hoping that, left on my own, I would grow tired and give up. When I didn't take the hint she banged kettles and cursed. She banged; I banged louder. She cursed; I cursed back.

"Get away from here!" she ordered, and I could tell that she didn't mean just to leave the kitchen. She wanted me to leave the Eden before I ended up as scorched and bitter as she.

This was the custom: the day before we opened we made five hundred blintzes – potato, cheese, cherry, blueberry and prune.

Nana always had commanded Operation Blintz, but her talents were limited to destruction – cracking eggs, beating them. She hated to depend on her son-in-law, but she needed his skill in the art of creation. He would stand beside the stove with a tiny curved ladle – quick dip in the bowl, a question mark of batter in the heavy iron pan, a shake of the handle, one, two, three, *flick* and a wafer of dough would float to the counter. As a child my task had been to spoon a gob of filling in the center of each crêpe. With his long heavy fingers, my father would fold the skin around the filling, fold, fold, fold, *tuck,* then he would flip the blintz and pat it as tenderly as if it were a just-diapered infant.

This year, I had intended to make the blintzes myself. How hard could it be? But the morning of B-Day I found my father by the stove and I didn't have the heart to say I didn't need him. He was waiting for my grandmother to finish whipping up the batter. In each hand she smashed two eggs like her enemies' heads, four brains at once spilling into the vat. She didn't heed the Jewish law forbidding blood-speckled yolks. That would have been too costly. And she wanted to keep her eyes on the two men who sat at the long enamel table, murmuring in one another's ears as if they were planning a liaison instead of a menu.

Which maybe they were. The fairer of the two, Jerry Blank, had been a few classes ahead of me at Paradise High. He kept mostly to himself, jotting notes with a fountain pen on three-by-five cards, which he filed in a box. Sometimes he invited me to sample his lunch – soups in which dumplings nestled within a forest of greens (I asked what these were just to hear him say "leeks, marjoram, sorrel," a savory poem), or lamb swaddled in grape leaves, or paté that left the flavors of ginger and pistachio on my tongue instead of burnt rubber, as Nana's chopped liver always did.

"And it's kosher," he assured me, thinking that I cared. "My father's suspicious, but really, it is."

Since fleeing Eastern Europe, Mr. Blank had become head chef at the Catskills' most religious hotel. He tutored his son in the complexities of *kneydlach* and *kashres,* and so he was happier with Jerry's decision to become a chef than most fathers would have been.

"I huf all pipple know tchef izn't kveer."

The second time Jerry heard his father say this, he couldn't help but mention that actually he *was* queer. He expected his father to quote the Talmud that the love between men was the evil for which Sodom was burned. Jerry was ready to answer that the crime wasn't love, it was rape, but his father didn't bother to buttress his case with learning. He simply threw Jerry out.

"Kveer izn't Chewish! Kveer izn't tchef!"

Jerry left Paradise to study at a famous culinary institute in France. He returned with a lover – a baker named Justin who shared Jerry's vision of a world in which "kosher" needn't be a synonym for heavy and bland. Hopeful with love, they thought Jerry's three-year absence might have softened his father.

"My tzon iz dead man!" Mr. Blank screamed from the door. "Only if tzon brink back vife iz he liffink!"

I ran into them in town not long after this encounter. Jerry's eyes were still pink and moist. He and Justin had been arguing about where to go next.

"I know we're not being very realistic," Jerry told me. "But we want a kitchen of our own. We're trying out recipes for a cookbook. Oh, we have such wonderful ideas!"

The ideas he related implied a belief that gourmet Jewish cooking – light, free of grease, flavored with the perfect bouquet of spices instead of the usual ten cloves of garlic – would bring anti-Semites to their knees pleading for thirds; bring too the Messiah, led by his nose from his chambers in heaven.

Never mind the Messiah. To attract younger guests I would need to serve food that fed their nostalgia. The problem was that young guests wouldn't *like* jellied calves feet. Mrs. Grieben was not, as Nana claimed, a pig. But neither was she a very good cook.

I hustled Jerry and Justin into Rosenblatt's Deli and plied them with Dr. Brown's Cel-Ray Tonic and visions of the Eden as an oasis of tolerance for all ways of life and *nouvelle* cuisines. But even as I said this my conscience cried out. Bad enough that my mother would pity two *feygeles*. If Nana saw Jerry touch Justin's knee this way, she would chop off his hand. And what retribution would Jerry inflict if he caught my grandmother slipping rotten tomatoes into a salad to save a few cents?

"It's a deal," Jerry said, and we drew up a contract on a place mat and signed it.

They had arrived at the Eden the evening before, drunk on the prospect of a summer together, cooking in peace. When I showed them to their garret in Rose Cottage, they exclaimed at the view of the mountain, the fan-shaped mirror above their bureau, the tassels on the window shades, the white chenille bedspread and the clawed feet on the tub. Now they sat with their yarmulkes bobbing together, a stack of recipe cards precarious as the Tower of Babel between them. They didn't notice my grandmother weighing two eggs in each hand. They didn't hear her mutter: "If no one else stops this . . ."

DON'T YOU DARE, I mouthed.

"Naah!" She turned away so she wouldn't see my lips.

I should have stayed to protect them. But I knew that if I pushed my grandmother too hard – if things came to a fight – she would win. Because I felt so helpless, I blamed Jerry and Justin for being the sort of people I had to protect.

I went to the pantry for a jar of prune butter. I had forgotten about my father, who stood staring at the less-dirty spaces on the wall where his photos and clippings had hung.

"Dad," I said. "Are you all right, Dad?"

"What? Yes? I'm sorry. Is your grandmother ready for me now?"

I waved toward the provisions. "Thanks," I said. "I wouldn't have known what to order."

He fondled a turnip. "I just hope your friends can use it. You don't think they'll scrimp? The guests don't know from fancy, they only care about filling."

"No one will starve. I've already told them: fancy *and* filling."

He shook his big head. "I'm sure you'll get along fine without me."

"Oh Dad," I said, "I won't. I'll have a hard time. But you need to get some rest."

He stroked a sack of pearled barley. "Your mother says the same thing. But I still . . . I haven't told your mother yet, but I volunteered to cook for the Meals on Wheels Program. With all this spare time . . ."

I once had found it funny that my underfed father was so preoccupied with feeding other people. He could boast none of Jerry's skills, but he had long been an expert at foraging for staples. I had asked him about his time as a mess sergeant in the Army. He claimed there was nothing much to tell ("It was Spam, Spam, and hash"), but my mother told me that he had been stationed in Poland when the camps were thrown open. I imagined him spooning his rich, meaty stew on the bones of the dead, the skeletons of Israel rising up and dancing. I wouldn't demand the truth, afraid that he would answer, "No honey, I told you, it was Spam, Spam and hash. That's all that I was fit for. I was too clumsy to fight." I could believe what I wanted, and, believing, I stroked his pendulous cheek.

I heard a thump from the kitchen.

"Jesus," I moaned.

"Wait." He coughed. "I want . . . She's an old woman, honey. She's worked her entire life. And the rest of us . . . I can't quite explain it, but we couldn't have been so . . . nice if she hadn't been so . . ."

"Nasty?"

A second corpse hit the floor. I ran in and saw my grandmother beating eggs with a whisk the size of a horse leg. Jerry couldn't understand why I kept asking if he and Justin were all right. Then the screen door banged open and a small man, black and crusty as an overcooked roast, staggered in with a crate. He dropped it to the floor near two others like it.

"Meat," he said, and went out for another crate.

I tore open the wax-paper packets: hearts, brains, intestines, and a slimy pink sponge I couldn't identify.

Jerry lifted the mystery meat to his nose.

"Lung," said the delivery man. He presented me with a blood-soaked receipt.

"There's been a mistake," I said. "I'm sorry, but you'll have to return all this."

"Mistake? Ain't no mistake. Been delivering for Mr. Fishie before you were born. This here's the Appelbaum place. And this here's an order from *the* Mrs. Appelbaum."

I waved the heart at my grandmother. "Who's going to eat this!" I shouted.

She looked up, her whisk dripping yolk. "Good, it came. For dinner the first night."

I heard Jerry gag. "Take it back," I told the delivery man. "Take it, or I'll never order another scrap of meat from Fishie's."

The man whistled. "Hooboy. I'll tell him. And won't Mr. Fishie be one happy butcher. Gonna dance his way home. Gonna give me a *raise*."

"You don't seem to be taking this very seriously."

"Me? I ain't serious? No, miss, I ain't. A person can't laugh at some offal . . . You want I should cry about some lousy piece a' offal?"

"Listen you." I thrust the heart toward his face. Juices oozed down my wrist. "I don't care what you do with this. Eat it yourself. Just get it out of here."

He licked his lips. "You know us black folk, we love that shit. Mm-mm, can't get enough of that de-licious offal."

"Raw?" I said. "You enjoy eating it raw?"

"Ain't my business what you do with that stuff. But if you ain't gonna sign this paper, guess Mr. Fishie can't make you pay. Hell, he can't seem to make you pay when you do sign. Just wish you'd said something before I drug all these big, heavy boxes in from that truck. Old man like me."

I pulled out some change.

"Yessir." He put the coins in the pocket of his white coat. "All this extra money, gonna buy me a *fine* mess a' offal." He wrestled the crates back to the truck, then climbed into the driver's seat. "Now, don't you be too hard on your granny." And he showed me his tail pipe, which backfired twice as he rattled down the drive.

Jerry and Justin were standing by the dumpster. My grandmother was guarding the door with her whisk.

"That meat was mine, naah. You want to get rid of me so these two . . . these two . . ." She waved the whisk at Jerry. "I won't eat the food that comes from the hands of an a-bom-in-a-tion!"

In their eyes I saw this: Another home lost, another expulsion. I had promised them a refuge. But if I fought Nana now, I would lose the chance to make the Eden a refuge for others.

"You want this shit hole? You want I should die? Fine, I'll stop eating, I'll die. But first you get rid of him."

I thought she meant Jerry.

"That *gonif!* That *yentzer! Toches leker!* He wants my hotel, so he tries to get you! All these years, he's just waiting until you grow up. But I see what he's doing! I'm smarter than a *shvartzer,* even a *shvartzer* who reads so many books. If he leaves, naah, it's yours. If not, you get nothing. A *makeh* you get. A *chalerye.* A *klug!* He's not gone tomorrow, naah, you leave too!"

She broke toward her bungalow, pushing me hard against the chest. She stopped beside her door and lifted her whisk as if it were Liberty's torch. It spun through the air. I ducked. It hit Justin. He seemed too stunned to move. Jerry touched his lover's ear and his hand came away bloody. This shocked me, as if I had seen only then how brutal human beings could be. Bad enough we butchered cows, chickens, lambs. We could turn against our own kind, especially if they were too gentle to fight back.

What could I have done? I was nineteen years old. I wasn't sure I loved him.

No. That's not right. I didn't love him enough. My grandmother demanded that I choose, and I asked Thomas to leave. I thought it was the Eden that defined who I was. Who was this man that I should relinquish so much for his sake? What would either of us be on our own in the world? He would understand, wouldn't he? He could find another job. He could come to visit, surely – she couldn't forbid that.

I avoided his shack. I told myself she hadn't meant what she said. When Nana repeated her ultimatum, I decided that I would be better off if he went. I listed his faults: He was self-righteous. Condescending. Arrogant. Too solemn. Too bookish. Too neat. I imagined saying, You *should go,* but I saw his face cloud, his eyebrows squeeze together, and I knew I couldn't say it.

But maybe I could.

I found him at his bungalow, staring at a sun so round and purple-red, surrounded by clouds, it was like a perfect beet-slice swirling in cream.

"Lucy – " he said, as if he guessed I had something dreadful to say. But I wouldn't let him speak. I had been rehearsing my lines and didn't want to be distracted.

"This isn't working. You were right. My being the boss and you the employee . . . My family, and Arthur . . . My grandmother, well . . . It seemed to me, maybe, for both our sakes, you should go."

He examined my face with the sort of puzzled scrutiny he used when he got stuck on a word he couldn't translate. "I have something to show you," he said. "I was planning to, eventually. Not tonight, but I guess this might be the right time after all."

Knowing what was in my own heart, I feared the intentions in his. But he wouldn't let me argue. He took my hand and led me down the road, away from town. He was skittish, his palm wet against mine. He kept glancing behind us. I had the crazy idea he planned to abduct me. If I wouldn't leave Paradise with him, he would take me by force.

We turned off the road at the hand-painted sign for Pospissil's Playland. I hadn't been there for years, not since I had come to watch Thomas fix the plumbing. The owner, Mr. Pospissil, had been old even then. Our last visit to the Playland ended with Mr. Pospissil weeping for his dead wife, Henrietta. Since she passed on, he hadn't had the heart to keep patching up the bits of buildings as they fell, or to cook, or even bathe. *Mr. Popsicle,* I called him, the ice melting down to the stick underneath.

Now the drive was overgrown with maples sprouting through the tar. The husks of prehistoric bungalows loomed before us like Stonehenge. The Playland's guests had been Orthodox. On the porch of one building stood an old ark for the Torah; its door, carved with lions, hung askew by one hinge.

"So," Thomas said. He lifted his arm like the Ghost of Things Future, showing me the ruins in which the Eden would lie. Then he smiled and I saw that the future he was showing me wasn't mine but his own.

"This is yours?" I said. "You bought Pospissil's Playland?"

He nodded. "I did." He said this as if he had purchased not only these falling-down buildings, but the very sky above them, that purple-red sun. He was thirty-four years old and he never had owned anything larger than a book. He had been able to buy the Playland with his savings from all those years working at the Eden, living in that shack, only because Mr. P.'s children finally convinced their father to move to a nursing home. "Didn't want to take advantage," Thomas said, "but, well, I figured . . ."

"It's ridiculous," I said. "What were you thinking? What would you want with an old Jewish bungalow colony?" I hadn't intended to stress the word *you*, or to add the word *Jewish*. In my anger, I forgot that minutes before I had kicked him out, fired him from a job he didn't want. "I don't get it. You don't have enough to do? You told me yourself, the Eden's porches are rotting away. Someone needs to check the wiring in the casino. And the fire escapes, some of them look like they're barely hanging on. And the chimney in the bungalow . . . One decrepit resort isn't enough?"

He spoke very distinctly, as if I had to read his lips. "The Eden's not mine. You just told me, didn't you. I couldn't ever feel at home there."

Of course he was right. Unless I changed everything, the Eden would remain a Jewish hotel. He was black, and a *goy*. That was how the guests and my family would always see him. And I would always see him as the recalcitrant handyman who wouldn't do what I asked. I didn't want an employee – or a lover, or a friend – who had his own future. But how could I admit this? If Thomas didn't belong at the Eden, my whole dream was flawed.

I was glad he'd gone, I told him. I wished he'd gone farther. Of all the many ways I betrayed him that summer, this was the first: I acted as if he betrayed me. "Are you going to run it?" I said. "Are you going to steal my guests?"

"Run it? You mean, like some sort of hotel?" He lifted his

hands. "Sure! Can't you just see? Uncle Tom's Cabins! Bunch of darkies strumming fiddles, cotton fields out back . . . Like that Disney place, you know? Except instead of talking to Mickey, you get to say hello to your favorite colored person. 'Hey, Aunt Jemima, how you doin' today? Hey, Sambo!'"

"You're making fun of me," I said.

"Lucy, I didn't – "

"You sound just like my brother. Has Arthur been talking to you? Is that what this is about?"

"Arthur? What would I be . . . Lucy, I didn't mean . . . How could I run a place like this? It's in terrible shape. It'll be all I can do to salvage enough to put a roof over my head. I'll grow what food I can. Do some odd jobs in town."

He wanted, he said, to become self-sufficient. (How ungrateful I thought him for wanting to build his future around his own self, not mine!) He talked about how the real Thomas Jefferson, if he truly had been great, would have pursued his happiness and invented his inventions without the help of slaves. The Playland would be his own Monticello, he said. Thomas had . . . a project. Maybe, if he got to where he had the time, he could work on this project. A man ought to have a project, now didn't he? He wanted to compile a collection of sayings from the world's great philosophers, holy men, mystics, visionaries, nuns, so that ordinary people could find enlightenment too. He described this project shyly, like a teenage boy describing a girl he might court. I had no right to be jealous. But still, at some level, I was hurt that his project had less to do with me than a bunch of philosophers whose names sounded like water gurgling down a drain.

"Lucy," he said, "you've got your reasons for not wanting me around the Eden, and I've got my reasons to leave. Let's just say it's convenient I have a place to go. But why shouldn't I stay in Paradise?" He took off his cap and rubbed his bald spot. "World recognizes just two kinds of black men – the ones you can scare, and the ones who scare you. I'm sure tired of being the former. And I'm damned if anyone's going to turn me into the latter. People around here, they know me. They call me Mr. Jefferson. They leave me alone."

"That's what you want? To be left alone? That's what you always wanted, isn't it. You bought this place without telling me. You promised you would stay. You promised you would help me keep the Eden together one more year. You broke your promise. Well, I'll be sure not to bother you again. I'm sorry I ever did."

The sun had gone down. All I could see was the luminescence of his shirt. I heard him stop breathing. Then I heard a sigh that sounded like a man letting out something sour and stale.

"I thought you would understand. I thought you of all people would understand why I wanted a place of my own."

And I did know. I *knew*. But I let him go on and apologize. I left him there, in the ruins of Pospissil's Playland, trying to figure out what he had said or done wrong.

Too nervous to sleep, I paced the Eden's grounds. Its squalor appalled me, but what could I do now? In just a few hours eighty-nine guests would walk beneath that arch, clamoring for food, amusement, clean beds.

I got in my car. I drove and kept driving, though in so many circles that just before dawn I found myself fewer than twelve miles from home, at the spot I had been circling unawares the whole time – the cemetery where three of my grandparents lay.

It was tucked beneath the last bunker of the championship golf course of the most famous Jewish resort in the world. In the weak morning sun the fairways glowed, velvet. I imagined my grandfather reaching up to pull this blanket around him, its colors so much softer than the afghan that his wife had compelled him to use.

Confused for a moment, I couldn't find our plot. This way? No, up there. How could I have missed it? There was room for twenty graves, though it held only four: ABRAHAM, VLADIMIR, BUDDY, LUCILLE. My parents would lie here – JULIUS and RUTH. But what about ARTHUR? And how would my own stone be distinguished from that other LUCILLE?

My grandmother, I knew, would try to live for eternity rather than allow herself to be buried in a hole from which she had to gaze up at the mock-Tudor mansions, the Las Vegas Niteclub, the tennis courts, ice rinks and Olympic-sized pools, the toboggan run and ski slope, the riding trails, row boats and small private airport of the magnificent resort that should have been hers. How galling that the matriarch of That Other Hotel should have traveled a road from the *shtetl* to here that paralleled Nana's own road so closely. God could have confused them if He had just crossed His eyes! They had been born within fifteen miles of each other in Galicia. Both their families had hopscotched from Poland to Liverpool, then on to New York, so, by age twelve, my grandmother and That Other Jennie each found themselves toiling on a bench in a sweatshop, the one trimming buttonholes, the other sewing on buttons. Eventually, each woman was whisked to the Mountains, one by her father, the other by her spouse. Each woman labored year after year, but one woman's labor produced a hotel so enormous it could have contained the two thousand inhabitants of the *shtetl* she had come from – though her guests were in fact America's wealthiest Jews – while my grandmother's work did little more than replicate the most miserable corner of the *shtetl* itself.

"Why!" she demanded. "What's the difference between us!" And she truly didn't know. She thought a woman's fate was determined by her birthplace, her family, her wealth, by the husband who chose her. What else but these facts could account for such a failure, such a stunning success?

I stepped over the rail surrounding the plot. Was the fence to keep vandals out? Or to keep the dead from leaving? Grandpa Abe had bought the plot so his relations all would lie here with him as their host. But no one except my father's grateful parents had agreed to be buried within the same fence that would someday hold Nana.

I suddenly felt so dizzy I had to lie down. Dew soaked my clothes until my very skin seemed to melt. What had I been born with? A family. A name. A religion. A home. What were these worth? After I died my name would be forgotten, my body only bones, my home a plot of grass marked off by a fence. Did I think it really mattered if I lived as a Jew, or a Christian, or a Buddhist?

No. I didn't think so. But if I were to admit that anything was possible – if I could go anywhere, be anything – then how could I choose where to go, whom to be? I would waste my life deciding. It was safer to live within the limits of *this* life, to make what I could of my family's hotel, to be certain that my name would be carved on this stone, if preserved nowhere else.

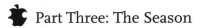 Part Three: The Season

Eighty-nine guests checked in that day and I couldn't have said how. Our bellhop, Sam Brush, was more concerned about getting his charges to heaven ("Jesus was a Jew! He came to redeem us!") than up to their rooms. One couple found a nest of mice in their bed. The drains in Rose Cottage backed into the halls. (I sent Cyrus to fix them; luckily, he was still sober enough to work a bucket and mop.) A crew of six people with lights, cameras, microphones and thick coils of wire that hissed across the rug took charge of the lobby and filmed every argument I had with a guest, every sneeze, every scratch. The woman who hosted *I Love New York* kept interrupting me with questions ("Where are your parents? And your grandmother, where is she? You have a brother, too, don't you? Why aren't they here?") until I nearly began hurling curses right on TV.

This was what saved me: I could sense Nana waiting, smug in the certainty that I would have to admit kindness didn't work, an Abe could exist only with a Nana backing him up. I retained my good humor, and, within a few hours, most of the guests were walking off lunch, admiring the zinnias or enjoying the pool. Is anything sweeter than finding out your talents are suited to the life you have chosen to lead? I had been training since childhood to run a hotel. I didn't need to think, only move, only *be*. I rushed here and there, light with the synchrony of body and mind, smoothing rough feelings with my grandfather's ease, mingling as he would. The mere words *to mingle* filled me with joy. *To mingle* was to be the person in charge, not alone behind a desk but in the middle of a crowd, shaking hands, introducing this man to that woman, telling jokes, solving problems, though I later found out it's easy to mingle with guests like oneself, to solve problems in which nothing more difficult than a clogged drain is involved.

The older guests squeezed my cheeks. *What a pleasure to see a young person keeping the old ways alive!* After dinner I held court, accepting good wishes for my new undertaking. I felt like Queen Elizabeth leading her retinue to the theater for the latest offering by Shakespeare, though instead of Ophelia or Juliet, Mamie appeared in a striped sequin gown and belted out her theme song:

> My yiddishe mamme, *I need her more than ever now,*
> My yiddishe mamme, *I'd love to kiss her wrinkled brow . . .*
> *Oh, I know that I owe all that I am today . . .*

"*Shmaltz*," sneered Mel Gold. "All those wonderful *mammes* are wasting away in nursing homes. But the children hear someone sing: 'How I owe!' and they think they've done something."

Mamie stopped in mid song. "You're saying I didn't take good care of my mother?"

"Don't take it so personal. He's talking in abstract."

"Not personal? My mother – "

"All he said was – "

The other guests rose to Mamie's defense. "If you don't like our Mamie, you should leave."

"An excellent idea." This came from Mel Gold, who led the Communist column as it marched from the room.

"Good." The guests sighed. "We enjoy now in peace." And they listened as Mamie sang a medley of folk songs, their stick-finger hands floating on the waves of each familiar tune.

"Promise us, Mamie darling, tomorrow you'll sing each song again, but all the way through."

"And promise you'll translate," begged a girl from the Yiddish class. "And sing each song slower. I couldn't understand any of the words except the titles."

Tears streaking her makeup, Mamie said yes, yes, she would sing each request, translate each word. "But now we must give the next performer his turn."

Lennie bounced from the wings. "Next. Next. I'm next."

Immobile, I watched as the audience and the camera crew were treated to Lennie's imitation of Groucho and his brothers hailing Fredonia in a scene from *Duck Soup*. The regular guests smiled indulgently, but the newer guests gaped. They had come for nostalgia, and what was nostalgic about an over-grown boy in a too-tight pink jersey and plaid Bermuda shorts reciting lines from a movie he didn't understand?

Lennie bowed and bounced off. Then his mother reappeared with her Fred Astaire dummy, a wheel on each sole of its black patent pumps. They twirled, dipped and squeaked – Fred's wheels needed oil – to a scratchy recording of "Begin the Be-guine." Inspired by the camera, Mamie spun on her toes. She was so tender toward Fred – after all, the only partner she'd had since her husband, Cecil, ran off – that when his neck snapped on a particularly vigorous turn, Mamie simply laid his head on her shoulder, patted his top hat and continued their dance.

Several weeks later I received word that the Eden would be fea-tured that night on *I Love New York*. I announced this at dinner, and, after they had finished Justin's amaretto mousse ("With-out milk!" the guests marveled, unaccustomed to eating such a creamy dessert with a meal containing meat), the older guests tottered on their walkers to the game room, the younger guests taking small steps behind. The Communists filed in and threw up a phalanx around the old Zenith, which hung from a cob-webby corner of the ceiling like a one-eyed black spider.

"I think this is very funny," said Comrade Levine. "Now that I'm toothless I can be on the television. When I'm young, mak-ing a movie about danger in the textile mills, they break into my rooming house, smash up my camera, steal my film – "

"Shah, shah, it's starting."

And almost before it began it was done, opening day com-pressed to three minutes: the guests checking in – without a single complaint, only outbursts of happiness upon finding that the Eden hadn't been sold – and a shot of the Communists reading aloud, their voices drowned out by the narrator saying that "each afternoon, the Yiddish Literature Society studies the works of Sholom Aleichem . . ."

"Sholom Aleichem!" Comrade Beck snorted. "This book from which we read is Karl Marx' *Manifesto!*"

"*Nu?* Tell a lie and someone might believe it."

"Psst, psst, *genug.*"

The host recited the Eden's history – an account she stitched together from stock phrases like "quaint Old World customs," "search for a place where the Jews could breathe free," "ethnic identity and heritage," all intoned to a soundtrack of "Tradition" from *Fiddler.* My chest tightened as if the Ark of the Covenant had survived the millennia and been installed in the lobby.

"Of course," chirped the host, "if not for the founder's wife, whom everyone here affectionately calls 'Nana,' the Eden would never have become the hospitable place it is today."

The sharp intake of breath of four dozen people drained the air from the room.

"An invalid confined to her bungalow, Nana no longer can tend to her guests as intimately as she would like, but she waves from her window to everyone who passes." And there she was, waving – though if you looked closely, you could see she was waving a fist.

No one said anything – the newer guests because they didn't know my grandmother, the older guests because they did.

Then the last thirty seconds: snatches of a folk song and a quick shot of Mamie dancing with Fred – not to the Victrola, but rather to a laugh track, as if Mamie's routine were *meant* to be comic.

"Where am I," Lennie wailed. "Where am I. Where am I." But his act had been edited out of the segment as smoothly as if I had gotten my wish and he never had been born.

"As the sun slowly sets on another peaceful evening in the Catskills . . ."

The Eden was draped in a gauzy pink veil like a bride whose worst features are being concealed. It was a distortion, a lie, but where was the harm? If anyone saw this show and came for a stay, only to find that the bride was a *mieskayt*, with a few more infirmities than the groom might have guessed, he could leave the next morning with no loss except whatever deposit he had been foolish enough to pay in advance.

Jewishness was in fashion that summer, at least among Jews. After years of being scorned as tasteless and out-of-date, *yiddishkayt* and the Borscht Belt had died of neglect. Now it was safe to revive them as quaint.

Within weeks of the Eden's debut on TV the number of guests had swelled to two hundred. The mail brought requests for reservations, good wishes from couples who had stayed at the Eden decades before, a letter from the makers of Nu-Scent Air Freshener, who believed that our hotel, with its odors of onions, sauerkraut and fish, would make the perfect setting for their latest commercial ("In addition to the extensive – and need we say free – exposure for your business, we would be willing to pay a significant sum . . ."). The Eden as a synonym for air so offensive it needed a *shpritz* from a can? I once had mocked my parents' method of judging current events: Would this earthquake or flood, this crop failure, space launch or slump in the market bode well for the Jews? Now I heard myself ask an even narrower question: Is this good for my hotel? I saw myself write: "Dear Sirs: We would be honored to allow you to film your commercial at our hotel, but the fee you are offering seems low . . ."

I wielded this rule – was it good for the Eden? – as a person wields a knife to slice intricate knots. I didn't have time to sip tea as Thomas untangled my moral dilemmas. I knew what he would say: The Eden should be an island where people like Nat and Shirley could read *Faust* to one another, a café al fresco where the Communists could contemplate the world's dialectic, a home for outcasts of every nationality, religion and race. Well, I couldn't stay in business running a retreat for scholars and saints, any more than I could obey Nana's wishes and manage the Eden as a factory that processed its guests like so many lemons, squeezing them for profit and discarding the rinds.

I thought of Thomas only when the meat slicer broke or the door to the game room swelled shut and sealed four elderly domino-players inside. Each week, the employment agency sent a new "handyman," none of whom could tell a pliers from a wrench. I fired all three, then decided to get through the summer without a handyman, not only to save money, but also to spite Thomas – each burned-out bulb and cracked window would be a reproach. If the Eden fell apart and someone got hurt, the guilt would be his. My family had given him work, a place to live, kindness. How could he say he didn't need us? How could he act as if the planet he lived on were more than a satellite circling our own?

He came to the Eden only once that first month, showing up after dinner with a bunch of flowers that looked like weeds. I set these on the desk, then ushered him past the guests milling on the verandah waiting for the show. Though Nana hadn't left her bungalow since starting on her hunger strike, I kept glancing around, afraid she might see us and launch a tirade. The younger guests stared. Who was this black man walking with the owner? The older guests asked Thomas if he would please fix their sinks, and didn't the lawn need mowing? We walked past the flower beds, which were littered with trash. I thought this would shame him, but he didn't pick up the wrappers, and the shame turned on me for thinking that he should.

When my mother finally learned about her own mother's hunger strike, she carried a plate of food to the bungalow. My mother tried her key, but Nana had added a chain. Undaunted, my mother slipped a note beneath the door. A few minutes later, this same note, in pieces, snowed upon her head. She left the plate on the porch and returned the next morning to find the applesauce and pureed beef splattered across the stoop. For a week this went on. My mother left a plate. Nana gave it a kick.

"That means she isn't dead," I assured my mother.

"Very funny." We both knew that Nana's stockpile of baby food couldn't last. "You can always get a new chef, but where will you find a new grandmother?"

I told my mother not to worry. Food kept disappearing from the pantry, though no one except Nana and I had the key.

"And if you're wrong?" my mother said. "Have you ever known your grandmother not to make good a threat?"

And so, late that night, I crouched in the dining room with my eye to the door leading to the kitchen. The floor boards groaned as they cooled. Moonlight dripped in through tatters in the drapes, splashing off the silver settings on the tables. Despite the support-hose my father had given me, my feet ached, as cramped as if I had just run a marathon. In another few hours I would have to run another.

"Naah, naah, naah."

The noises were coming from the kitchen. A cooler stood open; by its glow, I made out my grandmother in her bathrobe. Deaf to the clatter of jar against jar, she sampled soups, stews, soufflés. She dropped spicy chicken-wings in her pocket, stuffed an enchilada in her mouth. Then she scuttled to the bakery, where, I later learned, she poked her thumb in each of a dozen brioches. Back in the kitchen, she yanked Jerry's knives from their racks and pounded their blades against the metal counter until these were dull. She blew out the pilot on the ten-burner stove.

The fuses for the freezer, the meat-slicer disc, the lids from all the sugar bowls . . . had I thought they could walk off? I had attributed these mishaps to my lack of experience, Mitchell Brush's malevolence, gremlins and elves. But why think of gremlins when a flesh-and-blood Nana was so much more plausible?

"Naah! Naah!"

She dashed from the pantry, scattering rice across the floor the way a farmwife feeds hens. Then the screen door banged shut.

I slumped against the wall. I couldn't sit up late every night, could I? If I called the police, Nana could lodge her own complaint: "There's the ingrate who stole her grandma's hotel and kicked her out of the kitchen so two *feygeles* could use it to perform a-bom-in-a-tions!"

I would buy locks for all the coolers, the pantry and the bakery. What else could I do, short of driving a stake through her heart? Maybe she wouldn't wreak her vengeance on anything more precious than knives. Although the number of locks I was buying suggested that she already had.

 When I woke up most mornings, the moon floated in the sky, wrinkled and pale. By the time I was gliding across the hushed grounds (the guests still in their beds, just where I had put them) the sun had joined the moon and they hung in an arc like balls I was juggling. The Communists sat in a column of lawn chairs and wheelchairs, performing calisthenics. Comrade Beck, at their head, conducted their movements with his chewed-up cigar – *arms out up three four!* – so they resembled a giant bug on its back, clawing the air. When they sang the *In-*

ternationale in their shaky falsettos, the younger guests poked their heads from the windows. "Come on, we're on vacation! It's only five-thirty, would you let us get some sleep!" But what could they do, call the FBI? Punch Florence Steinburt in the nose? The Communists might have preferred this to being indulged as harmless fossils, but that's just what they were, so the younger guests contented themselves with slamming shut their windows and scuffing back to bed.

I soon became an expert at settling disputes about boom boxes disturbing noon naps, the pastry cook kissing the chef ("All right, it's a shame God made them that way, but I don't have to watch"), Sam Brush and his mission to open Old Testament eyes to the truth of the New. Every afternoon I visited the pool, where the matrons and widows were trying to get on with their mahjongg despite the anthropologist circling their backs.

"I thought they were only going to cut out a tiny piece," Ida Sklarr was telling her friends. "But when I came to, I was missing an entire breast! You've heard the joke? A woman is searching her bosom for a Kleenex, she says, 'I knew I had two when I left home!'"

My love for these women rose to engulf them. More than anyone else, they approved of what I had done. They had spent their lives cooking and caring for others, so running the Eden was a business they understood well, and they chatted with me across the front desk as they might have chatted across the laundry line with the young wife next door. My mother was right – these women knew death, abandonment, loss. Why had I thought they were trivial clowns – because they wore funny hats? Because, in their seventies, they felt they deserved to sit in the sun playing mahjongg and canasta? Because they spoke through their noses and sprinkled their conversation with *nu, takeh, nebbech*? If they had been elderly Chinese, I would have thought them exotic.

The anthropologist pressed Ida. "Don't you think it's unusual joking about cancer?"

She dropped her tiles, shocked that anyone would say "cancer" outright like that, without even adding *nisht do gedacht* – May it not be thought of here! – to keep the Evil Eye from punishing them each with a lump.

He started again. "Don't you think it's unusual – "

Ida stopped him before he could reach the dread word. "Better I should *kvetch* so much my friends run away? Or I should sit alone and cry?"

As he jotted this down, Ida surreptitiously touched both her breasts, the real and the false.

"And would you ladies also react in a humorous manner about a disease as serious as cancer?"

The women tortured their beads and the petals on their kerchiefs. I prepared to shoo the man away.

"You see," he explained, "we have to make certain it's not an isolated phenomenon, but a cultural pattern."

I envisioned the contents of his book: "The Importance of Humor," "Marital Habits," "Food," a chapter called "Death." Question after question made the women squirm, although they tried to be gracious to this handsome young Jewish professor from Columbia. Their only challenge was this: Why would strangers care to read a book about them?

Oh, but they would! A colleague had written a book analyzing the interpersonal structure of a nursing home for black senior citizens in Alabama. It was such a success that the inmates got fan mail. A documentary was filmed. Busloads of tourists began to show up.

Busloads of tourists? A few tactless questions, I decided, couldn't hurt. These women were strong. Perhaps they would even benefit from the attention.

It was harder to defend the scrutiny to which I exposed the old men. With their spindly legs and bulbous heads, they looked like pale fungi sprouting from the round petri-dish tables at which they played cards. The first group of Yiddish students had left, but another had arrived. The teacher of this class was compiling a lexicon of Yiddish proverbs, though he acted less like a scholar than a slouchy detective who wasn't above roughing up his suspects.

"Hey, wait, I missed that. That figure of speech, I want it."

Mr. Shuldik looked up from his cards.

"Why don't you ask the 'Literature Society' for their figures of speech?" Mr. Cox suggested.

"Oh, we tried them this morning," said an earnest young blonde, "but they said they were having an important private discussion."

Mr. Cox blew his lips. "What they discuss is, does Karl Marx think it's better to wipe your *tuches* with the right or left hand."

"I just love the way you talk!" Again, the young student. "It's so colorful!"

Colorful? I cringed. These men hadn't come to the Eden to be colorful.

"Come on now, I'm waiting," the professor told Mr. Shuldik.

"Say again for vot you vont it?"

"I told you, it's a book so people can learn Yiddish." He might as well have added *after you're dead*.

"Dis isn't a lenkvich a person learns from a book."

"Leave that to me. I'd like that idiom, please."

The men urged Mr. Shuldik to give the man what he wanted so they could resume playing cards.

"*Nu*, if you insist." He lowered his voice. "*Me tracht un me tracht, un nocher me b'macht*. Dos is my 'yiddy-yom.'"

"Good, good. Now the translation."

"You vont I should trentslate? If there's Inklish trentslation, for vot I need Yiddish?"

Mr. Shuldik was stalling – he was only ashamed that the saying was so vulgar.

"I'll wait all day if I have to."

"So then, I trentslate." Mr. Shuldik spoke into his cards. " 'You tink and you tink, and den, even so, you make a big stink all over yourself.' Dot's my trentslation. You go no ozzer kvestion?"

But the scholar kept niggling. I felt like a ranger in a wildlife preserve, keeping alive a near-extinct species so its members could be studied by zoologists with dart guns and Sunday safarians who poached feathers and tusks. I told myself I couldn't let the species die out, though if I truly had wanted to keep it alive – for its own sake, not mine – I wouldn't have sold tickets. I didn't want to be the savior of *yiddishkayt*. I wanted to be the little girl in the red polka-dot swim suit who even now was preparing to jump in the pool.

"Our hair!" the women shouted. "Tania, don't splash!"

"Mom! Hey, Mom, watch!" The girl ducked underwater, and even then, at nineteen, I couldn't resist counting. *Thirty-nine, forty* . . . The girl's mother pushed herself up on her elbows. *Fifty-eight, fifty-nine* . . .

A polka-dot depth charge burst from the pool. "I made it, Mom! I made it! Sixty's a minute!"

But I made it once to a minute and twenty seconds. I would have said this aloud if I hadn't been reluctant to disappoint the girl, whom I loved just for trying. I wanted to hug her to my gravy-stained blouse, sniff the chlorine from her sunburned neck and wet hair. I wanted to keep her at the Eden all summer, swimming in the pool like a very rare fish.

Except for her mission to bring Nana food, my mother stayed away so she wouldn't be around when the Evil Eye paid a call, the ever-present phrase "last Catskills resort" like a taunt: *Come destroy us.*

I didn't mind her absence. Scared herself, she scared others. The parents of the toddlers she had minded all those years used to complain that the children suffered nightmares. Since she had retired, her paranoia had gotten even worse. After scrimping and toiling so many years, saving toward the time she and my father could rest together in peace, she was terrified that the Angel of Death might swoop down and steal her beloved Julie. He was too pale and thin. She was sure he had leukemia, but the doctor refused to send my father for tests. My mother force-fed him milkshakes enriched with raw egg. When he gained a few pounds and his color returned, she found other fears to dwell on.

"Bad enough that you cook for these people, why do you have to drive to their homes?"

"They can't get to town, honey. That's why it's called Meals on Wheels. Most of these people are too sick to even get out of their chairs. If only you could see the *tsuris* – "

"If I want to see *tsuris*, I can look in my own house."

In fact, my mother saw so much *tsuris* in a house where no *tsuris* existed, I suggested to my father she ought to "get help."

She overheard my suggestion. "You just pretend I'm crazy so you don't have to come visit."

"I don't visit because it's the height of the season! You of all people ought to know what that means."

"I know you can spare yourself during the show."

She kept after me until I was forced to give in. When I finally drove to town to visit them one night, the lights were all off. My parents never went out. I was halfway across the patio when I stepped on my father's foot.

"It's only me," he said.

Why were they hiding?

"The man's a lunatic!" My mother's voice leapt from the dark and flapped around my face like a bat.

"Who is a lunatic?"

"That Hasid. They put him in jail for a few days, for writing bad checks, and by the time he gets out, who does he think he is? The Messiah!"

The Messiah next door? Good or bad for the Eden? On the good side, he might become a tourist attraction. On the bad side, he might harass the guests.

"He came to the synagogue," my mother said.

"Ruth, honey, I told you, it was harmless. He just wanted to talk."

My father had to be lying. The Hasid hadn't seemed harmless even before he had become the Messiah. "So what did he say?" I asked.

"I couldn't follow him, exactly. Something about a law being repealed. The only thing God forbids us is . . . sadness. We're supposed to serve God through . . . through pleasure, I think."

"And we know what *that* means." My mother's voice rose like a siren. "Bad enough he should tell such foolishness to us, but he goes to the churches. 'We should all be good friends and have one big party together!' As if everyone doesn't realize what kind of party he means."

I suggested that it might be less embarrassing to have the Hasid arrested than to let this go on.

"That's a terrible idea," she said. "Don't you remember what happened the last time?

"Last time? What last time?"

" 'What last time?' she says! The last time we asked the *goyim* to arrest some *mishuggener* Jew who thought he was God!"

The switchboard lit up. "Eden, reservations."

"Lucy? That you? A homey touch, kid, the owner answers the phone herself."

I felt the hesitation that comes of not knowing when you've last heard a voice, if it brought pain or pleasure.

"I'll give you a hint: I'd like to reserve the linen closet upstairs."

If I had been less naive – or more – I might have hung up. I thought I was safe. As long as I stayed behind that desk, I was safe.

"I guess you're pretty pleased with yourself, getting the best of old Jimmy. No need to deny it. You're in business, kid. I respect that. 'Oh Jimmy, poor me, I can't meet my premium.' And the next thing I know, you're a TV star and the Eden's jammed full. How can I help but admire the way you had me bamboozled?"

The longer he went on the more he convinced me that I actually was as clever as he seemed to believe. I had bluffed him, he said. He didn't like to be bluffed. But a deal was a deal. Why, just the other night his friend Miller reminded him that the Eden was due for a fire inspection. Miller owed him, Jimmy said. The guy liked to play poker, but he wasn't good at bluffing. Jimmy would forget the chips Miller owed him, and Miller would stamp the inspection APPROVED. That's how things worked.

He didn't mention the chips *I* owed him. Jimmy talked about the weather, how even the sun seemed to be on my side. He said he missed my company. I was busy, he knew, but come the long winter . . .

Winter! It seemed so far off, he might as well have asked if I wanted him to keep me warm in my grave.

And my luck seemed to hold. By all rights, more guests should have injured themselves that season than ever before. Those who had been old the previous summer were now even older. The younger guests weren't content to just sit: they played volleyball and handball, swam, went on hikes. Their children climbed trees. Yet I needed to report only two accidents, and both of these were minor. I didn't see my luck as random, any more than my mother would have seen a long string of fatalities as chance. I was certain that God so approved of my plans He would stretch His hand beneath any guest who fell. On the two occasions Jimmy did adjust a claim, he surprised me by acting in a businesslike way. I felt almost disappointed. I had come to enjoy evading him as much as he enjoyed giving me chase. I caught myself flirting, like a rabbit who so thoroughly eludes her pursuers she doubles back and taunts the hunters and hounds.

I knew this was only part of Jimmy's strategy. Sex was a game. Too easily won, it lost its appeal. Numbers enthralled him. Like me, Jimmy thought having an audience made him more real. He dashed about the grounds like a setter who's been locked in a city apartment and finds himself released in a field full of quail. He didn't care if the women were twice his age or half, *zaftig* or thin, fair, sallow, dark. I would still be in Paradise when winter set in. For now, there were dozens of other women at the Eden whose chips he might cash.

It was a Sunday afternoon. Half the crowd was checking out, the other half checking in. As soon as a guest handed me his key, he ceased to exist. But let a stranger take that key and I would do whatever he wanted, as a genie must grant wishes to whoever rubs his lamp.

Simon Lipkowitz paid his bill and disappeared from my life as abruptly as if a trap door had opened beneath him. I grabbed a key from a hook and turned to find my brother.

What did I feel? What any sister feels upon seeing the brother whose love she wanted as a child. He had done nothing then but taunt me. Still, a brother was a brother, one of the few things with which I'd entered this world. I didn't want to lose him, to leave this life poorer than when I came in. I thought he owed me his approval, as if being richer in years meant he was richer in love. I never once imagined that my brother might be seeking something from me.

Since I had taken over the Eden he had called me on the phone more than ever to tease. That show on TV, it made him throw up. Was the place really full? What kind of person under age eighty would come to the Catskills? Never mind, he could guess. They were Jewy Jews, weren't they. The women were wide hipped and full breasted and wore gold-plated Stars of David and didn't shave their legs. Their husbands were reedy orthodontists or overweight social workers with thick curly beards and spots of food on their ties. They had little boys named Josh and little girls named Rebecca. They gushed about God and how their lives now had "meaning" and what a blessing kids were. They felt sorry for Jews who didn't know the joy of a Friday night meal.

What could I say? Most of our new guests did fit this description.

It's fake, Arthur said. They need a gimmick to their lives. Everybody's got some ethnic shtick going on. Jews light candles and eat challah for the same reasons Christians decorate their trees and eat cookies on Christmas. It's nice. It makes them feel good. It gives them something to do. You call that religion? You really think God gives a shit whether people eat bread shaped like braids or cookies shaped like stars?

He was right, I see now. But how could I accept the truth when my brother delivered it in such a sharp tone?

Arthur looked around the lobby. "You dusted," he said. "The windows look clean." He looked around again. No, that was all. "Jesus, I'm exhausted." He rested on the desk. "I've been handling a big merger for the firm. Sunday afternoons, I drive down to New York. I spend the week running errands for a bunch of old farts in bow ties. Saturday afternoons I drive all the way back to Boston, then I turn around and start driving back. This time, I got as far as the Tappan Zee Bridge and I couldn't make myself cross it. I guess I ended up here."

The couple behind him sighed and studied their watches. I

had known this couple two weeks. My brother had been there when my parents brought me home – pinching me, it was true, but out of billions and billions of people on this planet, only Arthur and I had once shared the same home.

"You're a lawyer," I reminded him. "You work for the oldest law firm on the East Coast." I was only repeating what he had told me himself. "They're *prestigious* old farts. And once you make partner – "

"Maybe I won't make partner, okay? Maybe I don't even want to make partner. Maybe I slaved all those years for nothing. Doesn't that happen to some poor shmuck in the Bible? He works seven years, he gets his reward, except he finds out it's not what he wants. He gets Leah, and what he really wants is Rachel."

It took me a moment to realize that my brother had compared himself to Jacob. As far as I knew, he had never read the Torah. Grandpa Abe had pleaded with Arthur to be bar mitzvahed, for his sake, and Arthur refused. *I don't believe in it,* he said. *I'm not going to get up there and say words I don't believe.* My mother considered Arthur's refusal the height of conceit – a thirteen-year-old boy doubting God! I'd thought he was nuts. Given the chance to perform before an audience, I would have pledged my allegiance to Zeus.

"So what am I supposed to do?" he said. "All those ninety-hour weeks . . . I'm supposed to give up a million-dollar partnership?"

The telephone rang; I ignored it.

"You know what I would really like to do?" He ran a finger down the guest book. "I've got some money saved up. I could put a deposit on an inn on Martha's Vineyard, a nice bed and breakfast . . ."

The guests' grumbling had reached such an ominous level I barely heard what he said. "You want to run a hotel?"

"Why not? I never said I minded hard work."

"As long as the guests aren't Jews?"

The couple behind him started pushing. "Come on," the man said. "I've got to get back to the City before six. You want help with your problems, find a shrink."

"Oh, hold your tongue," another guest chided. "If you don't make it back before six, what will happen? You'll starve? You'll miss some *drek* on TV?"

A third guest whispered in a voice that could have carried to the moon: "It's the brother. The one who nearly let the Brush boy drown that time? It's been years since he came."

"The brother? The one that went to Princeton and works for that fancy *goyishe* firm? He's very nice looking. Is he married? Do you think he would like our Suzanne?"

"*Tattele*," said an old woman. She patted Arthur's arm. "Take as long as you want. We're not so important we should come between family."

Then the lobby went still. Everyone waited to hear what we would say.

"Arthur," I said quietly, "if our family had run an inn on Martha's Vineyard, you would have ended up hating WASPs." And, what I didn't say, that I would be nostalgic for glazed ham and croquet.

He shrugged. "I can't stand here arguing about who's more obnoxious, Christians or Jews. I'm about to pass out. You have a room or not?" He really did seem to totter. "If you're full, I could stay in the bungalow, with you."

I spent barely any time there. Why couldn't I give him what little he asked?

"I shouldn't have to beg. Half this hotel is mine, you know."

Looking back, I'm amazed that I suspected he would claim his share of the Eden, if not the whole thing. Let exiles return and a civil war starts. If I'd had enough power, I would have banished him from the Eden then and there.

"Not the bungalow. It's mine. I mean, I need some privacy."

His eyes widened – he must have thought Thomas sneaked

in my room to make love every night. I held out the key I had planned to give the next couple. The Pagoda, third floor.

Arthur picked up his briefcase. I started to say we could meet later in the kitchen. I would brew a pot of coffee. He could try one of Justin's *rugelach* and tell me about his job. But then, in a gesture as threatening as if he had raised his hand to slap me, he reached for the secret latch beneath the palms.

"If you're really that busy, I could try to stay awake a few hours and help out. You look like you need a nap more than I do."

Whatever he had done to make my life miserable, he offered me this. I could have accepted. But my grudge was so familiar . . . If my brother truly changed I would feel disappointed, as if Abel and Cain had shaken hands and made up.

I leaned my weight against the desk. I was fine, I said. I could handle the guests on my own. Arthur's face lost its light. He tossed the key on the counter, raised his briefcase like a shield, then pushed his way through the crowd in the lobby and left.

"That's her, over there."

The man whistled. "She must have been some beauty. So what's her name, Fiddle?"

"Feidel," I said. "Her name is Shirley Feidel."

I felt like a stoolie, though the man to whom I had revealed Shirley's identity wasn't a cop, just a harmless historian with a thick black mustache and frizzy black eyebrows. He had found out from an uncle that the Eden had been a haven for Holocaust Survivors since my grandfather placed an ad in the *Forward* that all Displaced Persons could stay there half-price. But they hadn't survived very well for Survivors. Unlike the Communists, who lived with their eyes on the future, the Survivors looked back. In the race against death, this weighted them down; they didn't see the dangers just ahead, at their feet. Only a handful still rented rooms at the Eden. I led the historian to each, and I hated to see how reluctant to speak these old people were.

Bringing it up will only give us nightmares.

Who wants to make the gentiles feel guilty? People don't like to feel guilty.

But each Survivor relented. Historians, after all, were God's scribes on Earth, and this one belonged to an institute that bore the name of Anne Frank. A vault of Holocaust stories wouldn't bring the Eden more guests, but I took pride in knowing that my family's hotel would be a footnote to history. I had kept these people alive long enough to deposit their secrets in that vault of recordings at Brandeis.

I introduced the historian to Shirley, then sat in a chair a little way off. The terrors she had been through gave her great dignity. She had witnessed an evil as immense as the Hebrews' captivity in Egypt. But she refused to tell her story. It was possible, she said, to be as vain of one's suffering as of anything else.

"If I can be honest," the historian said, "you won't live forever."

Shirley nodded. This was obvious. The wonder was that she had lived until now, that she was sitting in America on this fresh summer day watching the cottony plume from a jet dissolve to dots and dashes across a sapphire sky.

He ruffled his eyebrows. "But who will tell your story after you're gone?"

At least he hadn't said "dead."

"Story?" she repeated. "What I have lived through is not a story." She had just the breeze of an accent – a sibilant *s*, a thickly rolled *r*. Logically, I knew she had spoken English this way before living in the camps. But her accent seemed a scar, like the numbers on her wrist or whatever the Nazis had done to her womb. "Any words you could say would make it seem ... small. Something a person could understand if only he read those words enough times. A few familiar phrases. Those same photos, so small and harmless on the page. The naked men in the pit. The skeletons pressing against the fence."

"But I've told you, the book won't be what I say. You'll speak into this." He waved his hand above the slender steel recorder on the broad arm of Shirley's chair. "I'll just transcribe the tape."

"What if I haven't the words?"

"You speak better English than anyone I've interviewed."

Shirley leaned back, flattening her bun against the chair. "Someday they will add a verse to the *Tanach:* 'An enemy rose up and slew the six million. Their ashes and bones cried out to God, and at last He delivered those few who were left.'"

I was struck with awe, as if a chapter of the Bible had been written right there, on the Eden's lawn.

"Great. That's just great." The historian removed his glasses (I expected to see his nose and mustache come off too). "Then the gentiles can doubt the Holocaust really happened, the way they doubt the Jews were ever slaves in Egypt."

Shirley closed her eyes. "Perhaps it's better to test the world's faith than always offer proof."

"Don't you see? This is bigger than the Exodus precisely because we *do* have proof. Most American Jews stopped believing in the Bible a long time ago. They were ready to stop being Jews. Then they found out what was going on in Europe. The world wanted them dead? Ha! They would keep being Jews, out of spite."

"And is spite a good reason to keep alive a religion? Without spite, without being hated, is there really no other reason to go on being a Jew?"

"I would think you wouldn't mind a little spite."

She folded her hands. "Whether it is written or not does not matter. What I have been through is known."

"Maybe it's enough for you that it's written in God's mind how you suffered. Me, I want to leave something my children's children can read."

"What is written in God's mind I cannot know. I meant only my husband. He knows what I have been through. And that must be enough."

I did nothing that summer anyone else in business wouldn't do. I scrimped. I cut corners. I placed the Eden's survival above everything else. I argued with Jerry to use cheaper beef cuts. I stopped putting chlorine in the pool (dead or alive, a germ was invisible; what would be the harm if someone did swallow a mouthful of pee?). I had no time to weigh this claim, that defense, niceties of feeling, oughts and ought nots. Was it good for the Eden? No, no, and no.

When Mamie asked for a raise – should she get the same money for entertaining three times as many guests as she used to? – I didn't need to consider. What was the worst she could do to me, quit? Where else could a *tumeler* look for work if not here? Who would provide room and board for her son? She might try to be grateful.

Grateful! To someone whose dirty diapers she'd changed? When Lucy Appelbaum was a *pisherke* crying for attention, who'd given it? Mamie.

When she saw this didn't sway me, she changed her approach. "*Bubele,* I know exactly what you're going through." She nodded so emphatically her ancient fox boa – bald now on top, missing one eye – shook its head in chorus. "Since my nogoodnik of a husband ran off, I've had to pinch every coin. Always I have to worry what's to become of my poor baby. I try to make sure he can stand on his own feet, I try to develop my baby's one talent. And now I find out this talent is 'tasteless'! What I do is 'exploit'! I hear what they say. You think *he* hasn't heard?"

Lennie sat beside the front desk, mumbling and rocking like a yeshiva boy, though his prayer was a bit of dialogue from *Cocoanuts*.

Tell her that the retard scares away guests. Nana's voice filled my head, as if, in her deafness, she had found a way to be heard that didn't involve ears.

He's a human being! cried another voice in my head. *The boy is her son.*

Human? That's human?

You could have been him.

What could I do but turn Mamie down? If, out of pity, I fulfilled her request, the waiters and busboys would demand raises too.

Most of the staff were young Puerto Ricans and Vietnamese who had never waited tables. Mitchell Brush not only had taught them their jobs, he made sure they were prompt, efficient and neat. While my brother had gained his waiters' good will by procuring girls from town, Mitchell expected his soldiers to obey out of fear. With his sandy crewcut and planed, hairless face, he exerted the appeal of a steel-eyed Marine: *I'm strong, take my orders or you slobs might get hurt.* He hated incompetence. When Herbie spilled gravy on a guest, Mitchell delivered a cruel dressing-down and fired him, though I assured Herbie later that I was the only one with the authority to do this.

It was less that Mitchell was evil than he saw evil everywhere. Once, when he stumbled over my feet and dropped his tray, he accused me of tripping him on purpose so he would look foolish in front of his crew. When the leftovers of Jerry's goose-liver terrine gave Mitchell diarrhea, he stormed into my office and accused Jerry of trying to poison him.

"That's ridiculous," I said. "Why would he want – "

"Because he knows I hate fags."

Even the craps games Mitchell ran seemed less for amusement, or even for profit, than to teach his subordinates how much they stood to gain if they did what he said. I didn't have the grounds to ask Mitchell to leave, but I couldn't have my guests losing so much money they couldn't pay their bills. I couldn't have Herbie asking me for loans because he couldn't afford to buy razors.

"I was just trying to give them a chance for a little extra money," Mitchell said. "A little recreation. Their wages are so demeaning, I thought – "

"Their wages are low because they earn tips."

"You don't think it's demeaning to have to kiss up to a guest all summer, then beg for what you're entitled to? You don't think it's demeaning to never get a day off? To have to sleep in a slum?" Mitchell's mouth twisted. "Give them decent wages and one day off a week, let them sleep in the guest rooms, and there won't be a reason for the games."

"I said you should stop. That's enough reason."

"Why don't you just fire me?"

He knew that I had seen him try to drown his brother, yet I had hired him anyway. That meant I was desperate. And where could I find another headwaiter to replace him this late in July? "I do have the right to fire you, yes."

"Or why don't you turn me over to the cops? Isn't that what you'd really like to do? Like it never occurred to you the little twerp might have walked into the pool without any help from me? I was just six, for Christ's sake."

"I never thought – "

"Yeah. Right. Like you don't think I'm some sort of bully. Like it isn't even possible I might want to see my boys get what they deserve."

"Maybe you do. But I can't afford – "

"Like hell you can't. This place has more guests than it ever had."

What I had told him was true. I couldn't afford to pay the

waiters more money or give them time off, as I couldn't afford to admit I was working them too hard for boys of sixteen.

"That's it? You won't do it?" He turned on the heels of his polished black shoes. "You'll be sorry," he said, slamming the door so hard the next page of my ledger turned by itself. I stared at the blank columns in which to keep track of what I might gain or lose in the coming months, and by the time I'd gotten up and followed Mitchell to the lobby to tell him that I wouldn't stand for threats from my employees, he had been caught by someone else.

"Come on, Mitch. Please? Just tell me you'll meet him."

"Let go of my sleeve."

"Please? Just for five minutes. That's all it would take."

"I said to let go." Mitchell bent back his brother's wrist. "First it was Jesus. Now it's Reb Asshole. You're not very loyal, are you."

"That's just it! Rebbe Askold and Jesus Christ are the same guy. Well, sort of. They're brothers. They're both sons of God."

Mitchell rolled his eyes. "Poor Jesus Christ. We're both stuck with brothers who are assholes."

They stood in the lobby, exactly alike in their white shirts and black pants, except that Sam wore a wood crucifix on a thong around his neck and Mitchell wore a whistle. Watching them, I realized that if I had been born with a twin so placid and bland he would walk into a pool because I told him to do it, I would have hated him too.

"I'm not an asshole," Sam said. "I just have a hard time putting things in words. That's why I want you to meet the rebbe. He explains these things better."

"Let me see if *I* can explain things." Mitchell touched his brother's crucifix. "I don't believe in Jesus. I don't believe in this 'rebbe' of yours." He twisted the cross so the thong tightened around Sam's neck. "I believe in myself. In what I can see with my own eyes. In what I can do with my hands."

" 'Without faith, it is impossible to please Him, for he that cometh to God must believe that He is.' "

I had never heard Sam utter so many words at once. But then again, they were someone else's words.

"Cut it out!" Mitchell twisted the thong tighter.

" 'For by grace are ye saved, and not of yourselves. It is the gift of God, not of works, lest any man boast.' Ephesians, chapter – "

"Shut up!"

Sam smiled beatifically, confident of some truth beyond Mitchell's grasp.

"You asshole!" The thong snapped. The cross came off in Mitchell's hand. He stared at it, horrified. "Get out of here!" He threw the cross to the rug. "Get out of here, I told you!"

But his brother stood there and smiled. It was Mitchell who left.

I was so stiff and weary that even when I realized a man was standing above my bed, I couldn't move or cry out. The moonlight threw the man's shadow across the thin sheet that covered me.

"So, how's it been going?"

He had wakened me at two to find out how I was? "Is something wrong?" I asked.

"I should have known you'd be asleep." He moved toward the door; his shadowy double rolled off my bed.

"Don't go yet," I said. "Really."

"You're sure?" Arthur came back and sat beside me on the mattress. This filled me with love – until I remembered there were no chairs in the room; over the years they had been scattered to replace broken chairs elsewhere. This was the bed our parents had slept in from May through October for the past thirty-four years, except for those nights the Eden was so full they rented out their bungalow and slept in the lobby. (In the late 1950s, before my own birth, the Eden was so busy that Arthur might return to his room and find some strange couple sleeping there. Was it any wonder he didn't feel at home at the Eden? Why do we treat our families in ways we would never treat our guests?)

Haltingly, he told me that he'd fallen in love. He met the woman – her name was Maddy, or maybe it was Mattie, I was too tired to guess – about six months before, at the wedding of his freshman-year roommate from Princeton. She was a friend's sister's friend, a Quaker who taught philosophy of religion at Barnard. They had gotten to know each other during the weeks my brother spent commuting to New York, but now that his work on the merger was done, they saw each other weekends a few times a month.

"I mean, I could ask her to look for a job up in Boston, but she has tenure, for Christ sake. Professorships aren't easy to come by. It would be easier for me to get a job in New York, but I would have to start over. I would have to try to make partner at a new firm, from scratch. Besides, there's this religion thing. She's not so religious herself. I mean, she's just a Quaker. So fine, she won't sleep with me, I can handle that. It's just, well, that spiritual crap means a lot to her. Philosophy. God. She *likes* that I'm a Jew. She thinks it's . . . interesting. Interesting! She's always asking, 'Did you do this as a kid? Did your family do that? Do you really repent on Yom Kippur, or do you only pretend to?' You should see her face when I tell her I think it's bullshit. I mean, it's great that she cares about something other than how many hours she can bill. But what does she want from me? I'm supposed to pretend I believe in God and Revelation and all that I-and-Thou stuff? Just what I need – a wife who wants me to read Martin Buber. Never mind read Martin Buber, she wants me to *be* Martin Buber. Oh, never mind. You wouldn't understand."

No, I wouldn't understand how it was possible to love some-one because he believed in something higher than fame or success, yet despair of ever reaching that something yourself.

Arthur tugged at a slight tear in my sheet, ripping it further. "She wants me to play Martin Buber? Okay. Fine. I'll grow a beard. I'll wear my *tsitsit* hanging out. I'll tell her to convert. 'You want to marry me? Okay, shave off all your hair. You have to go through the whole *mikve* routine.' I'll tell her that we've got to make love through a sheet." He poked his middle finger through the hole and wiggled it obscenely.

I closed my eyes. "Arthur. They don't really do that." I wished the Hasids did; I had hundreds of holey sheets I could sell them. "Besides, I thought you said she wasn't really religious. Why would she want you to pretend to be an observant Jew?"

"Oh, I don't know, she thinks it's cute or something. When we're together, when she's looking at me, I feel like she's studying me. To see how a Jew acts when he's . . . you know, eating, when he's taking a piss with his genuine circumcised dick. She's interested in . . . authenticity. She goes around the country trying to find authentic religious communities. You know, Amish guys in buggies. Snake-handlers in some pa-thetic church in Georgia. She's writing a book on whether it's still possible to have an authentic religious experience in America, or whether it's all junk tradition, leftover culture. You know, people eating certain foods and saying certain prayers, but nothing's going on inside, they're not having an honest-to-God-authentic William Jamesian experience of the divine. Shit. You're asleep."

"I'm listening!" I jerked upright. "I wasn't asleep."

He got up from the mattress. Tired as I was, I hoped he wouldn't go.

"At least the food here is kosher. She can't criticize us for that."

"She's coming here – what's her name, Mattie?"

"It's Maddy. Two *d's*. Short for Madeline. And yeah, she'd like to come, if you can spare the room. Two rooms, actually – one for her, and one for me. That's why I . . . Listen. She wants to meet my family. She wants to see where I come from."

Did he mean that if we weren't Jewish enough, this woman wouldn't marry him? (*Come on, Fred and Ethel, let's help Arthur fool her! We'll wear wigs and black coats . . . It's just for two days.*) If Maddy judged us fakes, would she publish her findings in the paper, the way the State of New York published the names of restaurants that claimed to be kosher but surreptitiously greased their baking pans with lard or mixed dairy with meat?

"Lucy," he said, and this was the first time my brother had said my name without making it a slur, "I want you to know, I have no intention of mooching off you like Abe's brothers mooched off him."

"I won't take your money. You're family," I said.

"Yeah. I'm an Appelbaum. And in case I forget, somebody, somewhere, will be sure to remind me."

He bent down and stuffed something under my pillow. "Thanks," he said. "We'll be here this Friday afternoon."

After he was gone I reached beneath the pillow. The money felt like dead skin. I lay with the stack of bills on my chest, and in that moment between my brother's departure and my descent back to sleep, I tried to figure out why everyone I knew – Arthur, my mother, Thomas, Nana, Jimmy – made me feel like a whore.

When Maddy toured the Eden she professed to be charmed by everything – from the stain on the dining-room wall where Arthur threw his first *latke,* to the vine-woven trellis, which she circled as if taking its measure for a bridal canopy. She was a beautiful woman – tall, with straight brown hair and a clear, open face. When she smiled – which was often – I couldn't help but feel proud. My hotel was authentic! I was treating my guests as Thou's and not It's, the way homogeneous American chains seemed to do. Her only disappointment came from the Eden's guests, most of whom didn't keep the Sabbath or pray. The Fourth of July and Labor Day were fine, but why couldn't the Eden stay open to celebrate Rosh Hashanah and Yom Kippur? And what about that holiday with the wooden huts – Succoth? Where could such holidays better be spent than the Catskills, amid the rich autumnal colors of decay and rebirth?

And then, once she started, Maddy couldn't stop. Lunch tasted great, but Jerry's soufflés didn't seem . . . authentic. And maybe I could find a way so the staff didn't have to work on Saturdays.

I started to tell Maddy that half the Eden's waiters were Vietnamese and the rest Puerto Rican, but I knew this was flimsy. Even non-Jews deserved a day off.

"I didn't want to make a fuss my first visit," Maddy said. "But as Arthur can tell you, I'm not very good at keeping my opinions to myself."

I choked with resentment. Couldn't she see how much effort it took to serve a meal to two hundred guests?

"Come off it, Mad." Arthur scraped his bowl clean of mousse. Herbie, who had been hovering behind him, took away the dish. He and my brother exchanged awkward smiles and a promise to talk later, when things settled down. Then Herbie grew shy. He hoisted his bus box and ducked inside the kitchen, not to re-emerge for the rest of the meal.

Arthur turned to Maddy. "Listen, I'm all for waiters' rights. But these guys don't give a shit that it's Saturday. Even the Jewish guys. They want to sleep a few hours in the sun, not spend the day cooped up in some synagogue."

They started to argue. The other guests listened as intently as if they had been asked to judge the debate. I tried to make peace, but neither Maddy nor my brother wanted to stop. A

Quaker who loved to argue! That must have been the root of their love: each enjoyed a good fight.

"Never mind. Arthur, you just finish your lunch." Maddy wiped her mouth. "I'm going for a walk. That is the proper thing to do on the Sabbath, isn't it, take a walk?"

"Have a nice time." Arthur waggled his hand.

But three hours later, when she hadn't returned, my brother was so frantic he dialed the police. "She left her luggage," he told me. "Her things must have her scent."

I put my finger on the button and restrained him from fetching her brassiere. "I think I know where you can find her."

"Lucy, I swear, if you take me on some wild goose-chase . . ."

Despite his fears, he let me lead him to the Playland.

"Pospissil's? What would Maddy be doing – ?"

I didn't want to tell him that everyone I knew ended up here. The few times that month I had stolen time to walk up this drive to spy on Thomas, I always seemed to find someone else there – Comrade Beck, on his knees, hammering a new porch; Jerry exclaiming over a species of rare mushroom he had found by the pond; Shirley reading poems while Thomas painted the bungalow and Nat fixed the furnace. I had even found the Hasid and his disciple, Sam Brush, haranguing Thomas as he sat reading some heavy tome in his yard: "Study shrivels the spirit! Books confuse the heart! Solitude and study are sins against God! The Messiah himself could appear before you now and still you would read!"

We found Maddy and Thomas astride two cement sacks. Most of the bungalows at the Playland had been picked as clean as the game hens we'd served the previous night, but Mr. P's bungalow sported new windows, new doors and new paint. The Torah ark was gone; I imagined it in Thomas's bedroom, filled with khaki pants and shirts.

"Seems I recall some proverb about how a Jew is in exile," he was saying.

"Yes, yes," Maddy answered, "but that's a statement of fact, not a state to be wished."

"Ever think it's a kind of definition?"

"Semantics! If exile were desirable, why would Jews pray for the Messiah to end it and bring the living and dead back to Jerusalem?"

"Your folks go back to England, Lucy and Arthur head off to Israel, my folks go back to Africa. Call that redemption? Sounds more like Jim Crow to me."

The longer I listened the more I rebelled, as Lucifer must have felt his gorge rise on hearing the archangels sing their saccharine duets.

What my brother felt I can't guess; he was struck silent as if he had come upon his girlfriend discussing God with a bear.

"I don't want to interrupt you," I said.

They turned to us then like two guilty children.

"Oh, I am sorry, Arthur. We got so caught up in what we were talking about . . ." Maddy stood and stretched her legs, then held her hand for Thomas to shake, which he did. "I can't tell you how much I've enjoyed our discussion." She took my brother's elbow. "I haven't figured out how to serve food without waiters, but the sun is going down now, and I have to admit I'm hungry enough not to care." She tugged at Arthur's arm until finally his feet moved.

I lingered behind. I needed something from Thomas. Something I couldn't ask for.

He took off his cap. "Some surprise, mmm, you brother's friend."

I nodded.

"Lucy. I've been meaning to come see you, but time always seems . . . Like the rabbis say, Day's short, there's lots to do, the laborer is sluggish and the Master is . . . Well, I guess you don't care what a bunch of dead geezers have to say."

It pained me that he would betray those dead rabbis for my sake.

"Care to come in? Got lots to catch up on."

My heart eased a little. But I hated to feel like an after-thought. And now, of all times! Jerry had charged his pastry chef with using real butter and cream even in desserts that were meant to be *pareve,* an accusation that caused the lovers to stop speaking. The waiters were still grumbling about their wages. A klezmer band was due to arrive any minute to per-form in that night's show.

"I can't," I said. "I'm sorry," and I rushed off before he could guess my real fear: that after so many hours discussing phi-losophy with Maddy, he would find me homely and dull.

One evening I ran into Nat Feidel on the path to Nana's bun-galow. He held a bunch of daisies, a screwdriver, a little hack-saw, a covered dish and a heart-shaped box of candy. He knocked once, for form's sake. Then he screwed off the door knob, hacked the chain with the saw, and let himself in.

Five minutes went by. The daisies, I thought, were a sort of white flag. Though Nat was younger than Nana, he must have been her ideal. He was courtly. Successful. More important, he treated his wife like a queen. He wouldn't let her work. When the doctors said a child might ruin Shirley's health, Nat wouldn't hear of trying. The men called him arrogant, "impressed with himself, like all those Viennese Jews," but their wives praised his chivalry, not to mention his good looks.

In my mind's eye I saw my grandmother bent over some project. She felt a tap at her shoulder and jerked around, star-tled, to smack the intruder. Then she saw Nat. Did she curse him? Apologize? Did she think he was a dream? Flustered, she would find a vase for the daisies (a gallon-sized vinegar bottle covered with yarn). Then she would lead him to the parlor and pour him a shot of the hundred-proof slivovitz she'd brewed decades before from the Eden's own plums. Did they sit and drink in silence, or did Nat write her notes? Did they talk about me?

Ten minutes, no Nat. Nana had danced on the candies and even now was carving Nat into scraps. I preferred to believe this. If all it took to get my grandmother to eat were flowers and candy, I could have brought those myself.

At last the door opened and Nat emerged, whole and stately as ever, hands free of gifts. The way he looked then, framed in the door, brought to mind something else. My grandmother's portraits of all those earls, dukes and barons, even Henry VIII, sported the same silver mustache, the same square chin and straight nose as Nathan Feidel.

She started to haunt him. When Nat and Shirley went out walking, my grandmother followed. Most afternoons, Nana stood beside the pool watching Nat swim. Once, Shirley gestured for Nana to join them. Shirley repeated the gesture, but Nana shook her head and shuffled away, muttering.

In the twenty-five years since the pool had been built, she had never dipped a toe in. No one had taught her to swim. Why hadn't Abe bothered? He'd taught everyone else. I'd seen photos of him helping several pretty women float.

Day after day Nana stood there and watched, until, late in August, on the sort of afternoon everyone dreams of diving fully clothed into a pool, my grandmother took off her shoes. I had been trying to clean the filter but the air in the pump house was suffocatingly thick. I crawled out to splash my face. Shirley and Nat finished swimming laps and lingered in the pool. Their backs were toward Nana so they didn't see her sit on the edge of a lounge, unlace her black boots, roll down her socks.

Gey nit arum borves, I thought as she walked toward the steps. Her feet were misshapen. The hot cement might have scalded her soles if her skin hadn't been so thick. I found myself wishing she would go back to her bungalow so I wouldn't see her suffer.

Shirley and Nat climbed from the pool and toweled off. Nana watched them leave. Then she gathered up her boots and, still in bare feet, walked the same path.

It reached the point where Nana held vigils at the stairs, waiting for Nat to come down or go up. She never approached him. She had no social graces and probably she knew this. Or maybe she thought she needn't win his love. Nat loved her already; they only needed to wait for Shirley to die.

I asked the Feidels if they wanted me to keep Nana away, but I hadn't a clue how to do this and therefore was relieved when they said they didn't mind. Why make a fuss? The poor woman, Shirley said, had nothing left to do.

She hadn't meant to accuse me, but I still felt the need to plead my defense. If it weren't for me, the Eden would have closed and Nana would have lost the one thing she owned. But Shirley's silence implied that there wouldn't have been an Eden if not for my grandmother's hard work all those years.

When Nana ended her hunger strike and finally left her bungalow, I feared she would make trouble. Instead, she ignored me. She acted as if I were some servant she had hired to run her hotel. She ordered her meals to be served at Nat's table. Each night she came to dinner in her best red dress and pearls – or rather, dried chick peas, each painted white – and gummed down great helpings of Jerry's Szechwan beef. ("At least this has taste. Not like that pap your mother left by my door.") She couldn't make conversation but enjoyed asking Nat to pass the olives or the bread. The older guests paid respects; Nana sat and nodded regally. When the younger guests learned who she was, they filed past her chair with the deference they would have paid a wax figurine in Madame Tussaud's.

Each week she grew plumper, and with each pound that my grandmother gained, I lost two. I had no time to eat. I hurried through the dining room repeating tasks to myself ("More sugar for Table Three, diet peaches for Seven, tell Cyrus to wash more coffee cups"), swearing if anyone dared step in my path.

Still, I thought everything would turn out to be all right. After the season I would recoup what I'd lost. This merely would be a matter of getting a few nights' sleep and forcing myself to walk to the Playland and apologize to Thomas. I felt blessed by God, protected. Everything I put my hand to would prosper. When I saw a commotion one evening on the lawn, I thought we had become so successful that we no longer could accommodate all the guests in one shift.

Then I saw a sheet stretched across the porch. In red paint – or was it ketchup? – a four-word slogan was scrawled: NO RAISE NO FOOD. The waiters and busboys and most of the Communists were marching in a circle with placards that read: EDEN IS HELL! ONLY CAPITALIST PIGS EAT THE SLOP THEY SERVE HERE. A waiter named Ho wore a napkin as a sort of revolutionary's headband and shouted in a language I took to be Vietnamese.

The only employee who wasn't picketing was Sam. What comfort was that? He had been missing for a week, though he had left a note saying he was "visiting friends." (I found it less trouble to carry the guests' valises than reprimand Sam for extorting our guests to join whatever religion he belonged to that month.) Even Herbie was here. He wore a sign like a harness someone had yoked around his neck.

Mitchell was perched on the verandah. Comrade Beck, as zealous as if he had been given the chance to spearhead the fight against Triangle Shirtwaist, used his cigar to lead the strikers as they muddled through every verse of every song

Woody Guthrie ever wrote, including three complete renditions of "This Land Is Your Land."

At the end of the chorus Mrs. Heffer shouted: "What about my thyroid? If I don't eat I might faint!"

Comrade Beck raised his hand. "Say Lenin and Marx: for the good of the people, the bourgeoisie must sometimes wither away."

"He wants her to wither!"

"We paid for that food. If we have to, we'll serve it ourselves."

Even as I watched the mob surge ahead, I felt no satisfaction – after all, they had surged out of gluttony, not loyalty.

"Wait!" Comrade Beck stretched his arms across the steps; the arm that had spent all winter in a cast looked fragile and pale. "All of you, stop!"

Like most Jewish mobs, this one obeyed.

"Look at these boys! Like your own sons, they work hard to get an education, to help in the family. Seven days they labor, and for what? The Eden exploits these boys and you let them!"

"It's true," someone murmured. "That boy over there even looks like my Darryl, except around the eyes."

"I can't cross a picket line. I remember in the Thirties, our strike at the automobile plant . . ."

"Someone get the girl. She should meet their demands. Then we can eat."

"Never mind the girl." This last came from Mamie, who had mounted the steps. "That Lucy is worse than her grandmother. She even *looks* like the old woman, have you noticed? Not the way Jennie looks now. I mean years ago. That red hair. The angry face. She's even started cursing."

Mitchell looked down at me and smirked. And that's when I saw he wasn't as wily as he pretended to be. He shouldn't have left me with no choice except losing my home.

Mamie and the strikers joined hands and started singing "We Shall Overcome."

I sneaked around back and let myself into the kitchen by the dumpster. Two hundred soup bowls stood empty on the counter. Steam wafted from the kettles of mushroom barley on the stove. Jerry looked at me curiously; I put my finger to my lips and stole through the dining room, appearing on the verandah so quietly that the singing didn't stop.

"You're fired," I told Mitchell.

He cupped his hand to his ear.

"Fired!" I shouted. I pulled off his bow tie.

Mamie stopped singing. Everyone watched.

"Pack your bags and get out."

"Right," Mitchell said. "And who's going to be your head-waiter?"

If Jimmy's praise of my bluffing had been flattery then, now it was true. To bluff well, a person must have everything to lose and nothing left to wager.

"If you fire me," Mitchell threatened, "the others will quit."

"You're sure about that?"

"Go ahead and see."

I turned to the staff. "Here's my offer. On Wednesdays we'll serve a buffet lunch and dinner. Half of you can work, the rest get the day off. The following week, the groups switch. If the Eden makes a profit this year, I'll split it with you all. Take it or leave it."

"Take what?" Mitchell said. "An afternoon off every other week? And you won't see the money. Assholes! She can't get anyone else this late. If you quit, she'll come begging."

"If you quit I'll say fine, good riddance. I'll close the hotel. I'll close it, do you hear me? You won't get your wages and you'll forfeit all your tips."

This was more than Ho could bear. "If not tips, I poor guy! No college! No car! I already owe Captain Brush four hundred dollars for poker. I don't even got no way to get home!"

"Tips." Mitchell sneered. "*There* are your tips." He motioned toward the guests. "All right, listen up. Everyone who owes Ho a tip, if you'd please pay him now . . . Mr. Kroll, Mr. Flax, you've been here two months. A hundred apiece would be about right."

But the only tips these gentlemen seemed to care about then were the tips of their shoes.

"Mrs. Hope? Mrs. Heffer?"

Suddenly these women's shoes also became all-consuming. If the boys stayed and dunned them in the time-honored way by chasing their taxis and throwing themselves across the hoods, well, they would see. Watching those women, I almost forgot whose side I was on. I wanted to shake their handbags and see what fell out. I wanted to pick up a sign and start marching.

"Mr. Beck!" Mitchell said. "You sit at Ho's station."

A long pause. "Yes, well, we Communists believe tipping is wrong. It's a way for the owners to excuse paying lower wage."

Mitchell leaned down.

"But in this case, I suppose . . ." Comrade Beck rummaged in his pants. "A gift from the workers. To show support."

Mitchell unrolled the bill. "It's five fucking dollars! Ho brought you three meals a day for two months!" He tossed the money in the bushes. "If you quit, she'll come crawling. She'll double your salaries and you'll still get your tips."

It took me a moment to realize that I was this "she" who would come crawling. I repeated my ultimatum: If they didn't serve this meal I would send everyone home.

They looked at me, then at Mitchell, then back again at me. They let the sheet fall.

"Assholes! Don't do it!"

Nervously, they filed past me to the dining room. As Herbie walked by, still wearing his placard, I held out Mitchell's bow tie. "Here," I said. "You're in charge now."

"Oh, I couldn't." His nose twitched.

"Sure you could." I clipped the tie to his shirt. He brought his hand to his neck the way a young girl would bring her hand to her first necklace.

"Really? You think I could do it?"

I nodded and smiled. Herbie nodded and smiled back, then stood straight and marched in.

"Assholes! Wimps! *Gooks!* You stupid P.R.'s! I knew I couldn't trust you!"

But by then the last boy had slinked back to his post, and even the Communists decided to trade their placards for menus.

"All right," he said. "You win. I'm the bad guy and you're the hero. But why, would you tell me that? Because I wanted to help those poor sons of bitches stand up for what they're worth?"

"Come off it," I said. "You just like the power. You want everyone to follow you."

He smirked again. "And you don't?"

Mitchell jogged down the steps and headed toward the Horseshoe. I felt like calling him back. Without Mitchell Brush, some spell might be broken, some chain of events inexorably leading from *then* until *now*. If Mitchell hadn't pushed his brother in the pool, or, as he claimed, allowed Sam to walk in, I wouldn't have had the chance to pull Sam out and save him. I wouldn't have come to believe that I had the power to revive what was dead.

Late in August, Thomas appeared at my office with a lopsided basket and a burlap pouch. The door was open, but he knocked and asked if he could come in. He was stiff as any stranger.

"If you're busy . . ." he said.

I almost said yes – from habit, or from spite. But the way he looked, with that basket, made me think of Robinson Crusoe.

He was lonely, I thought. Then I remembered how many visitors he had. *I* was the one who might as well have lived on an island, hoping to discover someone's tracks in the sand.

"Don't want those berries to rot on us, do we."

Why not accept? The hotel was running smoothly (I rapped the wood desk). The waiters and busboys grumbled like the losers of any failed coup, but the rhythm of their work left them no time to plot, and the longer they worked under Herbie's command, the younger they seemed. They grudgingly joined him in softball tournaments and trips to town for ice cream. ("He good guy," Ho said, "but he driving me nut. Tell him he don't got to apologize for every bad thing G.I.s do in Saigon.")

"I guess I can spare an hour," I told Thomas.

I casually tried to steer him away from the places Nana was likely to be. When we left the main grounds I thought we were safe, but we came upon her suddenly, climbing the trail to the fields. We couldn't help but overtake her. Thomas touched his cap, but Nana acted as if we were two menial employees whose names she didn't know.

We passed the camp house, which I had boarded up and padlocked so the children couldn't gash their hands on cracked glass or suffer the rage of hornets. (Was my Old Testament in the cubbyhole? I couldn't recall ever taking it out.)

"It's a shame we can't use it," I said pointedly. "We have lots of kids this summer. When it's rainy, they don't have anywhere to play."

He stared into his basket. Repentant, I said, "I guess we'll get by for another two weeks."

We hiked on in silence until we reached the pond, where the Sunday Painters' Club of Union, New Jersey, stood beside their easels. Palettes hooked around their thumbs, the women dabbed at blobs that were meant to be water lilies, but the one man among them was painting a nude – a naked pink bather rose from the pond, giant breasts and waves of flesh flecked with green scum.

Just out of earshot Thomas roared to the sky. "Beats me what Abe would think of this place. I'm not sure he'd even know where he was. But that painting!" He wheezed. "*That* he would like."

Why did everyone use my grandfather to mouth their judgments of me?

"Better watch out." He tickled my neck with a blade of grass. "That frown could sour the whole berry crop."

I tried not to smile. But Thomas – and the Catskills – were at their most seductive. The maple trees rustled and tossed their heads. Locusts flew up before my sneakers like clods of dirt invested with life. I had spent most of the summer in my office or the kitchen; the simplest flowers seemed strange.

"What are those?" I asked.

"You don't know thistle? Or clover? You do know a daisy when you see one, mmm, Lucy?" He wove the stem through my hair, then ran his palm along my cheek.

I thought I might cry. Sadness and joy hung in perfect balance; I wasn't sure which to feel. An enormous turquoise dragonfly dive-bombed at my face. When I flailed at it, the insect split into two. They'd been mating.

When Thomas saw this he laughed and broke into song, gestures broad as a minstrel's: "O-o-o, I passed the bottle when she got dry, and brushed away the blue-tail fly." He danced farther up the trail. "Jimmy crack corn and I don't care, Jimmy crack corn and I don't care, Jimmy crack corn and I don't ca-a-a-re . . . My master's gone a-way."

I caught myself excusing his antics because he was so much younger than I was, that's how old I felt then. He reached the meadow first, and as soon as I got there I had to sit down. The air smelled of hot grass. Everything was green, except a single maple, prematurely red, like a messenger who appears at a party with news that can only be bad.

A few berries still were hard, with tiny green crowns, but most melted to jelly between my fingers. Stretched across the twigs were webs like quilts hung to air. I put a berry on my tongue; the rigid skin split, the warm pulp rushed out. I ground berries in my palm, plucked an Indian paintbrush and stroked the juice on my wrist, where it beaded like ink.

Thomas unfurled a blanket and spread it on the grass. "First," he said, "the salad course." From that same pouch he withdrew a handful of peas in their papery green pods, a bunch of frilly-stemmed carrots, snap beans, a small cantaloupe, a dozen purple plums from the trees behind his land. We plucked raspberries from the vines that crept around our blanket, each a red jewel. Thomas reclined on his elbows. "I've been working pretty hard. The house should be done soon." He picked at a berry seed wedged between his teeth. "I thought, well, in case . . . you might want to come see it."

"Halloo there! Hallo!"

Shirley and Nat strolled into the clearing. Thomas shrugged – it wasn't *his* fault. He stood and waved them over. Hurrying to join us, Nat tripped on something. He started to go down, but Shirley grabbed his arm and prevented him from sprawling, though she herself fell. Nat stood, helped her rise, brushed straw from her skirt. His hands seemed to linger. When they finally joined our picnic, both their faces were flushed.

"*Ach,*" Shirley said, "*so ein shöner Tag!*"

"And the smell!" Nat drew such a deep breath I could see his mustache stir. He looked around the field – good, they'd lost Nana, it *was* getting tiresome – then plucked the thighs of his trousers and sat.

Neither of them seemed to find it remarkable that Thomas and I should have been alone in this field. Shirley asked questions about my parents, nibbled a plum, then took a book from her pocket, leaned against a rock and started reading. I was tired and hot. I lay back on the grass and listened as Thomas and Nat started arguing about something, their voices distant and dull as the sawing of the locusts.

"Universal man! You sound like my neighbors in Vienna just before Hitler knocked at their doors."

"Never said I was trying to pass. Only said a man can be more than one thing."

"Pah. You think they come with an eyedropper, with a microscope? What they see from a distance, that's what you are."

"Just because a few fanatics see me that way doesn't mean I've got to define – "

"A few! Listen, Jefferson, life isn't a flea market. You can't pick and choose – a wise proverb by Confucius, selections from the *Sayings of the Fathers,* a witty parable from the Sermon on the Mount. You stitch together something like that – a person, a religion, what you call it, a 'project' – a stitched-together thing like that, it's a dead thing, a corpse."

"So if something's not one thing, all the way through, it's dead? You want me to be consistent? I'll tell you who's consistent. Himmler, he was consistent. Eichmann, now there was a consistent thinker. Göring, *he* was consistent."

The list of consistent Nazis went on. I forced one eye open, to see if Shirley was growing as impatient as I was. But her book had slid to the ground. Her skirt had ridden up, exposing her legs, which seemed beautiful to me then, white and smooth, with no veins. A beetle crawled across her thigh. The number on her wrist faced away from me, like a watch I couldn't read. Because of that number she could spend her days savoring the most ordinary things, and that would be enough. No one could chide her for falling asleep on a drowsy afternoon, her mouth gaping slightly and a noise coming out like the hum of a bee.

Before he left us that day, Thomas invited us to a housewarming party. I didn't want to go. I had no intention of sitting quietly while Thomas and Nat debated Talmud and Shirley read *Faust*. But, as it turned out, Shirley had a cold and Nat wouldn't go without her. I imagined Thomas waiting at his table, the tea growing chilled. I started to dwell on what it would be like the Monday after Labor Day, when the Eden was empty except for Nana and me. Already I had caught the first scent of fall.

When I got to the Playland, I was startled to find six or seven cars parked beside the road. I heard a Mills Brothers song, and I marveled that it should be playing on the radio on this of all nights. But once I got to the door I saw that the music was coming from a stereo, the old-fashioned kind with the speakers attached to the turntable like rectangular ears. Beside it lay a stack of albums so new they were still in their wraps.

"Lucy," Thomas said. He held out a glass of punch. "Glad you could make it."

The next guest came in and I stepped to one side. The bungalow looked much like the handyman's shack at the Eden, except that the toilet was inside its own room. I didn't think I knew anyone. Then a few faces grew familiar. There was Hwang, the one-handed chef who owned the Chinese diner on the outskirts of Paradise. I had eaten there many times, but I didn't recognize the chef now in baggy trousers and a yellow shirt instead of a white apron. He was standing beside the Puerto Rican clerk who worked at the fish store. I didn't know the man's name, but my mother once said his wife and sons had died when their apartment house on Main Street burned down. I had never heard the clerk or Johnny Hwang say a word – I hadn't thought they knew English – but here they were talking and gesturing extravagantly, Hwang with his good arm and the clerk with those delicate, tapering hands that could fillet a trout with one flick.

By the punch bowl, a young man with a goatee was drawing on the tablecloth. His name was Blake Fields. He had earned a physics degree from Yale, and then, for no reason, he'd come home to live with his aunt. He sat by the register in Fields' Hardware all day, sketching diagrams on bags, which he shielded from view. But here he was, showing a sketch of some gadget to the man who owned Doodie's.

The only guest I couldn't place was a wrinkled black man in a suit, though he seemed to know me.

"Got some de-licious offal cooking out back. Ought to try some." He winked.

The offal turned out to be barbecued ribs he had brought as a gift. All the guests had brought gifts: roast pork from Hwang's diner; the punch bowl, which came from Doodie's; some spicy fish stew; a lifetime supply of bolts, tacks and nails. I hadn't brought a thing. I'd thought my coming was a gift. How did these people know what sort of presents Thomas liked? They couldn't have become his close friends in the past several months.

He put his arm around my shoulder. He smelled different, I thought. Too . . . fruity. Too sweet. His shirt was stained with punch.

"Nice group of folks, mmm? Man loses his real family, got to put together a new one."

I started to say a family isn't something a person collects, like matchbooks or coins, but I didn't want to fight.

"Can the gentleman get the lady some punch? Old family recipe. Man's got a plantation, he ought to serve a bowl of plantation punch, mmm?"

I hated his gauzy expression, the way he leaned too heavily on my arm.

"Care to rumba?" he asked. He grabbed my wrist and twirled me. I started to fall, though Thomas was the one who flopped to the floor. He sat there and laughed.

"Friends." He held up his hands. "Friends, got a lot of good

food here. Lot to be thankful for. Thought it'd be fitting . . .
Thought if we tried we might be able to persuade a certain
young lady to sing us a blessing . . ."

"Oh, I couldn't," I protested. But everyone had gathered
around a guest I hadn't noticed. I thought I didn't know her.
Then I saw she'd just aged. Pamela Love had been in my class
at Paradise High. She had won a scholarship to Julliard, but
then she got pregnant. Her boyfriend, Boo Richards, went
away to college and died the first week, playing touch football;
no one was aware of the flaw in his heart. Now Pam worked at
Hwang's and sang in the choir at her church. She was here
with the baby, who had Boo's wistful eyes.

Pam gave in to the pleading and handed her son to the clerk
from the fish store. She wore a simple blue shift, her arms and
legs bare except for a gold chain circling one ankle. She was
darker than Thomas, not beautiful, but . . . poised. She kept her
arms crossed against her chest as if she were cold, or still
cradling the child. Thomas looked up from the floor, legs awk-
wardly crossed before him, his cap on one knee. As she sang,
he rubbed his eyes.

> T'was grace that taught my heart to feel,
> and grace my fears re-lieved.
> How precious did that grace appear
> the hour I first be-lieved. . . .

I let myself out quietly and closed the door behind. And I
knew I would hear that voice in my head each time I passed by,
recounting the many dangers and snares it had passed
through, and praising the grace that would soon lead it home.

Sometimes the Powers of Darkness doze off. The Evil Eye
blinks. A person's luck changes, though my mother believed
this was only a trick so she would let down her guard.

That summer, my parents bought the winning ticket at a synagogue raffle, the prize being Israel. My father had wanted to go there since he was a boy, but the closest he had ever come was his tour of the mess tents and pantries of Europe. The boundaries of his life were so . . . limited, I thought. I had traveled with him once to buy fish wholesale in New York. On the way home we stopped for lunch; a waitress with a thick New Jersey accent recited the desserts.

"How strange," my father said. "I can't imagine how that would taste."

"How what would taste?" I asked.

"Why, a borscht-and-cream pie."

No use sending him to Boston, all those Puritan churchyards with their crosses and their skulls. But the thought of my father standing on Masada, adjusting the black yarmulke he wore in respect for all those martyred Jews, made my eyes brim.

"We're not going," my mother told me.

"What do you mean? How often do you win a trip to Israel?"

" 'Win'! I get such a bad feeling when I think of this 'prize,' it's like a hand is squeezing my chest."

"For God's sake, Mom, it's the synagogue. You do trust the synagogue?"

"The synagogue I trust. The Arabs I don't trust."

"I just can't believe – "

"And such a long flight would tire your father. I still say he doesn't look well."

"You've got it backwards. Vacations are what overworked people need." I saw myself stretched on a lounge beside a beach, sipping cool drinks. I would stay at the fanciest Jerusalem hotel and let others serve *me*. "If you don't want to go, I would be glad to use the tickets." But whom would I take? Everyone belonged to a couple but me. Jerry had Justin. Mamie had Lennie. Even Arthur had a mate. (I had been startled from sleep several days earlier by my brother calling to find out if he and Maddy could get married at the Eden on Labor Day. "What's the rush?" I asked. To which he replied: "We're afraid if we wait we might come to our senses.") The world traveled in pairs, and the man I had been paired with was such a poor match I wondered if we might be the leftovers that didn't match anything else. What a mockery it was that Thomas knew Hebrew! I couldn't demand my mother give her ticket to *him*. Besides, we would have fought the entire time we were there. I would have begged to sleep late while he tried to drag me off to see this or that ruin. I saw him standing by some cave lecturing a crowd of Christians, Jews and Moslems who hung on each word, Thomas more at home in my homeland than I was.

"You could give the tickets to Arthur," I suggested. "For his honeymoon."

My mother considered this a moment. She couldn't convince her son not to marry a Christian, but Maddy's interest in the Eden and everything Jewish seemed a sign she would convert. A trip to Israel might speed that conversion. Still, my mother feared that her son and future daughter-in-law might be blown apart by terrorists. "What if they get kidnapped?" She clicked her tongue so loudly it seemed our phone line had been cut. "For a honeymoon present, I killed my own son!"

I told myself my mother wasn't really sick. And, even if she were, another two weeks of worry wouldn't kill her. After the season I would see she got help. As for my father, he had lived willingly with my mother for thirty-four years. If he hadn't seen her sleeping in the armchair that night, he would never have gotten married. Missing a trip to Israel would be a reasonable sacrifice for so many years of comfort, two children and a home.

The Torah proclaims it a mitzvah to help a bride and groom celebrate their marriage. Perhaps it seems odd, bribing guests to join a feast and wish the newlyweds joy. But envy strikes sharpest at weddings, I've found. Watching my brother marry Maddy, I felt spiteful and sad. I might as well have been the spinster aunt they didn't have.

Still, when I look back at that terrible year, I can say I fulfilled this one mitzvah. I was jealous. I was sad and full of self-pity. But at least I had the grace not to show how I felt.

The wedding was so rushed that only a few members of Maddy's family could come. They were a pale, quiet crew; though rich and well bred, they seemed pleased to have this chance to apply their Quaker tolerance to their daughter's new mate.

The klezmer band I'd hired began to play the wedding march. Maddy walked down the aisle. ("Look at that waist!" "Such lovely blonde hair!" I prayed I wouldn't hear a stage-whispered "*shiksa,*" and, happily, didn't.) Arthur met his bride and escorted her to the trellis, to stand beside me. Jays pecked the fat purple grapes overhead. I could smell Maddy's bouquet, her lemony shampoo, her bleached linen dress.

The rabbi leafed through his prayer book – he was an old friend of Arthur, a wild-living Wall Street trader who had gotten religion in his thirties, enrolled in seminary and been ordained just that year, still liberal enough to perform a wedding between a Jew and a Quaker, which none of the other rabbis in the Catskills would consent to. In his elegant suit and tie, he boomed out the service – in Hebrew, then in English – like a man calling out a bid on a new issue of bonds.

My mother, who stood beside my father, to my right, kept tearing at her handkerchief. She was glad that her only son was getting married. He might give her a grandchild over whom she could fret. But would that grandchild be Jewish? When my mother had raised this question, Maddy smiled and said she planned to give any child she had "a spiritual upbringing."

"Jewish spiritual? Or Christian?"

My brother answered for her. "Human spiritual," he said.

My mother made a noise that sounded like our ancient Hoover choking on a dustball. "Funny, when people say 'human,' they never seem to mean 'Jewish.'"

Maddy would have argued, but Arthur wouldn't let her. "Don't waste your breath. I could be marrying Golda Meir and my mother wouldn't approve."

She wasn't even happy about Arthur's new job – he had been hired by a fancy lawyer in Manhattan who'd made his reputation defending unpopular clients with names like Shapiro, Klugman and Levine. According to my mother, men like Ernie Dash gave gentiles the impression that the world was controlled by Jewish bankers and lawyers who schemed in New York. "Oh yeah?" Arthur countered. "Who else has the power to keep Jews from getting screwed if not lawyers like Dash?" This subject – getting screwed – was now near his heart. When he had told the secretary at his old firm that he was leaving, she confided that he wouldn't have made partner anyway. When Arthur pressed why, she said she had overheard Lee Treadwell tell Brad Hoar that Arthur's hair was too curly. "Too curly?" Arthur shouted. "I'll give them too curly!" My brother would have sued, but the secretary refused to testify in court and Arthur knew he couldn't win. Dash promised him a partnership, if things worked out, in a year. Besides, the lawyers at his new firm were so loud and abrasive that Arthur felt more refined than he ever would have felt at Treadwell, Mead, Hoar.

With all her objections, my mother was so happy that her son had found a wife she didn't wage as fierce a battle as everyone feared. As the wedding grew close, my mother worried less about anti-Semitic crazies gunning for her son than the crazy in our own family. Whom would Nana come gunning for if she learned her only grandson was marrying a *goy*? My mother slipped an invitation beneath the bungalow door, but my grandmother seemed not to understand what R.S.V.P. meant. And so, at the wedding, we stood beside the *chuppah,* glancing here and there – at the rustling hedge, the darting cardinal – hoping Nana wouldn't swoop down and stop the rabbi. Not that there was much she could do at this point – a friend of Maddy's parents had performed an ecumenical ceremony in a Greenwich Village chapel the weekend before.

The rabbi lifted the wine glass. He offered it to Arthur, whose hand shook so wildly he sloshed Mogen David to the grass. The rabbi blessed what was left. Arthur took a gulp, then passed the cup to Maddy, who sipped enough wine to moisten her lips. The rabbi was so new he lost track of where he was and skipped ahead a few pages to the service for a *bris.* Finally, he lifted an empty glass from the table; his instructions were garbled, but Arthur had attended enough Jewish weddings to know what to do. The rabbi wrapped the glass in a napkin and placed the bundle on the ground. (Was the glass our best crystal? I prayed Arthur had thought to use a cheap tumbler instead.) Arthur stomped on it, *plock!*

"Mazel tov!" cried Mamie.

"Mazel tov!" came the echo from everyone else.

Arthur lifted Maddy's headpiece and buried his hands in her hair. A long kiss. Another. He pulled off his yarmulke and tossed it on the trellis. Arthur's roommate from Princeton assumed this to be a Jewish tradition and threw his own yarmulke on the trellis. ("Artie," he had said when he'd first driven up, "what a quaint little place. All those weeks on the Vineyard and you never once asked me to visit you here!")

Maddy turned to me then. Her lips brushed my cheek. "You're a wonderful sister to help us arrange such a beautiful wedding, especially on short notice." She passed me on to Arthur, who gave me a hug – it was clumsy and brief, but the first hug he had ever given me, so I stood with my arms wrapped around my ribs long after the crowd swept my brother away.

The klezmer musicians played a flurry of Yiddish wedding songs. A plump little girl did a frenzied kazatske; the guests danced around her, clapping and stomping until their circle seemed to rise an inch from the ground. They placed Maddy on a bridge chair and lifted her above their heads. Her hair flew around her face. A slipper whirled from one foot. But she never stopped laughing, never lost her composure, and my chest swelled with gladness that such a graceful woman was now related to me.

Then it was Arthur's turn. The waiters hoisted him as easily as if he had been a tray of rolls. From Herbie they had learned he'd been a waiter like them; seeing him now, so well off and well rested, marrying a woman as beautiful as this, they gained hope for their own prospects and carried him off like the King of All Waiters.

The guests, old and young, formed a conga line and snaked their way among the tables, then on past the shuffleboard court, the Ranch, the Pagoda, the trellis, and around the pool before doubling back. Everyone they passed caught the end of the line, hands grasping the hips of the dancer in front. As the line snaked beneath the Eden's front arch, Thomas walked through. He didn't join the dancers, as though he were made of some substance the magnet couldn't pull. He was wearing a suit I didn't know he owned, so dignified and handsome I couldn't bear to think he was nothing to me now but a former employee.

The dancers bumped to a halt. The older guests stood staring until they recognized this stranger as the Eden's former handyman. The faces of the younger guests showed the sudden comprehension that nobody else at the Eden was black. If you wanted to bask in your ethnic tradition you had to give up the company of anyone who didn't share that tradition.

From her long years as a hostess, my mother greeted Thomas. I let him enjoy the guests' greetings. ("Oh, Mr. Jefferson, without you, the flowers turn brown in the sun!" "I said to my wife only this morning, 'Summer isn't summer without Mr. Jefferson.'") When only Shirley and Nat remained, I asked Thomas to dance.

"Can't!" He raised his voice above the clarinet and sax.

"Why not!"

"Don't know how to dance this Jewish stuff!"

I pointed to the younger guests dancing on the handball court. "Neither do they." One of the women kicked to the right when she should have kicked left; the circle tangled and collapsed.

"Doesn't matter. They're Jewish. If I fall, or even if I stay on my feet, I'll be, well, a colored boy dancing the hora. See – "

"No. I don't see. I don't understand why you have to turn an invitation to dance into a dissertation on why everything I do is wrong."

"Wait. I didn't mean . . . It's very nice. Really. I was working in my garden, and I couldn't help but hear the music, and well, someone *did* leave an invitation on my porch . . ."

I didn't have the heart to reveal it must have been Maddy. I looked around for Nana, but she wasn't there. Yet.

"They're playing a waltz now. Least I think it's a waltz." He slipped his hand around my back, where it fit like a key.

We waltzed. Or we tried to. I kept getting distracted. I had spent most of my life wishing people would watch me; now I couldn't figure out why I had ever made such a wish. I shut my eyes and counted. *One* two three, *one* two three . . ."

"Lucy, relax."

I tried to loosen up and swirl to the melody.

"That's better," he said.

The older couples on the court wore faraway looks and

faraway smiles. I could tell they were dancing in happier times – the Stamms, the Feidels, the Kochenthals, the Kirks. And there, beyond the dance floor, an apparition in red, like one of those fairies who comes to curse the bride with a hundred-year sleep. She had teased her hair – it stuck out like dandelion fluff. Her lips were bright pink, moving as if she were telling herself something to boost her resolve. She walked to the middle of the handball court and stood there, beside Shirley and Nat. The other couples lost the beat. Nana tapped Shirley's shoulder.

"I'm cutting in, naah!"

Nat looked at Shirley. She shrugged. "I don't mind." Nat took Nana in his arms, and they waltzed, in brusque jerks, the way the tiny figures on a jewelry box waltz. My grandmother wore boots. She wasn't used to letting someone else lead. And yet she looked prettier than I'd seen her before. With each rotation she seemed younger; I could see her as a girl, not glamorous or soft, but still full of hope, and I had to turn away so I wouldn't see that hope change back to despair when her partner released her and turned back to his wife.

The lawn lay deserted in the moonlight, tables and chairs neatly stacked. It was after eleven. In a few hours, the newly-weds would be on their way to the Azores, halfway between Martha's Vineyard, which Arthur had selected for their honeymoon, and Russia, where Maddy had wanted to search for our ancestors' graves. (What geometry of love could locate a point halfway between Thomas's world and mine?) Only Lennie was here now. He stood beside the trellis re-enacting the wedding: first the rabbi, *mumble mumble;* Arthur taking the cup; the exchange of wedding bands; the kiss.

I wanted to ask Lennie to re-enact the summer. Exhausted as I was, I would have preferred to live through everything again than face the desolate months that would start the next day.

I passed the kitchen, where the busboys were setting up for breakfast, the last meal before we closed. Maddy, Herbie and Arthur's roommate from Princeton sat at the enamel table, watching my brother stack plates on a tray. Arthur crouched beside the counter, slid the tray on one palm and straightened his knees. I almost went inside, to cheer my brother on, but Thomas rose from the dark, from the bench beside the door where Cyrus and the boys came to smoke between meals.

"It's done now," he said, and I wondered if he meant the season or his house. I never got to ask. He pulled me close in a way he had never done before. And even though he smelled anything but sweet, I inhaled a deep breath. He leaned down and kissed me, and I saw he didn't consider me a child any more. I felt his tongue, then his teeth, which clicked against mine. My knees weakened and shook, the way they used to feel after I had been swimming hours in the pool. I cupped one hand around his neck and started kissing him back.

"You have to choose," he said. His breath in my ear caused my skin to flush hot. "I know what she told you. I know why you asked me to leave."

"You'd already bought the Playland! It wasn't because of her."

He put a finger to my lips. "I let you have the summer. But I won't sneak around. I won't let your family think my intentions aren't honorable. You can't have it both ways."

Couldn't I? I wondered. There had to be an answer, if I thought hard enough.

"Lucy, you can tell me right now there's nothing between us. Or the two of us can march right up to your grandmother's bungalow and tell her what's what. If she changes her mind, okay. If not, let her do her worst. You can come and live with me. Walk away. Give it up."

I took a step back. "That's easy enough for you to say. What would I have left?"

I could sense his body stiffen. "If you don't know, I can't tell you."

He turned away. I was furious. I picked up a chunk of tar. I raised my arm to hurl it. Would I really have let it go? I've tried to guess but can't. I saw something red, by the dumpster.

"What are you doing here!" I asked sharply. "Can't you just leave them alone!"

"You think I didn't see! I'm deaf, naah, not blind! All summer, I know, you sneak around with that *gonif.* Get out of here, naah! Go with him! I'm selling it! I'll get rid of it! It won't go to you!"

Thomas stopped to look back, and I stood there between them, between Nana and Thomas, and I started to scream. I couldn't protest or argue. I just screamed, and kept screaming until I saw Nat standing there above me, in his blue-striped pajamas, on the grid of the fire escape attached to Room 12. Did he think the scream hers? Later I found out she had been coming here nightly to stand beneath his window. He must have wondered if she had reached a point of such despair she would wail and lament until he left his wife and came to console her. Did she mean to pursue him all the way to Brooklyn? Would she camp in their yard?

I glanced from Nana to Nat, to Thomas, back to Nana. "It's mine," I said quietly, and that's when I heard a terrific tearing of wood and looked up to see the fire escape pulling away from the wall. Nat lunged for the window, or maybe for his wife, who was stretching out her arms to grab him inside. But the fire escape lurched again. It hung by one bolt. I lifted my hands as if to hold this huge metal structure in place. Then that single bolt gave way, and the fire escape, and Nat Feidel, plunged in a terrifying arc to my feet.

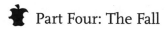 Part Four: The Fall

Of everyone who gathered around Nat by the dumpster, only I didn't believe his life could be saved. He had fallen free of the ladder. He wasn't bleeding. His arms were crossed against his stomach as if he were napping on a lounge. I might have called his name and touched him, but I knew that he was dead, as surely as I knew that whoever I had been until now was dead too.

That no one else accepted Nat's death seemed grotesque. My grandmother struggled to lift him. She wanted, I think, to claim the right to hold him before Shirley arrived. I didn't bother to stop her. What harm could she do? It seemed cruel of my brother to wrest Nat from her arms and push her so roughly.

Arthur said later he had been standing in the kitchen with those stacks of dishes on his tray and he couldn't comprehend why he heard the tray crash when he hadn't yet dropped it. Then Herbie ran to the window and started yelling out my name. They had heard me screaming, of course. My brother was so sure that I was the one who had been hurt, he didn't stop to put the tray down. He ran through the door – he was never sure how, since the tray was far too large to fit without tilting and the plates never fell.

Maddy called the ambulance. I stood and watched my brother kneel on the pavement and cover Nat's mouth with his own. That he knew only this one trick to save a life seemed pathetic – he reminded me of the "handyman" the employment agency had sent who tried to use a hammer to fix a leaking pipe.

When blood flowed from Nat's nostrils, Arthur looked up, confused. "He's still bleeding," he said, by which Arthur must have meant he thought Nat was still alive, though to me the blood meant life was fleeing Nat's corpse.

My grandmother, who sat where Arthur pushed her, pounded her head with her fist. I made no move to stop her and was surprised when Arthur's roommate squatted down beside her and captured her fist in his hands. Not knowing she was deaf, he told her, "No, stop." She allowed Arthur's friend to hold her, and I will always be grateful for whatever small comfort he gave her that night.

In the midst of this commotion Shirley came running up the drive. She must have run all the way – down the stairs, across the lobby, out the front door and around the Main House to the rear of the kitchen, where she found Arthur holding Nat. She lifted her husband's hand to her breast. In her lacy white nightgown, her silver hair hanging free, she seemed to be trying to seduce Nat from death.

The ambulance drew a crowd of guests from their rooms. "He'll be fine," the younger guests kept assuring one another. "*Olev 'a sholem*," Mr. Shuldik whispered, may peace be upon him, to which Mrs. Shuldik said, "Amen."

In the roving white light from the ambulance Thomas looked gray skinned and old. His hands moved through the air as if he could somehow fix Nat if only the medics would allow him to try. They lifted Nat on a stretcher, wrapped him in blankets, pressed an oxygen mask to his face. When they slid him in the ambulance, Shirley screamed: "No!" The medics beckoned her to join them, but who knows what memories this image provoked – the siren, those beckoning arms, a man's body being slid in the maw of a van. But she roused herself finally, lifted the hem of her gown and climbed in.

At one in the morning Arthur called us from the hospital to say Nat had died of a fractured spinal cord a few minutes after the ladder hit the ground. He was certainly dead by the time Nana reached him. Not that this matters. Not that his death made anyone's efforts to revive him as foolish as they seemed to me then.

Arthur drove Shirley back to the Eden from the hospital; she went up to her room without speaking a word to anyone. My brother and Maddy spent the first few hours of their marriage calming guests and relating the details of the accident to my parents and the police. I sat in the office, hoping that the officers would come arrest me. If not for the accident, by this time the next day the season would have ended and Shirley and Nat would have gone home to Brooklyn and I would have been sitting at this same dusty desk, counting receipts.

When I walked to the car the next afternoon to drive to Nat's funeral, I found my grandmother sitting in the back seat of the Pontiac in the same red wool dress she had been wearing at the wedding. She must have known the funeral would be some- time that day, Jewish law forbidding delay as it did; known also that Nat long ago had purchased a plot next to Abe's, an ironic arrangement too late to change now; known finally that no one would invite her to the funeral to pay her respects.

I didn't try to dissuade her. What right did I have to dissuade anyone from anything? Nana had loved Nat. Perhaps she blamed herself for causing the disturbance that brought him out on the fire escape. But she blamed the Eden more. It had killed Nat Feidel, the way it had killed everything she had ever wanted in life, although in my view the Eden was no more responsible for Nat's death than a pistol or a knife would have been.

My guilt for his death was simple and complete. Here was a man who had survived Auschwitz and Treblinka, and I had killed him with kitsch. Maybe if I could have served a long prison-term I would have forgiven myself. But my crimes would be charged against my grandmother and my parents. The insurance wouldn't cover a million-dollar lawsuit. Nana would be ruined. Even though my parents didn't own the

Eden, they would need to use their savings to pay my grandmother's debts.

My mother was home in her bedroom, sedated. She was mourning her own lost peace and financial security as much as Nat's death, but how could I be angry? How dare I condemn the madness of someone whom I had driven mad? I was angry at no one but Thomas – not because I blamed him for the wood being rotted, for the bolt coming loose, but because he blamed himself.

The few guests who stayed the extra day for the funeral stood beside the casket looking stunned and forlorn. (At least Arthur and Maddy were safe in the Azores. They offered to stay home, but I couldn't bear to think that the Eden would rob my brother of his honeymoon. Or that Arthur would give in to my mother's crazy pleading and come up with an alibi, some loophole of innocence through which I could slip.) Across a gravel path, flecks of granite in the monument in my own family's plot shimmered like stars light-years away. A moan floated down the hill – a long drawn-out *oooh,* then a rising *ahhh-ah!* I lifted my head and saw patches of plaid dotting the fairway. The details came back, foggy and small: today was the first day of the Paradise Ham-Am, a benefit sponsored by That Other Hotel so its rooms would stay full the week after Labor Day. All the comics who played the Borscht Belt were teamed with the county's best amateur golfers. Laughter rose from the bunker nearest the graves; I imagined a comedian I had always detested – he was elfish on film, but abusive in person – addressing the ball with a wiggling behind. And that wiggling behind seemed to represent the essence of the Catskills, the place I had grown up.

The rabbi arrived. Ancient, half blind, he was one of the many very old or young rabbis who passed through our town on his way to congregations far better than this. He moved slowly among the mourners with a carton of black yarmulkes.

My father took one from the box; I wanted to remind him that he was wearing one already, but my lips were too dry. He saw his mistake, then used the second yarmulke to wipe away his tears.

He was here despite a phone call from Jimmy Kilcoin warning us that attending the funeral might be construed by a jury as a sign of complicity in the death of "the claimant." Even an expression of condolence might be misread as an admission of guilt. But the moment Shirley came through the cemetery gate, my father approached her. He said something in her ear. Shirley brushed him away, and I almost fainted with regret for the pain he was in. I would have cried myself, but I was afraid someone would be foolish enough to console me. Even now Herbie watched, as ready to jump as a seeing-eye dog. He had worn his waiter's uniform – black trousers, white shirt, a skimpy black jacket he must have found in some drawer; with his melancholic face he looked like a mourner from Victorian times, paid to follow the hearse of whoever had died.

The rabbi glanced anxiously at the men and women knotting the grave, then tottered to my father and whispered a question, to which the reply was a diffident nod toward Shirley.

She stood by herself. Neither she nor Nat had a single relation on the planet. Nat had no son to say *kaddish*. ("Jefferson," he'd once said, "if we'd had a child, he should only, God willing, have turned out like you.") Even Shirley's friends kept a few yards away, afraid of her loss, of her terrible composure. Maybe she had cried herself out at the hospital, or alone in Room 12. But no one had seen this. Even when the rabbi whispered in her ear Shirley kept her gaze fixed on Nat's simple pine box. Maybe the rabbi asked the dead man's name, as was rumored he had done at funerals before. Or maybe he asked if she would like to move to the shade. But Shirley didn't acknowledge whatever she had heard.

I had always thought marriage was a puny ambition. Where was the glory in living your life before an audience of one? Now, seeing Shirley, I knew that to live in the sight of one other person was to make yourself real in a way that the gaze of millions of strangers, or your own gaze reflected in the mirror of self, could never assure. *My husband knows what I've been through. We have lived the same life.* And that husband was dead.

Applause tumbled down the hill. The rabbi took this for a welcome and started to mutter the funeral service. "Whether one lives a single year or a thousand, what does he gain? It is as though he never existed . . . Blessed be the True Judge who causes death and life. Blessed be He, for His judgment is true. His eye ranges over all, and He punishes and rewards each man according to the strictest account . . ."

Strictest account? The accountant was drunk! Why else would He debit Nat for my sins? To live through the concentration camps only to suffer a fate as trivial as this . . . The accountant, the judge, didn't – couldn't exist. The Earth was an absurd and desolate place where sinners like me were allowed to keep living and good men like Nat fell among trash cans and doddering rabbis blessed the dead to applause meant for a clown with a wiggling behind.

The rabbi started the eulogy. He hadn't known Nat, but he must have seen the numbers tattooed on Nat's wrist. He wet his lips and spilled easy phrases from his mouth – "worst evil of human history" and "six million dead" – until these lay about his feet like the pits of some fruit.

An agitation, a stirring – Thomas stepped forward, at once shy and compelled, as if someone had pushed him. His eyes were shot pink, his suit a sorrow of creases. (How had he gotten here? He must have walked the twelve miles. I caught myself wishing that I had walked too, as if repentance were a contest.) He took another step toward the grave, and something about the way he peered forward reminded me of the day I had taught him to swim. I remembered every detail – the water beading in his hair, the way his navel puckered, how his toes broke the pond's surface like ten tiny islands, pink and brown in the sun. Today, in the cemetery, in my long-sleeved black dress, I had to fight my desire to walk naked into that pond, to lift Thomas, hold him. To imagine this seemed a sin, as if Nat of all people would have wanted us apart.

Thomas took off his cap. Then he recalled he was at a Jewish funeral and put it back on. "I know it's not my . . . I was hoping I might say a few words, if that's all right."

The blackness of his suit drained the light from the sky. Only Shirley wasn't staring at him.

"It's just, well, it doesn't seem right to say that Nat Feidel was a man who knew evil. Nat was, well . . . yes, it's true he lived through the very worst sort of evil there is. But he didn't let that evil stop him from knowing other things too."

Thomas reached into his pocket, but he couldn't find a handkerchief, and he shocked me, though I had thought I was far beyond shock, by wiping his nose on his sleeve.

"A human being . . . he doesn't come ready made. Person has to gather the pieces himself. And Nat, well, he gathered a great many pieces. Learning, in his young days. Then wisdom. And yes, he was forced to gather up that knowledge of evil. Then the knowledge of love. And of dignity, and work."

No one moved except the gravediggers, who kept glancing at the rabbi for a sign they should lower Nat's coffin. One man, who was black, took off his dark glasses to get a better look at Thomas.

"Nat gathered up enough pieces, finally, to make himself whole. And then, for no reason other than the failure of one man to look out for another man, this good and whole person, this *mensch*, this human being, was dashed down and killed."

Shirley lifted her head. She regarded Thomas as if he had

roused her to consider some important matter she had neglected. Her face showed distress, then went rigid and blank.

The four men at last lowered Nat in his grave. One man's tattoo, a monkey, jumped every time his muscles tensed.

"May Nathan Feidels come to his final resting place in peace," the rabbi intoned as the four men stepped back. The one with the tattoo puffed his shirt to let his chest dry. The rabbi plucked a shovel from the dirt and offered it to Shirley, giving her the chance to turn the first clods of earth. But she drew back and balled her hands into fists. The rabbi turned to my father, wordlessly pleading for advice.

Not one of us moved. We stood there until Nana pushed forward. She tore the shovel from the rabbi's hands and raised it the way a priest holds a cross.

"I married the wrong man, naah! I should have had *him*!"

Shirley turned her back, as if she too were deaf. Nana watched her walk off, then hurled the shovel in the grave. It hit with a thud, but Nana kept peering down the hole like a child who's dropped a stick down a well.

Another burst of laughter rolled down the hill. Nana lifted her head. "Naah!" she wailed piteously. She clutched her sleeve and ripped the cloth so her shoulder showed through, white against red, the homage of bereavement she had neglected to pay at her own husband's grave.

The night after the funeral, my grandmother announced that she would die on Yom Kippur. She climbed into bed, still in the dress she had been wearing since the wedding. "And don't think you'll get it! I'll take it with me, naah, naah!"

I wanted to tell her to sell the damn place, but I couldn't say the words. I felt about the Eden the way I might feel about a dog that mauled a child because I neglected to feed it. I couldn't bear to destroy the Eden. I just had to make sure it wouldn't hurt anyone else.

After the funeral Thomas came to me and muttered how his pride had preceded another man's fall – not once, but twice – and it should lead to his own now. He quoted whichever rabbi had cautioned not to crave after the table of kings, as if buying a rundown bungalow colony and throwing a barbecue for a delivery man and a one-handed chef could have been construed as gate crashing at a royal party. How could Thomas think that he didn't have any right to quit as our handyman and lead his own life?

When I awoke the next day and discovered his good-bye note taped to my door ("I brought this on the Eden by coming here to hide, like Jonah on the ship"), I nearly ran after him to shout in his face: *Isn't it a little presumptuous to think God would kill Nat just to punish you?* But I didn't try to find him. Because after I had shouted all those accusations, I knew I would have begged him to take me along.

It rained and turned cold. The Eden covered itself with a quilt of colored leaves. Then summer came back, like a guest who's discovered he can't afford the rates at a better hotel. I caught myself thinking it was a good thing I hadn't drained the pool. Then I remembered I had to stay behind the desk, staring at the telephone, willing it to ring, willing it to be Shirley Feidel's lawyer, so the end could begin – the trial, then the judgment.

The sunburst clock above the desk said 4:30. I traced the silver dial of the phone with my thumb. After the accident, the phone had rung five, maybe ten times a day: a reporter from the local paper; tourists who didn't realize the Eden wasn't open all year; Jimmy Kilcoin and my mother with suggestions for appealing to Shirley's good will. Once, Linda Brush called to find out if I knew where her son was. Mitchell, she said, had run off to join the Army; he had lied about his age, and when Linda called the recruiter they sent Mitchell back home. But Sam never showed up. I started to say I wasn't responsible for my former employees, but I knew now I was. The twins were only sixteen. How could I have worked them so hard? Knowing Sam as I did, how could I have let him wander away without trying to find him?

In this way I finally hiked over the hill to see what the Hasid had done to Lipsett's chicken farm. But the Hasid wasn't there. He had gone to New York City to raise funds and find recruits; his disciples expected his return late that night. Scattered around the farm were a dozen men and women who seemed happy to have discovered something useful to do and someone who had given them a reason to do it. Among them I recognized several of the people who usually wandered Paradise ("lost souls," they were called, though no one ever took much trouble to find them). Sam was in the Lipsetts' kitchen on his knees, waxing the linoleum with a zeal he had never shown working for me. When I said that I had come to take him home, Sam shook his head no. The Messiah had taught him that going back to school would ruin his capacity for joy. He said to tell his mother that if she wanted to see him, she would have to come here.

Which is exactly what she did. Linda took the Shortline bus to Paradise, then a cab to Lipsett's chicken farm. When she called me that night, she thanked me not only for giving back her son, but for showing her where to find the man she had been searching for most of her life.

When the phone finally rang, I let it keep ringing. It was probably my mother.

But maybe it wasn't.

"Kid," Jimmy said, "she won't answer anymore. At least before now she always picked up the phone."

Jimmy had been calling Shirley twice a day to persuade her to settle out of court. I begged him to leave her alone but he couldn't seem to stop himself. He had to keep *doing* – planning, intriguing – and he already had done everything he could do at the Eden. He'd taken photos and sketched diagrams of the "scene of occurrence," interviewed every guest and employee who had been near Room 12 that night. There was no one left to interview, so he kept calling me. The only way Jimmy knew how to think was by talking out loud, and he didn't care who heard. His whole life, he said, everything he'd built was slipping away. Sure he felt lousy the old guy was dead. But Jimmy hadn't been the one to let those boards rot. He hadn't stood beneath Nat's window and screamed. Even if Jimmy had told the fire inspector to look the place over instead of just stamping the inspection APPROVED, Miller wouldn't have bothered to haul his fat ass up the fire escape. And, if he had, what's to say Miller wouldn't be the one in that coffin right now – Miller, who had four kids and who'd been a loyal member of Jimmy's weekly poker game for the past fifteen years – instead of some old Yid Jimmy barely knew from Adam.

So okay, he was sorry, but he owed his allegiance to the company. And to the insured – that was me. And to Miller, his pal, who was cowering even now in Jimmy's office, sloshing down whiskey from a Dixie cup and shaking. Miller had managed to keep his mouth shut about the phony inspection report, but who knew what would happen if the case came to trial?

Which didn't mean we wanted to cheat the poor woman. Even a reasonable out-of-court settlement would keep her cushy for years. We would be sparing her the strain of testifying, not to mention wasting her last savings on lawyers' fees. Hell, she'd be dead before this thing even made it to trial. If only she would give Jimmy a minute to explain . . .

"We're ruined, kid. You at the trial, me the day after. The

lawyers will prove you used sex to bribe me to lower the rates and fake the inspections – "

I hung up. Of course I hoped Shirley wouldn't sue. But not because I cared what a lawyer might say about me.

Just before five Mamie came to the office to call her agent in New York. My parents always let her stay on at the Eden until she found another engagement for the winter. This year, Mamie had bragged, things would be different. Hadn't she been a big hit on TV? After her appearance on *I Love New York,* a Broadway producer had booked her for a revue of old Catskills performers. But the invitations had dried up as quickly as the fad for the Borscht Belt. Now she scuffed to the office twice a day in her gold mules to check with her agent and pressure her friends in the business for tips. Her brashness was dull, her bravado had drooped. How could a woman who sounded this weary get a job as a *tumeler?*

If it hadn't been for Lennie she probably would have crawled into bed and given up, like the other old guests who had seen Nat that night, crushed beside the dumpster. In the week since the funeral two guests had faded. Comrade Beck had fallen a second time and broken his hip, which was another way of saying he had six months to live.

After Mamie left, Herbie came to the office door and asked if I wanted Jerry's "spaghetti carbon something," left over from dinner the previous night. I couldn't bear Herbie's solicitude, but he had nowhere else to go. His parents could barely care for themselves. He'd told me what had happened in Israel that time. He had shot an Egyptian. That's all he would say, "I shot an Egyptian," and then he just stood there, a sort of living lesson as to what guilt and self-punishment shouldn't be permitted to do.

"The spaghetti is fine," I said. "I'll be there in a minute." And he left, beaming gratefully for this, the first smile I had given him all week.

A taxi drove up. As it idled beside the arch I saw a shadowy woman leaning forward to pay. I struggled to open the desk – I had to warn the driver the Eden was closed. But before I could do this the woman slid from the cab – shapely legs, maroon dress, platinum bun – and the taxi drove off. She walked beneath the arch. Then the lobby door swung open and there Shirley stood, toying with the clasp on her purse.

"Please, do not say one word. I will not discuss anything."

Her lawyer would have warned her not to speak to anyone. Then why was she here?

"I know you are not open for business. But perhaps you could rent me a room? It is only for this one night."

"A room? At the Eden?"

Shirley nodded impatiently.

"Upstairs?" I asked. "But there's no . . . It's not safe."

"Safe." Shirley shrugged.

I was too shocked to think. Instead, I went through the motions of a hundred summer days: I turned, found the key, filled out the proper forms. Did she have luggage? No? Would she wait while I got the room ready? The sheets were still . . . stale. I hadn't changed the linens . . .

"The old sheets are fine. Better, I think." Shirley opened the purse.

"Oh no. I couldn't possibly accept – "

"I insist," Shirley said.

I let the bill lie there, a filthy green carcass. The phone rang. From habit, I slipped the plug in the switchboard.

"Kid," he said, "listen, I've got it all figured out. I'll drive down to Brooklyn and – "

"Jimmy," I said.

"Okay, okay. I've been there before and she wouldn't let me in. But this time – "

"Jimmy, she's here."

"Where here? The widow's with you?"

Shirley was staring at the staircase as if she saw someone walk down.

"Lucy, are *you* there?"

I nodded.

"Can't talk, huh? Just tell me this – is anyone with her?"

"I don't think so," I said. No one else had come in. I just wasn't used to seeing Shirley by herself.

"You don't *think* so? Come on, is she by herself or isn't she? I can't believe she'd be foolish enough . . ." The sound of a slap. "I gotta stop dreaming." Another slap. "Okay, just give her the phone. Don't say who it is."

"I can't."

"Why, she left? You let her get away?"

Shirley must have guessed I wanted to hold a private conversation – she had walked across the lobby and stood looking out the window.

"She's still here. I just don't want to bother her."

"You what! Listen up, kid. Maybe you don't care about saving my ass. But think about your parents' asses. And your grandmother's. And Miller's. Not to mention your own ass. Why, just yesterday, Eicher – "

"Jimmy, I won't do it."

"You promised me a favor. You hear me? I'm calling in the chips."

I didn't care about my promise. *That contract belonged to the Devil,* I thought. Then why did I give in and do what Jimmy asked? I suppose it made sense. Nothing I could do would bring Nat back to life. If I helped Jimmy settle the case, Shirley would get a fair amount of money without ruining my parents' lives. And maybe, just maybe, I did what I did so I wouldn't have to listen to Jimmy's voice any longer.

"Mrs. Feidel." I held out the phone. "Someone would like to speak to you, please."

"Yes? What? To me?" Shirley jerked from the window.

"It's Mr. Kilcoin," I said, covering the receiver so Jimmy couldn't hear. "From the insurance company?"

"The insurance? Ach, yes, the man who's been so . . . What does he want now? Why won't he leave me alone!"

"He just . . ." I waved the receiver.

Shirley shook her head.

"I realize it must be hard. But if you don't speak to him on the telephone, he's liable to try to see you."

"Here? He would do this? I cannot even come here . . ." Her expression grew clouded. "Yes, yes. You tell him to come. You tell your Mr. Kilcoin I have something very important to say to him, but he must come here to know what it is."

"You're sure?" I said. "If you don't really want to – "

"No. You are right about this. I must finish this business or he will give me no peace. Isn't that true? He wants, how does he put it, to 'negotiate' with me. He wants to negotiate so he can give, how he puts it, 'compensation.' Isn't this right? You tell your Mr. Kilcoin that Shirley Feidel wants to see him in person to . . . negotiate the proper compensation for . . . the loss of her husband."

She was toying with her purse clasp – twisting it open, clicking it shut. Though the sun was going down and the lobby was cool now, her upper lip and forehead were dotted with sweat.

"Are you there? Is anyone there?" Jimmy's voice wafted from the phone like the voice of a man crying in the woods.

"She said she'd see you," I told him. "She said she'd negotiate."

"Just the two of us? Holy Mother of God. I'll be there in twenty minutes. Don't let her . . . Lucy? She isn't nuts, is she? Any release I could get her to sign wouldn't hold up in court if she turned out to be . . . Does she look nuts? Is she doing anything, you know, funny?"

She was clicking the wine-colored beads at her throat.

"I don't think so," I said.

"I'm out the door, kid. Don't let her get away."

I hung up. "He's coming," I told Shirley. "If you want, I can give you a ride to town. You can catch the next bus."

"I'm very tired," she said. "If you don't mind, I'll go upstairs now." But she remained by the window.

Five minutes went by. I willed myself to say, "Mrs. Feidel, I want you to know how sorry we all – "

"Please. I have asked that we do not discuss this. I have said I will negotiate with your Mr. Kilcoin. You will please send him up."

She climbed the steps heavily. I heard the ceiling creak, heard the door of Room 12 open and shut.

A few minutes later Jimmy rushed in. "Where is she? You didn't admit anything, did you? You didn't, you know, let her go poking around?"

"She rented the room. She's up there now, waiting."

He banged his briefcase against the ashtray beside the desk, spilling sand. "That won't make it any easier, settling the claim in that room. How am I going to convince her the Eden's solid when the plaster's dropping on our heads? I'd better get up there."

"Jimmy. She might have a gun. A little one, in her purse. She's planning something. She's up there, waiting for you."

He stopped halfway up the steps. "Come on. You're just edgy. You're not used to playing for such high stakes. She's a harmless old lady. She probably wanted a minute to freshen up her lipstick, or to go to the toilet. Talking about money does that to some people, makes their stomachs go all flooey." He leaned down over the banister. "I'll handle her, okay, kid? After it's settled, we'll go to town and celebrate. Just you and me." This prospect gave him the energy to bound up the steps.

I collapsed in a chair.

Then I jumped up. What had I been thinking? Shirley needed my protection – though I have since learned that women like Shirley Feidel rarely need protection from women like me. I climbed the stairs but Jimmy had already disappeared into Room 12. I knelt beside the door. The keyhole was huge, but everything inside seemed distant, unreal. At the foot of the bed, the blanket seemed blood drenched. And there, on the pillow, lay Shirley Feidel.

She was dying, I thought. She had gashed her wrists, planning it so Jimmy would find her corpse.

"Mrs. Feidel!" He took a step forward and put his hand on the blood. And that's when I saw it wasn't blood, but her dress. "Mrs. Feidel?" he repeated.

She patted the mattress beside her.

"You're joking," Jimmy said. "Mrs. Feidel, this is business!"

"Of course this is business!" Shirley sat up, clutching the blanket to her chest. "Is just what I ask in return for my husband."

"Are you crazy? *Mishugge?*"

"Whole world is crazy, so why not me?" Her eyes gleamed like clock dials. "Here, give me your paper. The paper I am to sign?"

He opened his briefcase and removed a pad of forms.

"Now a pen." Pinning the blanket to her sides, she turned to the night stand and wrote. "There. I am not liar. I will put this paper here, underneath my pillow, and when you have done this thing I am asking you to do, you will take away the paper and never see me again."

What went through Jimmy's mind? From what he said later, I think he believed she wasn't crazy at all. She and dear Nathan hadn't had sex for the past twenty years. She had plotted and dreamed, and now she would get her last satisfaction before she was called to follow her husband to a heaven where sex was even less frequent than it had been on earth. Such propositions had come Jimmy's way often enough, and he'd never thought twice before hopping into a claimant's bed before. So why not hop now? Would he have been so aghast if a woman in her late forties had consented to sleep with a man in his sixties? She had been wily enough to keep herself covered. *Imagination,* Jimmy thought. That was the ticket. He would think about . . . me.

He took off his jacket and his shirt. Shoes, trousers, socks. Without looking once at Shirley, Jimmy walked toward the bed.

"Get away!" she cried. "Oh! Oh! Get away!"

Jimmy stopped where he was. His face showed the shock of a champion bluffer who doesn't believe he's been bluffed.

"How could you possibly . . . How could you think I would want you to take my husband's place, here?" She pounded the empty half of the mattress. "My husband!" she sobbed. "My husband is killed, and what do you say? 'We give compensation.' Is this what my husband was to me? One hundred dollars? Ten million? What my Nathan was, you cannot give me. My Nathan was this!" She lifted her arms so the blanket fell away. She clapped her hands to her breasts again and again, saying, "This was my Nathan! This was my husband!"

Her breasts weren't the withered tea-bags of most elderly women, but round, white and full. Her shoulders were smooth. The beads of her necklace stood out from her skin like drops of burgundy wine, her platinum hair fell and pooled on the bed. Anger had burned away the slackness of her face so her cheekbones stood out. Her lips were red coals.

"What could you give me? Nothing, I say. Would be awful! Who will ever make me feel such a way now? Not you. Oh, not you."

Awful? No feeling? Jimmy stood in his underwear. Shame seemed to make him too heavy to move.

"We are sleeping together in the same bed, as always, and suddenly my Nathan is outside the window. I reach out my hands, and the next thing I know is a terrible noise, and when I look down, there is the ladder, and there, on the pavement, next to the garbage, there lies my Nathan. I run as fast as I can, but already my Nathan lies still, he won't speak.

"And before I can get the stench of his death from my nostrils, a man calls me on the telephone, nice and polite, and says: 'Compensation.' I ask this man's name, and when the man tells me, 'James Kilcoin,' I have no surprise. I have watched this James Kilcoin, seen the look on his face as he leaves all these rooms. Even the linen closet I have seen this man leave, with that poor, innocent child Lucy!"

I wanted to protest – I wasn't poor! I wasn't innocent! But what could have been more innocent than thinking you've been clever when you've been so naive?

"So many women," Shirley was saying, "as if one is like another. But this does not concern me. I do not interfere. Only when this James Kilcoin asks what I want in return for my husband, how much money I want – the Appelbaums' money, to punish them for something they could not mean to do . . .

"I do not want their money! I want nothing but to be with my husband. If I were stronger, if I believed in life beyond the grave . . . But I know that I will never see my Nathan again, and this drives me so . . . so . . . I think, if only I can lie in our bed, the place we spent the first and last nights of our marriage, the room where my Nathan last was alive . . .

"But no! Even here you will not let me be. Even here you say 'money.' You say 'let's negotiate.' You say 'compensation.' And suddenly I am filled with this hatred I have not felt since I am offered what they call 'reparation' for what I lost in the war. Not forgiveness, but what sum I will take! Both times, they say, 'We know we cannot pay to make up your loss.' But such an insult even to try! So much for one Jew, so much for another . . .

"Thirty-four years I am living with my Nathan. How many days is this? Is more than twelve thousand. You know what twelve thousand days is? I show you. I count them."

She started to count, steady, intense, and with each number

she recited Jimmy seemed weaker, until, when she stopped, her voice dying out into hoarseness and sobs at one hundred twenty, Jimmy's knees gave way and he knelt beside the bed.

Shirley lifted her pillow. "Here. Here is your paper, your release. I want nothing. You are right what you said. I *am* crazy. If a man does not know what a human life is, can anyone teach him?"

Jimmy didn't move. The release was right there, but he didn't pick it up.

"Go," she said. "There is nothing, so go now. Please, or someone will miss you."

"No," he said, "no one will miss me." He buried his face against the mattress and knelt there like a man expecting a blow.

Shirley lifted her hand. "Nathan. My Nathan." She stroked Jimmy's hair. "*Mayn lebn.*" My life.

I barely had dragged myself back to the lobby before Shirley came down, smaller and older than when she had arrived. Hair straggled from her bun like yarn from a skein carelessly wound.

"Please to call a taxi," she said, then refused to say anything else.

After she left I rushed back upstairs and found Jimmy slouched on the bed. His arm dangled oddly. I thought it was broken, but he only had neglected to slip it through his sleeve.

He motioned toward the slip of paper on the mattress. . . . *do hereby release and hold harmless . . . zero dollars and cents . . .*

"Zero? No money? What happened?" I asked. And I wasn't pretending, I really didn't know.

Numbly, he told me, as best as he was able.

"Kid, I don't feel so good." He snaked his arm through the sleeve. "It's time old Jimmy went home."

I locked up the room. I couldn't bear to touch the sheets, the hairpins on the pillow, the mother-of-pearl comb on the night stand. Several days later a letter arrived from Colonial Conn informing me that our policy had been canceled. I called to beg Jimmy to keep the Eden insured until my parents could sell it, but the receptionist said, "Mr. Kilcoin isn't in. And he isn't coming back," whether because he had been fired or he had quit I never found out.

Mamie left first. She had gotten a job as the social director at the retirement home for Jewish vaudevillians down the road. The contract stipulated that, after Mamie's death, Lennie could remain as long as he lived.

I hefted three trunks of costumes and props into my parents' station wagon. Another two trunks of mementos wouldn't fit.

"Don't worry, *bubele,* my room there's so small I wouldn't know where to put them." To escape from that graveyard she would have left everything except Lennie behind. "Store the trunks in the cellar. I can always come back and fetch what I need."

Strolling about the grounds of the Thespians Retirement Home were elderly ladies with bursts of rouge on their cheeks, high-sculpted hair every color but gray, boas of every feather and fur. The men – there were fewer – sported candy-striped vests, suspenders, cravats, and rakish fedoras on their age-shrunken heads. They struck tableaux around the flower beds, which were stiff with brown stems.

"Look at them, wasting their talents. Such prima donnas! Nobody wants to organize, only perform. They're simply fading away."

The inmates lifted their heads. Flicking boas and canes, they drifted toward Mamie like starving cats that scented fish.

"People!" Lennie clapped, then crowed out the opening of *A*

Day at the Races: "Free bus to the sanitarium! This way to the Standish Sanitarium! Free bus!"

The next day, Jerry and Justin asked me to drive them to the bus station in Paradise. Each cradled a file box – identical copies of their recipes in case one set got lost. With the money they had saved working at the Eden they planned to start their own catering business.

"Gay kosher parties," Jerry confided. "There's greater demand than you might think."

The bus driver jumped down and stood beside the door, clicking his hole punch.

"I know we didn't always see eye to eye," Jerry said, "but you did give us our start."

"Bah, I didn't do anything," though my heart brimmed with gratitude for pretending that I had.

"All aboard for New York . . ."

Each of them kissed me – dill and paprika, almond extract and cloves. Justin squeezed Jerry's hand. The driver clicked his hole punch as vengefully as if he were punching holes in them.

"Bye!" I waved, "good luck!" They climbed past the driver, who spat on the sidewalk where their feet had just stepped, and I offered a wish that someone would afford them the protection I couldn't.

I returned to find Herbie rolling around the empty hotel like the last piece of candy in a dish. He could have gone with Jerry and Justin to serve at the functions they were hoping to cater – he could sleep on their floor, until he found his own place – but Herbie declined.

"In the City," he confided, "the windows have bars."

But even a prison would have been cheerier than the Eden. I tried convincing him that his loyalty was wrongly bestowed: he loved the Eden because it was the last place he'd been happy and he thought he owed me something for letting him come back.

"I *used* you," I said.

"Oh, I like to be used."

"You're fired," I said. "Go on, I'm kicking you out."

"You haven't paid me in weeks. You can't fire a person unless you're paying them, right?" He smiled at his own joke.

I took a dollar from my pocket. "It's pay day." I jammed the bill in his shirt. "*Now* you're fired."

"I don't like thinking about you living here all alone." The wind poked its chilly fingers through the cracks in the kitchen walls and set a shelf of cups rattling. Herbie's nose twitched. "But I guess, if you don't really want me to stay, I should leave."

I felt the first ease of gladness I had felt since Nat's death. But where would Herbie go? I didn't want him sleeping on a steam grate and begging dimes for ice cream. He needed an orderly life. Companions. Fresh air.

I searched the classifieds until I found just the thing: a counselor's job at a school for retarded Orthodox children in a neighboring town. Herbie agreed to apply. When the principal asked Herbie for an interview, then told him that he was hired, Herbie couldn't hide his glee. Someone had hired him! A person he didn't even know! I drove him to the school and helped unpack his suitcase in the quarters he was to share with two other aides. These boys loitered outside, eager to welcome their new cabin-mate as soon as his girlfriend went home.

"Are you sure you'll be okay there?" Herbie asked.

I nodded, then I told him good-bye, then I hugged him and said good-bye again, until Herbie seemed more anxious for my departure than I was.

The next afternoon, when I drove back to the school to make sure he liked his job, he was romping in the yard with ten or twelve children, playing Follow the Leader. The children looked normal, only slightly uncertain and heavy in their movements. Someone had raked a mound of leaves. Herbie rolled toward it. The children, barking hoarsely, did likewise. Some veered off course but the rest disappeared with Herbie into the pile of leaves until it came to resemble a many-legged beast with a calico hide.

That night, eating a can of beans from the season's last order, I almost wished I hadn't convinced Herbie to leave. Every wail of the wind, every squirrel in a gutter shot ice up my spine. Shirley drifted through the lobby, disheveled and pale. Each time I passed the dumpster, I looked up and saw Nat tumble from the fire escape.

I pureed some boiled chicken and took it to the bungalow, where my grandmother lay moping in that same red wool dress.

IT'S STAINED, I wrote on a napkin. WHEN YOU DIE AND NAT SEES YOU, HE'LL TURN UP HIS NOSE.

But she wouldn't let me wash it. The dress grew fetid and rank. I sprayed the bungalow with a can of Nu-Scent Air Freshener.

"If you don't like my stink, don't come back."

I set the food beside her bed.

"Tasteless." She spit the chicken on the plate.

WHAT'S THE MATTER, I wrote. SHIRLEY DIDN'T SUE.

"She did it to torture me! This shit hole swallowed everything I ever had. She wants I should keep it, naah, I should lose something else."

WHAT ELSE CAN YOU LOSE?

I thought I heard "you," but when I asked her to repeat herself, she sat up in bed and screamed: "Look at you! You're nothing but a nursemaid!"

I hacked giblets from the freezer and brought Nana a tray. She took a bite of lung stew, but the rest of the organs grew rubbery and cold as they sat there, untouched.

Seeing my grandmother like this, so quiet and small, made

me feel tricked. She wasn't one of the Furies, just a toothless old woman in a wrinkled red dress, refusing to eat. My mother's mother, Jennie.

"I can't stand the sight of you!" She hurled the liver to the floor. "Get out of here! It's still my hotel, naah! I forbid you should stay!"

I cleaned up the liver, but every time I came back she screamed and threw dishes. I stocked her refrigerator with soft foods and drove down the road to the Playland. The door wasn't locked; I let myself in and stretched out fully clothed on Thomas's bed.

I spent the ten days between Rosh Hashanah and Yom Kippur alone at the Playland. I ate little but some crackers I found on his shelves and corn and potatoes from his garden. I rarely went outside, unable to bear the splendor of the leaves or the rich, smoke-cured air. If Thomas's neatness once oppressed me, it now gave me peace. The spirit of the house no longer seemed to bristle each time I walked in but accepted my presence like a dog who stops barking and nuzzles a friend it mistook for a thief.

On Yom Kippurs before, when I thought God was watching, I sneaked food the way a child sneaks a cookie from her mother's cookie jar. Now I fasted for myself, and I didn't have the slightest impulse to eat. Alone late that night, light-headed from hunger, my mind spun out memories beyond my control: the camp house and the pool, the cabin with Thomas (maybe, like Herbie, what I felt wasn't love, but merely nostalgia for the wholeness of youth). But these memories brought no peace. I took down his Bible – not to read, just to touch. I sniffed the leather cover, ran my thumb along the spine. The book opened to a page Thomas must have earmarked; in the margin was a thumbprint – I imagined him nibbling a slice of Mrs. Grieben's seven-layer cake and sipping tea as he read.

The Song of Songs, which is Solomon's. O that he would kiss me with his lips! Surely your caresses are better than wine . . .

I recalled him reading me this poem.

I am dark yet I am comely, ye maids of Jerusalem . . .

I read the passage again and realized that the woman, not her lover, was black. Still, I thought. Still.

Like an apple tree among the trees of the forest, so is my beloved among the young men. I long to sit in his shadow. His fruit is sweet to my taste.

He had read this same book. He had slept on this mattress – the sheets held his scent.

On my bed at night I sought him whom my soul loves. I sought him, but I could not find him. I will rise now and go about the city, in the streets and in the squares I will seek whom my soul loves. I sought him, but I could not find him . . .

I had known Thomas would leave and I hadn't tried to stop him. His presence made me ugly, so I hoped he would go. Even if the accident had been partly his fault, how could he think that God would condemn him to a sentence so much worse than the one he'd already served? If Thomas didn't merit forgiveness, who did?

I stepped into the yard, verses from the Bible churning in my head: *sought but couldn't find . . . sought whom my soul . . .* And then I looked up.

That so many people had seen the stars as proof of God's existence didn't deter me from seeing them this way myself – the truth of a thing doesn't depend upon how novel it is. I felt small and alone, but I also felt a pride and importance so vast I barely could contain it. Not pride in myself, but in the whole human race. From hot formless gas swirling across an infinite sky to those bookshelves inside . . . Maybe there wasn't a god who kept watch from a bench high in heaven, a god you could blame for the evils here on earth, an accountant, or a judge. But there might be a god who created order out of chaos, instilled a knowledge of good in each human soul – although, like all knowledge, this was easy to lose, or forget, or ignore.

I stood there a long time, in Thomas's yard, and I slowly grew aware of a noise in the distance, like a harp's high-pitched strings. An orange glow lit the trees. And then I smelled smoke.

I ran the half mile down the road to the Eden. The Main House was already livid with flames. Smoke leaked through the walls; tar-paper bats swooped and soared on the drafts. As each *whoosh* of sparks shot high and disappeared, I grew lighter and happier. This must have been why owners burned their hotels – not to collect the insurance, but to free themselves of burdens they still loved but could no longer support.

The verandah off the dining room sagged, sending waves of heat across the lawn. The outlying buildings also were in flames – the Ranch and the Pagoda were supposed to be fireproof, but the stucco was melting like skin to expose the plywood bones underneath. How had these other buildings caught fire? Unless you believed in spontaneous combustion, half-a-dozen buildings igniting at once . . .

The Pagoda's third story fell through the second, and then through the first, with thunder loud enough to wake the dead.

But not to wake my grandmother.

I raced to her bungalow – but not quickly enough to outdistance the suspicion that she'd set the fires. I banged the door open, or perhaps it wasn't locked. The flames were confined to her workshop – *the turpentine,* I thought, *she must have used the turpentine* – so I didn't feel much danger standing by her bed, waiting for my grandmother to open her eyes. Her face was shapeless as a sock with no foot inside. Even when she saw me and started to fight – "Leave me, naah, naah!" – she was so weak I could carry her, squirming and punching, down the hill to the road.

I was afraid to put her down. I decided to carry her to the

Playland, put her in my parents' car and drive to Paradise, where I could call in the alarm.

I took one last look. The trellis was a pyre. The oak behind the Ranch wore an orange kimono across its outstretched arms. Adam and Eve and the Paul Bunyan golfer shriveled and turned black, the cows howling in terror as the flames licked their hooves.

I was turning away when I saw the ghoulish figures materialize from the smoke. They gathered in front of the main building, listening as if the hissing tongues spoke God's word. A fountain of flame burst skyward through the roof (I panicked for a moment, thinking Shirley and Nat still slept in Room 12), and the flash pierced their bodies. I saw straight to their bones.

Far away, in Paradise, the sirens started bleating. I laid my grandmother on the lawn. "Naah," she muttered, "naah," and curled up on one side.

"We were waiting for a sign," Sam told me. "He said it would come on Yom Kippur, and Yom Kippur's almost over."

Linda Brush was furious. "I said, 'Never mind redeeming all those women in New York. Why don't you just stay home and redeem *me*?'" She tossed back her hair. "Men!" she said angrily.

The fire engines shrieked and clattered to a stop beside the Eden's arch. Men jumped from the trucks and began hacking away the brush, searching for the hydrant. Most of the buildings had already burned. In a moment I would seek out whoever was in charge and decide what to say. First I checked on Nana. I hardly expected her to be there, but she was lying with her hands pressed beneath one cheek, like a child who's dozed off at a family reunion and will have to be carried gently to bed.

A few devoted golfers were playing the course above the cemetery; their striped umbrellas floated through the drizzle like hot-air balloons. The only mourners besides my parents were my brother and his wife – Arthur tan, Maddy burned. When the rabbi came around with his box of black yarmulkes, Maddy put one on too.

The memorial service was shorter than the Pledge of Allegiance. The rabbi offered no eulogy – perhaps he suspected that a demonic *naah, naah* would rise from the grave to deny his kind words. He shoveled a teaspoon of dirt on the coffin and motioned the gravediggers to quickly fill the rest.

My father said *kaddish*. His voice quivered with sympathy. "She had a difficult life. She deserved to be happy."

My mother swiped her nose. "If she wasn't happy, that was her fault. She wanted too much."

I heard everything through a haze of shock and fatigue. Staring at the ground, I saw Buddy and Lucille edging away. Nana protested too. She would move up the hill to lie next to Nat.

That's his wife's place, Abe said. *Your own place is here.*

You worked me too hard, naah. We were poor all our lives. I always was ashamed.

From Abe's bones, a sigh: *In the grave there's no work. And look at our plot! It's larger than anyone else's, with a beautiful stone. You only were ashamed for sixty-six years. Now you'll be proud for eternity.*

Nana fell mute – perhaps this convinced her, or the clods of dirt choked her voice.

I lifted my head. I wasn't crying, but Arthur acted as if I had sustained a great loss. He put his arm around me and led me to his car. A golf ball dropped from the sky, hit one of the headstones beside the parking lot and bounced.

"You look exhausted," Arthur said.

"So do you," I told him.

"I'm helping Dash negotiate a plea bargain for this guy accused of mail fraud."

Negotiate. The very word made me cringe.

"She doesn't look tired," Maddy said. "Only older. You were pretty before, Lucy, but now there's something else. Now you look . . . beautiful. Doesn't she, Arthur? Hasn't Lucy changed?"

"Beautiful?" he said.

"It was a great thing you did."

I said she didn't understand.

"What's not to understand? My sister-in-law is a hero."

A hero? Was she joking?

"It's a fucking shame, that's what it is." Arthur scooped up the golf ball and pitched it toward the fairway. "You carried her out of a goddamn inferno, and then how does she repay you – "

Maddy pushed him toward their car. "This isn't the place."

"She'll have to find out."

"I can wait," I told Arthur. Besides, I already had guessed.

"She left it to me! I tried to talk her out of it, but you know how she was. All those years of Mom and Dad slaving for her like that . . ."

"She didn't ask them to do it."

"You're defending her!"

"Well, she can't defend herself."

"All she left *you* was the insurance. Which, even if the policy hadn't been canceled, wouldn't have paid a dime on such obvious arson."

"She didn't know that it was canceled."

"You're saying she burned it to give you the money?"

"To get me away from here. To give me a start somewhere else."

"Come on. She wasn't a fool. She knew they'd figure it out."

"Lots of people burned down their own places and still got the money. Maybe she didn't realize you had to be subtle about how you did it. She wasn't famous for her subtlety."

"Or her generosity. Look, if you want to believe she was some kindly old lady, go ahead. You never were much for seeing things plain." He got in his Camaro.

"Come visit us," Maddy said.

I nodded and waved.

Arthur rolled down his window. "If you need anything, any money, just to tide you over."

"No, no, I'm fine."

"Listen, it's better like this. You never should have tried. It was . . . Well, it was fake."

He said this in a gentle, brotherly voice I didn't know he had, and the notion that my brother had been right all along shocked me as deeply as if I had learned the crazy Hasid was in fact the Messiah. If you believed, it was one thing. If not, it was fake.

After the funeral I stopped at the Eden to salvage what I could. So little remained . . . it reminded me of some soft, spineless creature that wouldn't leave a fossil when it died. The rain drummed against the shingles, impatiently waiting for everything to rot.

Mamie waded through the jumble that had been the Main House. "I'm so sorry, *bubele*. And your grandmother! I still can't believe she's gone. I keep thinking she'll jump out from somewhere and scream I should keep my hands off."

I said I felt the same way.

"A friend drove me over." A blue Cadillac with fins was parked beside the gate; the old man inside wore a white scarf and red beret. Mamie's toe nudged a picture frame. "The memories of a lifetime, gone up in smoke."

"*Mamme! Mamme! Mamme!*"

Mamie shook her head. "If I'd known how all this would upset him, I would never have come."

"I'll go talk to him," I said. "You finish here."

Lennie, in yellow galoshes and a slicker, was stomping through the wreckage of the casino, picking up pieces of melted equipment – spotlights, a microphone. "Me," he said. "Mine."

"It's not you, Lennie. It's nothing. It's just a light bulb. Don't cry."

He jerked here and there, acting out scenes from the summer before – imitations of guests, the staff, even me, all mixed with bits of Marx Brothers films, until he slumped against the charred baby grand and fell dumb.

After they had gone I unlocked the fence around the pool. A layer of sooty leaves coated the surface. If I wanted to drain the water (one pristine pool in a rubbishy field), the filter would clog.

The long-handled net hung from the fence. Just to keep from thinking I started skimming up the muck. Mouse corpses. Toads. Orange salamanders like remnants of flame. When a mound of ashy compost lay on the deck, I knelt beside the ladder. My black dress cast shadows; my hair, reddish waves. I lifted the image of my face to my mouth, put my tongue to the bitter water and drank.

My parents sat *shiva* for Nana, and each night that week our neighbors brought casseroles in place of the kind words that might have consoled us but wouldn't have been true.

For nineteen years I had heard these people complain that their hotels were bleeding their money and youth. The tourists were vermin, an annual plague. Please, they begged God, send us a buyer so we can lead normal lives. This had all come to pass. Their own small resorts had been sold or burned down. Now the Eden was gone. The town was convulsed with rumors that the giant resort on the hill had been bought by developers who planned to blow up the Niteclub and sell the guest rooms as condos for businessmen who liked to get away from the City now and then to play golf. Everyone in Paradise was angry and scared. At least in the past they had been able to boast they lived in the Borscht Belt; now, just a town. And so, all that week, they stood beside our rubber plant and told loving anecdotes about the old places, especially the Eden, which quickly became "the finest, the last."

Then my father shocked everyone by insisting that he and my mother use the tickets they had won from the synagogue raffle. My grandmother's death made my father feel mortal. If such a strong woman could die, what of him? While he still had the strength he would travel to Jerusalem, stand beside the Wall and ask forgiveness of God, as if God could hear better from Israel than here.

And my mother gave in.

"I never told you," she said. "Just before his stroke, your grandfather bought two airplane tickets to Israel. And she wouldn't let him use them! She made him put the money toward the mortgage, so she shouldn't have such a millstone after he was gone. In his whole life, he asked just this one thing. How could a wife deny her husband's last wish?"

And so, at the very end of October, I drove my parents to J.F.K., timing our arrival as close to take-off as possible so my mother wouldn't have the chance to fret and change her mind. All we had to do was find the right gate, which seemed to keep moving farther away the longer we walked.

"I hope we don't (puff) have to spend forty years (puff) wandering the airport before we find the Promised Land (puff)."

In both their long lives, neither of my parents had once left the ground. My father wanted to pack a lunch of hard-boiled eggs until I explained that the airline served meals. "A kitchen on a plane?" His heavy face lightened. A meal served on wheels was miracle enough, but a meal in the air! Already I could see him begging the stewardesses to let him help serve.

We reached the metal detector. I kissed them each hurriedly and gave my father a push. He ducked beneath the arch, then turned and smiled to reassure my mother. She closed her eyes and charged, like a child darting past her friends in a game of London Bridge.

A sour alarm. A Goliath with an Uzi stepped in her way. "Empty your pockets," he ordered. I rolled my eyes and motioned her to do what he asked.

"Here," she said, and gave the soldier a plastic-coated tag – her name and address, in case the plane crashed in the sea and the rescue workers needed to identify her remains.

"Nothing made of metal?"

My mother held up her palms.

"Come this way." The soldier gestured with his gun.

"No! I remember." She unbuttoned the top button of her blouse (the Orthodox men in line turned away) and fished out a *mezuzah* big as a perch. "For luck," she informed him.

The soldier shrank within his uniform; sheepish, he let her pass.

A few minutes later I watched from the terminal as their 747 backed from its gate (another moment and my mother would pop open the emergency exit to see if it worked). The jet sniffed out its runway and hurled itself skyward (my mother, I knew, would be digging in her heels and gripping Dad's hand).

They never came back. On top of Masada, as the tour guide explained how nine hundred Jews turned their swords on one another rather than let the Romans capture them as slaves, my mother said, "Oh!" and sat down. They had skipped breakfast that morning, rushing for the bus, and my father was so sure she'd fainted from hunger that even as a psychiatrist from Cleveland knelt beside her, feeling for her pulse, he kept asking if anyone in the group had a sandwich or fruit.

Later, in the hospital, the doctors did some tests and discovered that the hand my mother had complained was squeezing her heart was a warning that she shouldn't climb a cliff in the desert on such a hot day. I might have blamed myself for ignoring her premonition, but no matter what I did she would have found a way to prove the world to be a dangerous place. Sometimes I think she simply got too near the Forces of Darkness – through two thousand years she could still see those mothers slaying all their children, the husbands murdering their wives. She tried to end her life at this monument to the world's hatred of Jews, as a baseball fanatic might attempt to be buried at Cooperstown, or a Moslem at Mecca.

The damage to her heart wasn't severe (thank God), but nothing could convince my father to risk flying her home. The trip would be a strain, as would returning to the town where my mother's life lay in ruins. At my parents' instruction, Arthur sold the house in Paradise, though he still owns the land on which the Eden once stood. He and Maddy and their children visit Israel often – Maddy to conduct her research, my brother to conduct transactions with his clients, many of them wealthy Russians and Israelis who supervise their questionable deals from Tel Aviv. Despite my father's babying, my mother found a job a few hours a day caring for the children of immigrants from places like Yemen and Ethiopia; she worked there until she retired last year. Once a month, my father writes to describe the mountains of potatoes he peels at the refugee camp where he volunteers. As always he asks, in the same halting lines, why I can't manage a Holiday Inn in Jerusalem as easily as I can run one in Washington, D.C.? Each time I write back I tell him that I love him, but I'm not an

Israeli; if I can't find a way to be at home in America, I can never be at home anywhere else.

After I dropped my parents at the airport I didn't want to leave. Better to crawl through that labyrinth garage for the rest of my life than spend another night alone in Thomas's bed. I tried to stay lost, but the car found the exit. I handed the attendant a five-dollar bill. The metal arm rose and the driver behind me pumped his horn. The girl in the booth said, "Lady, could you please cry someplace else?"

On-ramps and off-ramps, tunnels, U-turns . . . Headlights and tail lights swam before my eyes, huge and distorted. I passed the warehouse at Pool World, which was being transformed just then into Christmas World. A crane lifted Santa toward the roof, where he swayed from a hook like a man who's being lynched.

I turned the car south. I sped through New Jersey, filled my gas tank in Delaware, stopped around three at a diner outside Baltimore, where I savored the meat loaf, carnal as flesh after so many meals of corn and canned beans. As I entered Virginia, rain began to pour, the wipers falling like truncheons.

I pulled into Charlottesville just before dawn. A garbage truck rolled slowly past the stately brick homes, four black men in work boots following the truck at a worshipful pace. Black women with scarves around their closely cropped heads waited on corners for Volvos and Mercedes to stop and pick them up. The tips of white shoes poked from paper bags, sleeves of uniforms dangling as if whole other bodies might be crushed up inside. I wandered the university, trying to imagine the Thomas Jefferson I knew so angry he would push an elderly professor down a flight of stairs. I sat on a bench and watched the sun's rays stroke the nap of plush courtyards and ivory domes as pleasantly curved as a young woman's breasts. The chimes from a church sang "de-COR-um, de-COR-um."

Two elderly ladies in plaid skirts and taupe stockings passed my bench and nodded. I wished them good day, then realized they weren't nodding, they were inspecting my tangled hair, torn jeans and scuffed work-boots – the same boots the garbage collectors had worn.

I started to walk, my eyes drawn to every black man, many of them in caps, none of them him. In Manhattan, when I'd met the gaze of a black man, he'd murmured, "What you want, girl?" or "Like what you see?" Here, they kept their heads down or averted their eyes. Everyone in Charlottesville – black, white, in between – treated each other with exquisite civility ("Excuse me," "No, *my* fault") as if the slightest jolt or jostle might cause the whole town to crack.

The only stores I found around the university were ladies' boutiques, haberdasheries, book stores, beauty shoppes and gift shoppes and markets that sold gourmet wine and cheese. Whom would he know here? Where would he be staying? He'd told me that his mother lived in a nursing home just outside Charlottesville – he sent her checks now and then. How many elderly black women named Jefferson – if that really was his name – could there be in one town?

I needed somewhere to think. In the Monticello Diner a waitress in a petticoat and a frilly white cap offered me a menu on fake parchment. DECLARATION OF TODAY'S SPECIALS, it said, the specials being pork chops, baked ham with mashed potatoes, and chicken-fried steak. As I waited for my coffee I studied the place mat – a laminated photo of the real Monticello, just three miles away.

Back in the Pontiac, I followed signs past elegant farms on which thoroughbreds grazed, so graceful and sleek they hardly seemed real. I parked beside a tour bus, then climbed the steep path past the huge fenced-in plot in which the President lay beside his family and favorite slaves. More than the mansion or the land, my grandfather would have envied that plot.

Below me lay the Commonwealth, fanned like a cape, plains embroidered with pastures and a crewel work of trees. I crossed to the other side and looked toward the city, the Blue Ridge Mountains beyond, as if all the blue atoms had settled from the sky, leaving the air that much fainter above. Then I paid my two dollars and toured the estate, room after room, some with beds stuck in alcoves (how inconvenient for changing linens!), some for dining or playing cards, others for playing music (the parquet floor in the music room was even more impressive than the floor at Fein's Hillside), rooms for reading, raising flowers, storing wine, cooking. And those gardens, and that fish pond, the magnificent view of land without end – an eighteen-hole golf course would fit neatly right there, and a tennis court, *there,* and a swimming pool, or two, trails for hiking, trails for riding . . .

Trust that a Jew would want to turn Monticello into a hotel. Thank goodness we didn't let that Levy person keep it.

"Levy? What Levy?"

"Why, as I was saying" – the guide lost the cadence of her memorized spiel – "after the President's death, a man by the name of Uriah Levy, through various unfortunate circumstances, came to take possession of Monticello. The estate was in shameful disorder. Unspeakably shameful. And Mr. Levy used his fortune to restore its former grandeur, for which all of us, as citizens of the nation, forever will be grateful, though the citizens did not, at that time, think it appropriate that so historical a monument should reside in . . . private hands, which subsequently caused a subscription to be undertaken . . ."

I giggled so hard the other tourists shushed me. Allow a man named Levy to keep Monticello? What would come next? Levy's Fish Store and Levy's Deli, Levy's Pawn Shop and Levy's Shoe Emporium, right on the grounds! (There was, in fact, a town not five miles from Paradise that was named Monticello, though the residents pronounced the word Mont-i-*sell*-o. That seemed fitting, I thought. People in the Catskills knew plenty about selling, but none of them could tell a cello from a tuba, let alone a violin.) The citizens of the nation had to make it clear you couldn't buy a heritage. Thomas Jefferson – the real one – might have been brilliant, of great mind and soul, but what would young Tom have done without all those slaves, tutors and books? And, given such gifts, couldn't *my* Thomas Jefferson have built this fine mansion, invented that clock, planted gardens like these?

The tour let us out near the slave quarters – a long, low, white building like a cut-rate motel. Parents posed their children in front of rooms in which maids had boiled the President's laundry; they paused to use the toilets or buy a souvenir. A black man in a jockey cap was sitting to one side, facing the grave of Uriah Levy's mother. I drifted from the tour group, and even before the man turned around, I knew who he was. Where else could he have been? If not today, then tomorrow, or the day after that.

"Lucy," he said.

Eyes burned my neck – from the gaggle of tourists, the ghosts of masters and their slaves. Hard enough at the Eden to overcome our history as handyman and child; here, history was measured in hundreds of years. Hard enough at the Eden, where the guests were aghast that the owner's daughter and the handyman were crossing the lines between gentile and Jew, black and white. At least at the Eden we were Lucy and Mr. Jefferson crossing those lines.

"Can we go for a walk?" I asked.

He took my arm and led me along the paths, bushes shielding us like bodyguards. I could almost hear my hoop skirt and crinolines swish. This was our home. The man who built Monticello was showing it off to me, his new mistress, his bride.

"*Zizyphus jujuba*," he said, caressing some nondescript shrub. "The Common jujube, in other words. And this here's the Haw." And this, Bastard indigo. This, Balm of Gilead.

Golden crownbeard. And this is Honesty. Love-lies-a-bleeding. Hearing his voice was like hearing the song your mother sung to calm you, except that my mother had never sung me songs. "And this here's my favorite. It's called the Sensitive plant." He touched the ferny leaves, which withered from his hand. "First time I did that, I thought the leaves pulled away because I was colored." He skimmed a stone at the fish pond; it hopped across the upside-down reflection of the mansion and came to rest on the opposite shore. "See all that masonry? All that woodwork? You notice all that fancy-work in town? God, how that ate me. My great-grandparents *built* that damn university and I couldn't even set foot there."

And it ate at me too. Why did blacks and Jews feel so out of place? We had helped build this nation. We had kept it afloat since earliest times. We didn't need to tiptoe like guests or poor relations. After nearly three centuries, wasn't it time we felt as much at home as anyone else?

He skimmed another stone. I tried skipping one too, but as soon as that stone kissed the water, it sank.

"Thomas?" Even then, his name felt strange to my mouth. "Where are you staying?" Though what I really wondered was where he'd go next.

"With an aunt. Great-aunt, actually. An old, frightened woman. Thinks I'm some sort of criminal. Which is a whole lot better than what my cousin thinks. Thinks I'm some kind of hero for killing this white guy – "

"It was my fault," I said. "I don't see why you keep – "

"Lucy, I promised I'd check those fire escapes. I promised I'd help you take care of that hotel. Then I got so busy with my own foolishness – "

"I told you to get out! I didn't hire anyone to take your place because I wanted to save money."

"And why'd I quit in the first place? Because I preferred to live by myself, with my vegetables and my books. You know what my mother said? I went to that nursing home, I found her and I said, 'Mother, I'm your Thomas, I'm your son, I've come home,' and she told me, 'My son's a professor of something or other at some college up North. He don't ever come home. He loves his books, not his family.'"

"That's not true. She's your mother, but it isn't true."

"Isn't it?" He studied the mansion so long I thought he must be recording every lattice. "Damn fool, trying to imitate something like that."

"There's nothing wrong with building – "

"There is. Yes, there is. Every world you create, it has to have borders. Has to have rules. Has to have someone making up those rules, someone in charge. Only God creates worlds. One world. He made it. Create your own world, you get punished."

"God didn't kill Nat. I neglected the upkeep, the wood rotted and the bolts fell out. You're not being religious. Maybe there is a God, but He sure doesn't sit up there minding every bolt and screw and who does or doesn't tighten them. All your science and your books – "

"It's a fine line between – "

"Superstition!"

"Think so?"

"You're worse than my mother." I said this as if being my mother were a crime. "You're worse than any old *yenta* in the *shtetl*."

"No coincidence. That's my *shtetl*, down there." He pointed toward the valley, past a fork in the road.

"You left that village a long time ago."

"Lucy, I'm not perfect, okay? Maybe you thought so when you were a little girl. Maybe I was flattered and tried to hide my . . . weaknesses. But the simple fact is, I felt guilty as hell over Nat's death. And I am . . . superstitious. How could we hope to lead any sort of life . . ."

"The Playland," I started.

"Poor imitation of this, don't you think."

"No. No, I don't think. It's remarkable you even – "

"Never been anywhere. Never seen anything. Because I was scared. Scared I'd get lost. Scared I wasn't smart enough, I'd turn out to be . . . nobody. Nobody at all. So I sat in my cell and I never . . . Just talk. 'Universal man.' What a load of bullshit! What can you do with a few lousy acres? You need a whole country. Got to scavenge what you need . . . Not boards from a few bungalows . . . You need to talk. Get ideas. From all sorts of people. Can't sit in one place. Can't just keep nailing those same old bits and pieces together."

"He was rich," I said. "The real Thomas Jefferson was rich. That's how he could afford to travel."

He folded his arms. "I can earn my own way. Doesn't cost much money to talk to people, or to listen."

"You're not Jesus either."

"I never said – "

"Do you think you can start some new religion, like that Hasid?"

"I can't go back there. That's all there is to it."

"All right then. We'll travel. Wherever you want to go, well, we'll go there." I imagined us walking across the Great Plains, then on through Death Valley. Maybe if we found some town we both liked . . .

"It won't work. Forget it."

"Proof's in the Bible. Ecclesiastes," I said.

"Ecclesiastes?"

I quoted: " 'Two are better than one, because they will have a good reward for their labor. For if one of them falls, the other will lift his fellow. But woe, *woe* to him that's by himself, because if he falls, he doesn't . . . he can't . . . he hath not another to help him up.' "

"But that isn't what the Bible . . . Your interpretation's all wrong."

"Shut up. Whoever quotes can interpret. Besides, I'm not finished. 'If two lie together, then they have warmth. But how can one person be warm by himself?' There. Now I'm finished." I smiled as sagely as I knew how. "Winter will be here sooner than you think."

He looked like a man who has been beaten at a game he invented. "Okay, yes, it's warmer sleeping with two. But during the day . . . What are you going to do to keep occupied?"

"I'll have plenty to do."

"For instance."

"For instance . . ." I glanced around for a hint. And nothing I saw, not even the grass, seemed the least bit familiar. I felt the vertigo of a sleepwalker who wakes to find herself at the top of a high building. I fought the urge to lie down, or to run to my car and drive home.

But then, like a tourist who stops complaining long enough to sample the sights and dishes set before her, I decided that I might acquire a taste for travel after all. The place I'd come to was no stranger than the place I'd just left. The only truly comfortable home was the grave.

"For instance," I said, "I need to learn the names of flowers. And the names of trees. You saw yourself, I don't have a clue what anything's called."

"Stop talking nonsense. Two weeks out there, nothing to look at but some trees – "

"And birds. I don't know the names of any birds."

"Even birds! You're watching the birds, you're hanging around the cheap part of town with this no-account Negro . . . I don't want you whining how you're bored. Or a few months from now, there's spring in your blood and the season's about to start . . ."

I let him go on. Then I said, quietly, "It's gone. It burned down."

He stopped. It sunk in. I told him everything. He took a

breath. "Hooboy," he said. "If life isn't . . . Life . . . " He swatted the air. "Hell, I don't need to tell you about life anymore. You know as well as I do. Life is . . . a motherfucker." He considered, then nodded. "It's a motherfucker all right. No two ways around *that.*"

If he meant this to scare me, the strategy failed. The unredeemed world that lay around my feet seemed more evil and threatening (its evil was real and couldn't be explained by Forces and Eyes), more conducive to feats of miraculous strength than any small kingdom I could ever dream up.

"Thomas?" I said. But he was crossing the lawn. He hadn't said good-bye. I assumed he would be waiting by my car when I got there. After all we'd been through, after my good fortune finding him here, how could he leave?

For a while, he sent postcards – from Memphis, Salt Lake City, Minneapolis, Detroit. He promised to come see me, which he now and then did. *I'll come back,* he kept promising. *Someday we'll settle down.*

In the meantime, for his sake, I did what I could. The hotels I helped manage attracted a clientele that often needed favors: men with no luggage who looked as if they had only swum ashore that morning; disheveled, red-eyed women with sleepy children in tow who kept glancing at the door and asking that I not tell a soul where they were; teenage kids who signed names like Mickey Jagger or Madonna and were too young to be given rooms, though I disregarded that rule. I couldn't solve their problems. But I tried to remember something Thomas said – that the only true refuge for a person in pain is in another person's heart.

It took years to save the money to buy my own place, and, more than that, to be sure that owning something wouldn't get in the way of saving my soul. But finally I decided that being in charge meant I wouldn't have to hurry. I could listen, I could talk, whichever seemed to set a guest most at ease. Rules are easier to bend if you've made them yourself.

In the quietest hours between three and five A.M., I sometimes browsed through the books Thomas had left in my care. I still found it hard to concentrate on things that didn't concern me, but more things concerned me than they had when I was young. I needed something to remind me life entailed more than filling out forms and pleading with plumbers to repair leaking pipes. I was sure that being Jewish meant more than being fearful, as my parents believed. It doesn't mean you've been chosen. If anything, it means that you have to keep choosing. You need to pay attention, to see the world as it is, to bless what needs blessing. Other religions may teach these same things. But I was born Jewish. You have to start with who you are. Though who you become later is more important, I think.

I needed years to learn this. I made my share of mistakes. It's hard to stay honest without someone to correct you, as Thomas used to do. While he traveled I fell in love with several other men. It's easier to love a man who doesn't feel the need to teach you lessons, though you can't learn a thing from a man you don't love. He was right, we weren't ready – not back then, not so soon, with both of us so battered and the world as it was. Thomas needed to become less perfect than he was. I needed to become better.

But that day at Monticello, I thought all I had to do was to follow him, catch up, find the words to convince him. And just for that moment, before I hurried to the car, a flash caught my eye. The gutters and windows and spires of the city, the enormous steel gas tanks, the rivers and lakes, the fenders and hubcaps, the swimming pools and manholes and golden-red leaves caught the sunlight and glowed. I scooped these reflections like so many gold and silver coins and flung them to the sky, hoping that they might rain down upon everyone in a shower of sparks.